Flawed Thoughts Ink presents

“Over Time”

by

W.A. Gordon

ISBN: 978-1-387-48877-3

Table of Contents

Acknowledgements

I would like to first off give glory to Jesus Christ, Lord and Savior of my life. He is the reason why I live, having given me chance after chance because of His work on the cross. All of my work, therefore is done in tribute to Him, using the gifts He has endowed me with to glorify His name and let people know of His goodness.

Thank you to my beautiful wife, Syiedah. Your support means so much to me and has encouraged me to go even further. I am so grateful to have you here as another project is finally completed. I love you!

To my loving parents – thank you for being a perpetual support for me in so many ways. Words fail to express how much I love and appreciate you. I often thank God for choosing to pair me with you in my journey here on earth. I only hope to make you proud in all that I do. I love you so much!

A heartfelt thank you to Pastors De'Juan Kelker II and Stacey Kelker. Your leadership and mentorship have meant so much to me, providing me with both spiritual and natural guidance in my journey since our introduction together. May God continue to bless you both in your divine calling to "effectively affect the world" – and I will continue to be there to help!

To my brother, Carlos – your encouragement is a mainstay, no matter how far or close we are in distance. My projects were cheered on by you, years ago. For that and more, I thank you!

To all those who I have not named specifically named, charge it to the page count and not my heart. Thank you for supporting me, my writing, and the Flawed Thoughts Ink brand. There is so much that I have put into this and every bit of encouragement that I have received has helped me in one way or another to get to this point...and to continue even further on this literary journey. I hope that this book provides you with moments of reflection, entertainment, and introspect. May God bless you all!

Chapter 1

"If Mel turn that ball over *one* more time...", mumbled Carter. "My fault, y'all. My bad," yelled Melvin to his teammates, piercing the irritated ear of Carter. His teammate had once again passed the ball carelessly in a basketball pickup game at the Reynolds King Recreation Center. Playing on the top court of the legendary four full courts at the "King" (as everyone called it), no team could afford any turnovers, less they'd be forced to sit 3 games or more in waiting for another chance for redemption. Carter, as close as he was to Mel, was sometimes more of a competitor than a friend, especially when the time and place was at the King.

So it came down to game point. Both teams were tied, 15 to 15, after an unknown visiting hooper to the King Center had stolen Mel's pass and ran down for an uncontested layup. The game was close, but probably should not have been. With Carter playing his last game before he would go back for his sophomore year as the star swingman at Cuyahoga Valley State University, he felt that he had to leave his mark, maintaining his claim as the next one to make the pros. Contributing 13 of his team's 15 points with an array of long-range shots and a combination of athletic layups and dunks, he could not lose now. It wasn't enough that he had a small, picturesque shrine at the King, that everybody walked past in awe of - a collection of photos, newspaper clippings, trophies, and plaques showcasing him as young as 12 years old. Carter always played as if he had everything to lose - because in his own mind, he did.

Carter ran under the hoop to Fred, the 15-year-old taking out the ball that they picked up to fill out their team - a last-minute fill-in to get the game going when someone left earlier than expected. He said to Fred sternly, but confidently, "Let me get that, homie. It's game time and these scrubs ain't getting one over on me." Fred happily gave Carter the ball with a soft, easy toss and ran to the other side of the court, less as a teammate, but more as a witness to what U.C. (Unstoppable Carter, as he was known as) would do in, what many thought might be, his last game before a "farewell tour" en route to declaring himself eligible for the big leagues. Another crossover, killer jumper, posterizing monster dunk - who knows what was going to happen. Everyone (both teams, the crowd, the team in waiting) were all ready to find out.

Carter sized up the man guarding him, Rell, dribbling meticulously at the top of the three-point line, looking at him eye-to-eye, doing his customary dribble between the legs, while deciding his plan of attack. The other teammates, including Mel, cleared out the space, to allow for Carter to stack another win amongst his many, since he started playing the game that he saw as his life's calling. Always the crafty ballhandler, Carter immediately faked a quick dribble to his right, to which his defender saw and immediately bit on. Carter smirked and saw that this was easy prey and yet another victim, doing the same dribble fake with his opposite hand. The small crowd of people who surrounded the baseline conversed with each other, speculating how U.C. would win yet another game.

Carter went into attack mode, dribbling now with his left, towards the hoop, but the defender received help when Mo stepped up in a zoning effort with Rell, cutting off the penetration. Carter, now surprised, crossed back over to the right, but Mo and Rell had a determined defense and beat him to the spot he would attempt to get to. Q, Mel's younger cousin, broke out of his spectative trance and yelled "U.C., G's up, G's Up! Let's go!" Carter and Mel recognized the call, and the mysterious play went into motion. Carter whipped the ball to the right wing to Q, Mel pushed off his man, sprinting to and planting at the left elbow - his usual spot in the go-to play. With everyone surprised that apparently Carter had given up his game-winning opportunity to whoever else had the courage to steal the show, Carter spun around Mo, preparing to leap off the baseline for an alley-oop pass from Mel.

Mel, in that split-second, however, had a strong remorse for his mistakes in the game. He knew that his last bad pass put his team in this situation and if he could make things right, this was the time to do it. As Mel contemplated his move, he heard a familiar cheer and noticed Regina with her 2 younger siblings in the far corner near the neighboring court watching the game with the rest of the crowd. He wondered how long she had been there. How did he not see her? After all, this was the love of his life, or so he thought, anyway. Regina and Mel had known each other since they were kids, living in the same neighborhood, going to the same church, and even being classmates for a few years. They just had another one of their breakups and one, if not both, was still not quite over it. This unexpected appearance threw Mel off, but gave him an idea.

Always one wanting to impress, Mel resolved in his mind almost immediately that he could (or should) be the one to win this all so-important game. Mel thought to himself, "If she saw that dumb pass that I did to cause this, I gotta get this shot in. Can't go out like that." And with that thought in his mind, Mel set himself in motion for what would potentially be a game-winning, left elbow, free-throw shot. This shot was a no-brainer, as far as he was concerned, and the pros far outweighed the cons. In just one shot, he would make amends on-court with his best friend Carter and gain redemption points off-court with Regina. The time was now!

Mel vetoed against the standard "G's Up" play that was carried out initially by Carter and Q, and now only needed one more role to be played. As Carter went up looking for the pass, he saw while he was mid-air that Mel was not in a passing motion, but rather a shooting one. He, as everybody else in the vicinity, wondered what would become of this apparent audible of sorts. Against his frustration that he was not getting the glory of the final, game-sealing shot, Mel was wide-open and ready to send their seemingly lucky opponents home. "It's whatever, I guess," Carter thought, as he descended down from the aerial move that was seemingly in vain.

The basketball left Mel's hands, in a confident and textbook motion, certain to make even the sport's founding fathers proud as it floated in the air towards the hoop. All eyes were fixated on the stretched measures of time, with everyone wondering why he took the shot, but just as anxious to see the end result. It floated, rotating towards the paint-chipped hoop, with a slightly aged, off-white net. As the ball projected from the hands of Mel it landed just above the hoop, hitting the back iron, then bouncing straight up about two feet into air, almost reaching the height of the top of the backboard. The ball then made a slow descent down to the center of the hoop, but made a slight move towards the right side of the hoop, causing what was seemingly a game-winning shot to be an unwanted miss.

With every player and spectator's eyes fixated on the missed shot attempt, the rebound bounced high off of the right-side. The players on both teams were almost frozen in place, assuming that the game would be over after that shot. Mel's heart sunk, seeing that the decision that he made was indeed the wrong one. Despite his best intentions, the game would continue, and there was no telling where things would go from here. Q stood with daggers in his eyes aimed at his cousin, with Fred letting out a sigh combined with rolled eyes at the missed shot. Carter, however, was the only figure moving in a frozen portrait of this moment in time at the King. His ability to jump again immediately after his own descent, allowed him to catch the rebound in full palm with his right hand. He then did a power dribble and a basic layup on the right side of the backboard with no opposition, finalizing the game. Mission accomplished.

"Told y'all that I got this! That's game! Who got next?" Carter yelled loudly, but deep down was relieved that he had pulled this one off. Despite the miscues from his running buddies, Mel and Q, he was able to pull off another one, extending his undefeated streak today at the King. Amidst the finality of the game, Carter walked over to all of his teammates offering up "good game" and hand slaps, reserving a dap and hug with his best friend. Mel returned the embrace in equal relief, but also in distraction. Over Carter's shoulder, he noticed Regina and her siblings heading out, leaving the courts. Mel simply could not get this girl out of his mind. Regina was that one that he could not pull away from, no matter how much he tried. Guess his attempt to talk would be reduced to another quick text or online message later on.

Carter, feeling the embrace was a bit weak and going a little longer than normal, pulled away and asked Mel, "Bruh, you good? Holding on a little too long, man." Mel shook off the daze that he was immersed in and responded, "Yeah, yeah, I'm - I'm good, man. Just glad that shot I took didn't lose it for us." Carter held nothing back, "Yeah, about that - what was that? You already know when it's 'G's Up' I'm punching out, putting these lames on notice. Had me touching the sky, looking like Blake Griffin jumping over cars for nothing." Mel laughed, responding, "Yeah, and here I come with the Bill Cartwright jumper thinking it was a wrap. My fault, man. For real, for real, I just was trying to shut it down quick, fast. You saw how open I was, right? But, you got that, we called the play, shoulda ran with it."

"It's cool, Mel. Gina woulda dug seeing Bulls number 23 instead of 24, though," Carter replied slyly. "Man, what you talking 'bout," asked Mel, with an embarrassed tone. "You think I ain't see her in the cut watching us hoop? I knew what it was. I'm cool, bruh. Just trying to get your shine on, whack jumper and all," Carter said with a few chuckles. As Carter went to the side to check his cell phone for missed calls or messages, Q came up to the two and said, "Hey, the next team ready. Let's go, y'all!" Almost within seconds, Mr. Waltman, the King Center's building manager came up and yelled in his familiar bellow, "Alright young cats, time to shut it down. It's late, I gotta date, and I don't think this one'll wait." The remaining crowd of people at the courts laughed in response, but respectfully made their way off the courts. Everybody loved Mr. Waltman. He was a neighborhood legend, in sports and every barbecue, going from dunking in people's grills to eating off of them. He was always friendly, but when he said it was time to go, it was time to go.

As Mel and Carter wrapped up their conversation, Mr. Waltman walked up to them and said, "And don't think I didn't see you trying to make that shot to impress Gina, Mel!" Carter howled, "See, I told you, man. Everybody knew what it was! Quit trying to act like you were all slick with it. With that ol' Matrix-looking shot you threw up. That girl still got you swinging." Mel started humming the song of the same title, as Mr. Waltman continued the barrage. Mel looked away and shook his head with a smirk, almost like the one of the kid who gets caught with his hand in the cookie jar. "Yeah, it was cute, but U.C. had to bail you out, as usual. Have to admit, though, shot wasn't that bad. If you just put a little more arc on it, like I keep telling you..." exclaimed Mr. Waltman. Mel interrupted, "Yeah, about that arc, you trying to school me on that is what messed me up in the first place when I was in high school. Still trying to work that *out* of my game." "Yeah Mr. Dub, you tried to trap me, too. Good thing I'm hard-headed and stuck with my natural God-given talent," Carter joked.

"Yeah, whatever. You young cats stay hard-headed. Can't tell y'all nothing. Don't say that I didn't try," Mr. Waltman said, having slight nostalgia of his own athletic exploits in his younger years. He tried, sometimes overbearingly, to impart his knowledge of both sports and life in general. He often felt an impressive obligation to do this, due in part to his own shortcomings in life, due mostly to combinations of poor decisions and times "when life happened", as he would call them. Having grown up in that same neighborhood, he was no stranger to local fame, and saw several who would come close, but Carter was quickly becoming an eerie doppelganger. Whether Carter liked it or not, Mr. Waltman would make sure that the same wrong moves would be avoided, on and off the court. He loved all of the kids who came to the King, but took special interest in Carter and Mel, having seen them grow up as close as brothers and King Center stalwarts.

"It's all good, Mr. Dub. Just clowning. You know how we do," Mel reassured their mentor. "You know we couldn't have made it without you, for real. But, we rolling out. I heard you dropping that old school player line on us trying to get us out. You got something lined up for tonight?" Mr. Waltman transitioned into a proud look on his face and responded, "Well, as a matter of fact, I do. Might mess around and get her surf *and* turf, if she play her cards right. We'll see what the business is and wha...hold on, what you need to know all that for?" The two young antagonizers chuckled, as they packed their belongings, transitioning out of their basketball shoes into their sandals, relieving their tired feet. "Just taking notes. Just taking notes, Mr. Dub. We know you got game and we'd be foolish to not be taking it all in. We need that good recap, ASAP, when we see you next time. Just make sure that your shoe polish doesn't melt off of your head and face while you're out laying your game down," said Carter, barely able to keep a straight disposition as the last words exited his mouth.

"Well, I'll be cool. Y'all just get moving. Gotta get moving in a few minutes," Mr. Waltman responded, walking away running his hand on his remaining hair, checking also for any residue from the alleged hair dye that Carter alluded to. As he left out, Carter went back on the offensive with Mel saying, "So how long will it be this time, man?" "What 'chu mean, C", Mel responded. "You know what I mean. With Gina," Carter said matter-of-factly, "Y'all do this every few months. On again, off again. Almost like you and Q's whack jumpshots. For real, though, what's the business with y'all now?" Mel sighed, as they began their exiting steps out of the facility, "Man, I'm not on it. We good. She's doing her and I'm doing me. It's cool." Q sprinted past them, towards the door, yelling "Alright, fam! I'll get up with y'all. Good run. I'll hit y'all, my girl trying to go to this new movie. Peace!" "Alright, Q! Be safe, cuz!", Mel responded. He welcomed the break in conversation, hoping that it would altogether deter Carter's interrogation. It wouldn't.

"Do you need me to sit y'all down and give y'all the talk again? I'll tell her how you're slow and don't know what you're doing. I'll throw on a few R&B lines, begging on your behalf, and you should be all good. Don't tell me you don't know the routine by now. We've been through it how many times?" Mel chuckled, responding, "C, for real, we good. If I need to talk or need for you to do whatever it is you call yourself doing, I'll let you know. I think we just need some time, and that's even assuming that we even get back on anything." Carter's side-eye look initiated immediately, "*If* y'all 'get back on anything'? Bruh, please. Anyway, I'm about to go get cleaned up and kick it tonight. You rolling through?" "Naw, I'm at the house tonight. Might go online and hit up some hoop games and live out my number 23 fantasies on these dudes," Mel said as he laughed, "Besides, I'm going to rest up this knee. We'll get up, though." As the two walked out of the King, approaching the parking lot, Carter responded, saying, "Alright, man. Well, you let me know how your conversation with Gina works out. You ain't fooling nobody. I'll get at you tomorrow." There was no way to convince Carter that Mel wasn't going to covertly seek out his on-and-off again flame.

Chapter 2

"Gina think you cute. Do you like her? Yes or 'No." The half sheet of notebook paper freshly ripped out of Karina's notebook in an effort to play matchmaker finally reached Mel's hands in the lunchroom. Of course, it passed through several hands to get from point A to the final destination - starting at the girls' table, amidst gazing eyes and shy giggles, going from Karina, folded and transferred to Melissa, handed under the table to Maria, who then conveniently had to go to the trash can next to the boys' table. She handed the tightly-folded grade-school love inquiry to a confused Carter finishing off a can of orange pop, to whom she whispered, "Give this to Mel. You-know-who like him." Carter immediately looked over to Mel, who was mid-bite into a bologna and cheese sandwich and whispered, "Mel...Mel...psssst. Look!" Carter motioned lower under the table, reaching over to Mel with the small letter of mystery.

Mel, intrigued to say the least, reached down and grabbed the school-certified letter and covertly read its contents under the table. "Gina likes me? Regina? Is this for real? Somebody playing games," Mel thought. There was no way that the new girl in the class that all of the boys drooled over was interested in him. From the first day of school at Southview Point Academy, Regina was the object of everyone's attention. Seventh grade at the small private school was looking to be the same lineup of interests for the boys - a new basketball season to get pumped for, landing the one and only Mr. Dewels (the coolest teacher in the school), football games at recess, and getting to see the new kids (specifically the girls) joining the class.

Mel, still skeptical of the authenticity of the letter, was being asked via whisper by Carter again, "Dude, what you gon' do? I know you not passing that up. Cuz look, if you don't, I will." "Alright, alright," responded a hurried Mel. He knew that he liked Regina, but who would have known that she would approach him and not the other way around. "Hey, Darryl, let me use that pencil, real quick," Mel asked his classmate sitting two seats down the table. Darryl stopped in the midst of drawing comic book characters he obsessed over. "Alright, hurry up. I'm trying to finish up this Mutant Mash scene," Darryl said, still trying to be helpful. Mel was one of the few kids who treated him well, so he took little thought to interrupt his own work to help out, even if it was just a pencil. Mel took the pencil, quickly scripted his response, re-folded the paper, and handed it to Carter saying, "Can you run this over there for me?" Carter nodded, saying, "I'll hand it to Maria when we get to the playground. Keeping this top-secret, for real."

Lunchtime was over and all of the kids made it to the playground, as usual. The same girls involved with the transport of the letter stood in a small huddle under the short row of trees on the edge of the playground. Carter, one of the last to get to the playground, had the letter in hand, with a few drops of water from the water fountain he stopped at before exiting the building. Before the girls were in clear view, he decided to take a peek at the note and see what decision his best friend had made. It was obvious, right? The new girl - the *cute* new girl that every boy had fallen head-over-heels for - would be the girl he would "go with", as they called it in their grade school conversations. And she was bold enough to approach *him*? He would be a fool to not take her up on the offer. Although no one in their class could do it on an actual basketball court, as of yet, this was a slam-dunk if there was ever one.

As he peered at the letter in feigned curiosity, his eyes widened as he saw neither box was checked, but in familiar handwriting, the words, "I'm cool." Carter was beyond shocked and immediately scoured the playground for Mel. What in the world could he be thinking? This was a no-brainer and his friend was going to pass up the opportunity of a seventh-grader's lifetime. Within seconds, Carter saw Mel walking over to the group of boys from seventh and eighth grade gathering for the all-important team selection for the daily football game. Carter ran past the girls, with all of their eyes following him in inquiry, and swiftly pulled Mel to the side, in the midst of the playground football draft. "Dude, are you serious?!?", Carter exclaimed. "About wha...you looked at the note didn't you? C, I'm cool, man. Gina cool and all, but something's not right about this man. I'm not about to get played," Mel replied.

"Yeah, you right. Something isn't right - her feeling you and not some other dude in our class or the eighth grade. I don't know why she like you, but you can't say no to this, man," Carter reasoned. "You know how many would love to be in your spot? Fix this before she changes her mind." Mel sighed, in nervousness, but was perceived by Carter as annoyance. Mel really *did* like Regina, but had been pranked before in a similar incident in the previous year. Karina engineered the ruse, just as she appeared to be doing with this situation, that time using Nicki as the "admirer". Mel, having liked Nicki, responded with an excited "yes" on that piece of paper, and as the group of girls received the response, they howled in laughter on the playground. Carter, seeing his friend confused as to what was happening, walked over to his friend and said, in short, "You just got played, man." With the same participants in play, the writing on the wall seemed all too clear and his ego was not going to take another blow like that one.

"I know what happened last year, but trust me, I'm not going to let you get played. I got you," Carter said reassuringly. As the last words left from Carter's mouth, Karina walked over in her delegate role and inquired of the two boys, "Mel, it's a yes or no. Quit playing like it's so difficult. Either you like her or you don't. It's really that simple." "Fall back, Karina. Me and Mel just talking right now. Nobody need you getting in the middle of all of this," Carter said in defense of his best friend. "We'll get at you before recess is done." "Naw, man. I'm good," Mel said in a surprisingly confident tone. "Karina, tell Gina to meet me after school at the bottom of the church steps across the street and we'll talk then. But like Carter said, just fall back. You already know don't nobody trust you anyway." Karina put on a shocked look, "I was just trying to help your whack self, but whatever. I'll tell her what you said, but I can't guarantee anything." She walked away back to her group, to report her findings.

Mel said to Carter, "Alright, man. Let's see if we can get into this game. They already started without us. We only got, like, 20 minutes before it's over." "Yeah, let's run this real quick. Now that all of your little drama is for after-school, we can get some run in," Carter said with a chuckle. Carter was happy for his friend, while Mel still was a bit unsettled. Well, at least he bought himself some time by negotiating a face-to-face meeting. There was no telling if this was for real, but this would probably be his best way to find out. Also, in the meantime, he would have an opportunity to show off his athleticism in the football game that was always watched very closely by the girls of the school. If she did not really like him, she would start to after the performance he intended to put on. Mel loudly yelled to the quarterback, "Hit me! I'm open!"

Chapter 3

Mel got out of his car, still slightly damp from the workout at the King. He was surprised to be able to enjoy a dry day, as rain was a constant in the local forecast, causing even some causes for concern of flooding in nearby areas. After a workout at the King and a reasonably dry post-game arrival to homebase, it looked like a relaxing evening was in tow. His parent's house sat empty, to his surprise, and was quiet with one lone light on, showing through the kitchen windows towards the back of the house. As he walked in through the back door and entered the kitchen, a note sat on the table, catching Mel's eye. It read:

"Melvin,

Sorry for not telling you before, but your father and I got tickets to a jazz concert from a radio contest I won (yay, me!). It's going to be nice to get out and enjoy ourselves after the Noah's Ark flooding that we just endured. I left a plate of food in the microwave for you to eat. Help yourself. See you when we get back. By the way, Regina called for you. You might want to give her a call back and fix whatever you guys have going on. Just apologize for whatever you did and get back with that girl. Your Mom knows best - she's a keeper! Besides I saw you two in a dream, with you on one knee. Don't start doubting my prophetic gift now. We'll talk later.

Love you,

Mom"

Mel, shook his head with chuckles and a smirk. He knew his mother always wanted to see he and Regina together. That dream probably came from one of her TV shows she fell asleep watching on her DVR. His mother, however, was a sharp critic of his girlfriends, even in spite of the fact that he brought a minimal number to meet her, in fear that she would eviscerate the young unsuspecting women with her on-the-spot interrogation. No one was good enough for her Melvin, with Regina being the sole exception. That was a part of what made it so hard for him, knowing how close she was to her family, specifically the most important woman to him - his mother. The pressure for reconciliation with Regina only built even greater.

Mel put his gym bag on the floor, went to the microwave to peruse the meal left behind for him (grilled salmon with asparagus), still a bit warm, as his parents probably did not leave too long before his entry. He could still smell the dueling fragrances of his Father's cologne and his mother's favorite perfume close to the doorway.

Not wanting to wait too long, Mel pressed the "60 second quick cook" button and went to wash his hands in the sink. Mel dried off his hands and prepared his drink of choice, water with lemon infused - a drink he adapted from his grandmother and father, who always kept fresh lemons freshly sliced, readily added to their cups of water.

They fancied it a family tradition during Mel's childhood, but his mother spilled the beans once he approached his senior year of high school. “Your Dad's family swears by drinking lemons to keep them rail-thin as they are all are. Truth is, when your Father was a boy, they were so broke, they could barely afford Drink-Ade, much less even sugar water, so they got as many lemons as they could from the food pantry in their neighborhood and that was their special drink." Mel did not care a bit. Since learning during a science project his junior year the benefits of adding lemon to water, he ran with the idea and it became even more of a mainstay in his regular diet. The 60-second cook time went by quickly, as he finished in time to enjoy his home-cooked meal. Mel sat down and began to eat one of his mom's signature dishes.

The meal was incredible, as it always was. This sure beat the cold pizza that he had become accustomed to while away at college. One of the things that he missed most when he moved out was Mom's home-cooking. Mel was nostalgic for watching his mom cook and prepare his plate, setting a standard that he had yet to find anyone come close to matching. No doubt, Regina, or whoever his girlfriend would be, had some big shoes to fill, or in this case an apron.

Finishing the meal in little to no time, Mel took his plate and cup and placed it in the kitchen sink with the rest of the dirty dishes that he would have to conquer before his parents returned. As he sighed with the annoyance of still doing chores even as a young adult, Mel always reminded himself that it was a much lower cost than that of paying actual rent. This was made clear when an actual deal was made with his Dad that his stay between semesters would not be a free ride, but that he could earn his keep by simply doing the things that they would have to pay a housekeeper to do. When he weighed the options, being an unpaid servant was the lesser of two evils, by far. Taking the trash out weekly, doing the laundry, washing dishes - all of that paled to the inevitable reality of hundreds of dollars of rent and all of the other bills that he saw his friends struggling to keep up with.

While walking upstairs with his gym bag to his room, he heard a text alert from his phone. As the beeps continued, he grabbed his phone from his bag and saw a message from Chris, the youth pastor from

Blessed Hope Missionary Church. "Hey, Mel. You still coming through tonight, right? The kids are already amped," the text read. Mel threw his head back, with a defeated "awww man", instantly remembering that he had agreed to help run the kids' game night at the church. He looked at the time on his phone and he had less than 20 minutes to get cleaned up and still make it in time for the 8:00 start. Looks like the online basketball night-in would have to be called off now.

Mel sprinted to the shower, shortening his notoriously long body cleaning to give himself a chance to make it to the church on time, or at least close enough. The kids looked forward to this monthly event, not only to play games, eat food, and hang out all night, but to spend time with Mel and some of the other volunteers who helped run the show. To Mel's surprise, he had become quite the role model for many of the kids at this church. Many of the young boys grew up watching he and Carter play sports at school and around the neighborhood. Amazingly, they managed to keep clean public profiles amidst all of the attention, which garnered local endorsements from the parents, as well.

Mel, himself, had distanced himself a bit, inadvertently, from going to church, but this to him was not like what he had grown up in. There was something different about this church, a lot different from his learned notion of what church was supposed to be, anyway. Needless to say, Mel got as much, if not more, out of these events. As long as he was not being forced to have to go through the routine of having to go to church again, like he was most of his childhood, he had no problem helping out. Besides, he knew that he was doing a good thing, and that above all mattered.

Tripping over his gym bag and laundry basket in his cluttered room, Mel hurried to get his clothes together and run out the door get to the event at Blessed Hope Missionary Church's gymnasium on time. He went to his closet and grabbed a gray polo shirt to pair with his dark blue jeans and gray low-top sneakers. Even in a rush, Mel knew he had to be a fashion statement for anyone there – especially if Regina found her way there. While it was a long-shot, he knew that she could possibly be dropping off one of her sisters there and they could run into each other. That slight possibility of crossing paths was even more incentive for Mel to get going to the game night event.

One of the challenges that Mel always faced was creating a dividing line between "church Mel" and "regular Mel". Growing up, he always felt the need to have two different versions of himself to accommodate the different environments that he found himself in. Growing up in a household where it was commonplace to be in church, almost as much as home and school, the multiple identities were almost a must-have for survival. The way that Mel saw it, being "saved" while being cool was a social trick that he worked hard like many of his peers to pull off. The old, Baptist hymns that rang in his house from Dad's turntable, atop the family stereo system was a stark contrast from the hip-hop CDs that Mel cautiously stashed away in the back corner of his dresser drawer. It was a stash that had music and lyrics that Mel's parents were hard critics against, but kept him relevant in conversations at school and in the neighborhood, for the rare times he was allowed to play with his peers on Forest Ave. Little did he know that this struggle would continue on throughout his life.

Mel, having learned much about himself since those times, did his best to provide an example to his mentees and admirers at Blessed Hope. Mel's mentee was Carrell – a 12-year-old boy from the same neighborhood as Mel, who was the son of a close friend of his parents. He was the youngest of 3, having two older sisters, living in the upstairs of a nearby two-family home blocks away from the church. Carrell was a student at Southview, just like Mel, having been forced to go because his mother had it under good authority from Mel's parents that it was a much better option than the local school district. With Carrell's older sisters having gone to the local public schools, he often wondered why his path had to be so different. Mel, having traveled a similar path, always tried to ease Carrell's nerves. Not one game night at Blessed Hope would pass without Carrell's complaints, including "Why I gotta wear a shirt and tie every day?" and "It's hard to play football in these tap dance-looking shoes. I fall every day."

Yeah, the more Mel thought about it, the responsibility to be there at Blessed Hope was too high for him to miss out. As he began to dart down the stairs from his room and race through the kitchen, he saw the unclean dishes in the sink. He quickly took the same piece of paper on which Mel's mother left him her message and wrote on the back apologizing for not getting the dishes done. To add a dash of sincerity to the message, he made sure to mention that he was headed to Blessed Hope, which he was sure would earn some mercy points before their iron fists would come down on him upon his return. Mel dropped the pen and laid the note in the same place where it originally was placed. As he rushed out of the door, his phone beeped an alert for a text message. It was from a number he had never seen before. "Hey, Mel. This is Karina. From Southview. You busy?"

Chapter 4

Southview Point Academy's final bell signaling the end of the school day finally concluded its ringing cadence, echoing inside its hallways and resonating in extended proximity throughout the neighborhood. The moment of truth had come, and Mel, while protruding a calm demeanor on the outside, had a stomach tied in boy-scout quality knots on the inside. At this time, everybody was prepared to line up to walk out of the classroom as normal, with the boys in one line and the girls paralleled in another, all with their bookbags in tow. Carter surveyed the moments leading up to the final line up for exit and already figured out that Mel's nerves were hitting a fever pitch with his meet-up with Gina.

Being the last to pack up his bookbag and finding himself by what seemed to be a classroom-length away from his friend at the front of the line, he bartered with Kevin to cut, as he was second in line. "Kev, you still want those Sour Squeezes from lunch? I got a whole pack of cherry left," Carter asked. Kevin, never one to turn down the candy of choice amongst all of the kids, took Carter's offer and his cue, allowing him to step in front and assume his spot in line. Clearing his throat, inconspicuously he said, “So, you ready, man?”. Mel turned around slightly startled and responded with a nervous sigh, “Yeah, I guess so.” As the words left his mouth, Mel could see Karina in the middle of the girls’ line talking with Gina, who was holding the folded paper from earlier. Both girls briefly paused their conversation and looked over in the direction of Mel and Carter, immediately emitting a small laugh before returning to their current topic.

Mel, still having flashbacks of the previous debacle he fell victim to from Karina’s meddling before, immediately confided in his friend. “See, Carter, it’s all a little game to her. Let’s just hit up Red Hot’s and chill on our way home. I’m not about to look stupid again.” “Chill, Mel, chill,” Carter reassured Mel. “Look, if it makes you feel any better, I’ll go with you. Let me run game on Karina. That’ll leave you to be able to chop it up with Gina and see what’s really happening. I got you, man.” Only seconds after Carter’s pledge to aid his friend, the school bell rang out again, allowing for the kids to begin their exit out of the school. “Ok, young scholars. We’re headed out. Don't forget the tests that we have tomorrow in Math and English. I'm not curving scores this time. No matter how many packs of Sour Squeezes or rare sports cards you try to offer me." Mr. Dewels looked at Carter and Mel via his peripherals with a smirk, while small laughs could be heard from their classmates.

Mr. Dewels was indeed the coolest teacher at Southview – a sports legend to the boys and the center of attention to the girls. Having grown up in the neighborhood, many knew him and his family from his exploits on the hardwood and football field. After a star-studded rise through the high school and college ranks, his professional career was cut short by injuries. Wisely heeding the advice of his parents, who were community educational stalwarts and known professors at nearby Cuyahoga Valley State University, he pursued degrees in education and became a teacher once his athletic aspirations dissolved. Mr. Dewels had taken resolve in the fact that he was looked up to by so many and, in his short tenure at the school, was revered by his peers on the staff and throughout the community.

It was no secret that there was value in the fact that Mr. Dewels also stood out the way that he did. As one of the few male figures within a staff predominantly staffed by women, the spotlight on him brightened, being immersed in a community where positive male figures were not as present. As a result, many single mothers readily signed up their children for his afterschool program he founded, providing mentorship and additional tutoring. It also was in his favor that many of those same mothers set their sights on him as the top bachelor in the area. There were many declaring their attraction to the former star-athlete turned teacher who managed to closely maintain the physical attributes that drew additional attention during his high school and college years. This same attention garnered the school-girl crushes and admiration of many of the boys in his classroom well throughout the school. Mr. Dewels was the teacher everybody wanted to be around.

As the school bell approached its final dings, Derrick, the student with the class' highest grades, ran up to the front of the line flailing a stapled set of papers. “Mr. Dewels,” Derrick exclaimed with an inexplicable shortness of breath from a mere 4 or 5 steps of movement. “You forgot to collect the Math test from Monday. I know that I only got an A-, but I got my Mom to sign it after she made me promise to do better. Here’s mine!” Several of the students let out a collective moan of disappointment, in hope that they had escaped the need to return the test that the class had taken earlier this week. Because of the overall poor performance and the pressure to improve the math skills overall in the seventh grade, this was especially important since it was the year before the mandated state testing. Mr. Dewels gave the test results to the students for them to take them home to their parents and have them signed. Somehow, Mr. Dewels had forgotten to collect these tests earlier, leaving the concerned students to believe that they had gained unmerited reprieve. Derrick, in his zeal to redeem himself in his own self-assessed failure, would not allow that to happen. Clearly, many of his classmates were not on the same wavelength.

"Wow. Thanks, Derrick. Very responsible of you to remind me of this one. Scholars, please hand these to me before you walk out." Mel thankfully remembered to get his test signed. It wasn't his worst work, but certainly not his best. The C+ that he presented to his parents was met with a removal of his video games and no access to his bike for one week, but could have garnered a much harsher punishment. Mel handed his signed test sheets to Mr. Dewels, meeting his look of respect with his own of disappointment. Carter, bent on one knee in front of his bookbag, furiously looked for the test unable to find it. He quickly sped to his desk to see if it was somehow misplaced in his organized confusion of a filing system. As the lines filed out of the classroom, almost everybody managed to meet the given objective, to the surprise of many, including Mr. Dewels. Meanwhile, Mel stood across the hallway waiting for his friend and interference-runner to join him for his rendezvous with Gina. It was not looking good. To make matters worse, when Regina had gotten to the front of the line where Mr. Dewels stood, rather than hand in the test sheets, she began to offer an explanation. Carter was unable to clearly hear most of what was said, but what rang out clearer than anything was

Mr. Dewels saying, "Well, Ms. Vincent, you have detention today for one hour. Responsibility nets rewards, recklessness nets repercussion." The infamous "RNR Speech" always spelled doom for anybody who was the intended audience of it. This definitely spelled doom for the after-school plans of whoever was on the receiving end of it today. Apparently, it was a two-for-one opportunity, with Karina pleading her case right behind Regina, minus the usual confidence she wielded beyond her 12-year-old parameters.

With the majority gone, the "RNR Speech" had now been targeted at four students, which included Gina, Karina, Darryl, and Carter, who snuck a gaze past the group to his now-abandoned friend in the hallway. Within that same moment, as other classrooms completed their exodus out of Southview Point Academy, Gina mouthed to Mel, silently, "Sorry." Mel was "sorry" too, disappointed that he would still be left with no answer to the question that lingered since recess earlier today – "does Gina really like me?" As Mr. Dewels ushered the students down the hall to the detention room in silence, with their belongings in tow, Mel walked in the opposite direction, looking over his shoulder, almost tripping over the extra desk that was placed in the hallway beside the sixth-grade classroom for students displaced for a period for bad behavior. Mel was disappointed and confused, all at the same time. Tomorrow, or maybe next week, depending on the punishments that could come out of this, could not get here soon enough.

Chapter 5

Mel stood perplexed. It had been a little over five years since he had even seen Karina, and to further confuse matters, he had not had this phone number no more than a few months. He recently changed it due to a rash of blocked calls that became too much to live with. The $15 fee to change his phone number was a drop in the bucket compared to the ocean-sized annoyance that had picked up in the months leading to upcoming elections. How did she get this number and what could she want? With time ticking away, Mel decided to revisit the questions around this unexpected text message, tucking his phone back into his pocket, exiting the back door, and jumping in his car to head to Blessed Hope.

Upon parking, before he could get out of the car, Carrell, spotted him almost 20 feet away from the rec room entrance and raced to Mel. "Mel, I thought you weren't going to make it. I heard you and U.C. were still hooping at the King," said a relieved and excited Carrell. "Someone was at the game and was showing it live online. How you miss that easy shot, man? It. Was. A. FREE-THROW!" With a brief laugh, Carter replied, “Rell, give me a second to get out of my whip, man. Sheesh, it’s not like you have much going on with that little ‘can’t get right’ looking jumper you got.” “Whatever, man, I can still cross you on the court. I been working since the last time we hooped. Hope your ankles ready for that work this time,” exclaimed Carrell. Carter immediately retorted playfully, “Video games don’t count, little scrub! Especially since you play on ‘Rookie’ level.” Immediately, Carter gave dap and embrace to Carrell. The exchange was a normal dynamic to their relationship at almost every meeting.

The two walked into the rec room and gymnasium at Blessed Hope and were immediately greeted by Chris. “Mel, what’s good, bro? Glad you could make it. Got a little worried when I didn’t get a response from my text earlier. Plus, I saw you brick-laying at the King online. You leaving school and pursuing masonry, huh?” he playfully asked. “You got jokes, huh? Ok, ok,” Mel responded, while giving a similar handshake with Chris. “But for real, glad you could make it because I might need to step out for an emergency meeting that Pastor is calling me into. Gonna need you to hold things down tonight for game night, if you don't mind. Same stuff as usual." Mel nodded, "I got you, brother. Just hold *me* down and call my Moms to let her know that I had to put in extra work at the church. Call it even, then." Chris chuckled, "No doubt, man. Anything to keep the 'work for food and shelter' agreement going. I already know." Chris handed a small set of keys to Mel, looked at his phone and began to walk to the Pastor's office, in the direction of the church's administrative area, leaving Mel and Carrell.

Mel walked into the open doors, leading to the gymnasium and saw all of the other children and fellow mentors running around. There were almost thirty mentees in attendance, with a little more than half of mentors in number. Mel was relieved to be one of the few mentors only committed to one. This program was growing, so he realized that it was more than likely that his role would balloon to one or more additional mentees. As much of a handful as Carrell could be, especially on game night, just the idea sometimes caused a hypothetical face-palm. Mel loved what he was able to contribute, but sometimes felt drained from the commitment. However, he found himself rejuvenated when he saw the smiles on their faces, not to mention the frequent text messages that he would get from Carrell, updating him on his grades and other 12-year-old exploits.

With no actual games being played, Mel immediately went to the sports equipment closet to retrieve the ball basket, giving the crowd tools to enjoy the monthly affair. Basketballs bounced and chit-chatter slowed down, being drowned out by the excitement that was about to take place. The freshly-redone gymnasium shined under the newly-installed LED lighting, making this grade-school sized venue a basketball paradise for hoopers, even at Mel's age. This monthly meeting was an event that every mentee looked forward to, as most of them were aspiring athletes and many were intent on getting on the hardcourt. While a few sat on the chairs, focused in on their phones or tablets, the majority of the children clamored to the court, first challenging their mentors, in an effort to show off new moves learned since their last duel. Mentors like Mel refused to hold back, standing up to the youthful challengers, regardless of the age gap.

Mel felt the familiar tap on his back. "Carrell, I already told you that there's not enough ACE bandages to help those ank..." Mel's words faded into a halted stop, as he turned around and realized that the tap on his shoulder was from none other than Regina. "Gina, uh...what's up? I didn't expect to see you here," Mel effortlessly lied. "Well, I'm up here to help with game night. Chris asked me to help cover for him while he took care of some important business," Regina replied with a slight smile. "Was this a set up", Mel thought to himself. "I knew that I was hoping to see her, but what kind of strings was my guardian angel pulling to make this happen." Mel quickly replied, "Well, I guess he got you caught up, too. He just went to the back for some meeting he had to get to. You staying the whole time?" "Yeah, I guess I can do that now, especially since my sisters are using me to get out of the house from being on punishment. You know, my parents lighten up a little when big sis is in charge. I've never been put in charge of this before, so what all do we have to do," Regina asked with a slight confused look. Mel confidently replied, "Aw, its nothing much. Let the kids run around, we pull them in for the Halftime Huddle, our Mentor/Mentee one-on-ones, and then we grab whatever pizza or food they get delivered here. I got you, though."

Mel knew that this meeting just had to be predestined. As he walked to the scorer's table that sat at mid-court of the gymnasium, the basketball bounces became less audible, with echoes of the good memories that he had formed with Regina. As vivid moments between the two played as an instant cinema in his mind, he was interrupted by Carrell, who excitedly brought his expected challenge to Mel. "Play me in 21, Mel. Bet you twenty that I get to at least 10 this time!", Carrell confidently exclaimed. Mel offered a slight laugh before responding, "But that's not winning, C. I'm not about to front you twenty for participating and this is church, fool. Just take the ball out and let's get this run in real quick. Gina, I'll be right back." Regina slyly responded, "Ok, Mel, don't let your mentee have you looking like you did at the King. You know I got Carter on speed dial." The day was not even over yet and he still could not live that pickup game down. Mel dropped his head playfully, then looked at Regina saying, "Now see, you just got lil' man shut down to no points for that. Carrell, you can blame her for this beatdown.

I'm blocking shots, ripping you, showing no mercy! Let's go! Take it out." And Carrell dribbled in to start their game, with the night beginning to take shape.

Chapter 6

"Melvin! Telephone!"

"Telephone," Mel wondered. His curiosity kicked in because as far as he knew, he was still on punishment and had absolutely no access to the finer amenities of life, which for kids his age included being able to talk on the phone. "Melvin, come get this phone before I change my mind," his mother yelled. As Mel rushed down the stairs to the cordless phone base, his mother handed him the phone. "It's Quincy. You have exactly fifteen minutes. He has to go over those scriptures that you need to recite for the program at church. From what he said, the ministry team changed them up and won't have another rehearsal in time. Here," she said as she handed the phone to Mel. Mel was overridden with confusion still, but accepted the phone with a respectful "ok" and proceeded back upstairs to see what all Quincy had to share.

"Hey, Q! What's up, man?" "Yo, Mel, you'll never believe how it went down after you left today, man!" That voice was *not* Q – it was none other than Carter. How did he manage to pull this illicit call off? His mom knew the voice of every person who called their home – it was a short list, after all. “Carter? Is this you?” Mel asked. “And, me, too. Carter needed to call you and you know your moms’ll let you talk to me, especially if it’s got something to do with church,” Q chimed in. It all made sense now. Carter obviously called Q, then Q called Mel on three-way to get the call through, and *voila*, they pulled it off! This is only the second time that they have tried this and Mel was afraid that they were pushing their luck, testing the prophetic and discerning gifts that Mel’s mom seemed to have. Mel could hear the tick-tocks of the fifteen minutes he was granted for this forbidden mission, so he chose to act fast.

“Mel, Mel, Mel…”, Carter said in a stretched out manner, drawing in Mel’s anticipation. “You won’t believe what went down today in detention. I gotta be quick because my parents went out to the store real quick and they’ll give me the business if they catch me on this phone.” “Ok, so spit it out, man!” Mel demanded. Carter reveled in Mel’s anticipation. As great a friend as he considered himself, there was a twisted satisfaction in being in possession of something Mel was on the edge of his seat to know. However, he knew his time was limited with the penitentiary-type chance he was taking by reaching out to his friend. “Bro, Gina is for real…” Carter started. Mel interrupted with wonder and excitement, “For real?” Carter finished, “…I think.” Mel went from the mountain top of hope to the valley of despair, in one fell swoop. Q could not sit on the phone idle any longer and inquired, “Hey y’all, who is Gina?” Carter rebounded, “Q, only the baddest girl in our class, man! And she’s feeling Mel…I think.” “There you go again! Carter, what happened, man? You really trippin’ right now with this *I think, I think*”, mimicked Mel in a deep exaggerated voice.

“Aight, aight. What I’m saying is that for the half-hour of being stuck in detention…” Carter started. Mel immediately interrupted, curious, “Half-hour? How did you get out early? That hour is brutal, bro!” Carter, beginning to become irritated with the interruptions, responded, “If you’d let me finish, I’ll tell you. What I was trying to tell you is that my mom came up with the signed test, since she signed it, but forgot to give it back to me after that super-long lecture she gave me about test grades being important and blah-blah-blah.” Carter cooled down as he continued, “She gave Mr.

Dewels the test and he let me out early when she told him that she knew." "Pfft...you got off easy then!" exclaimed Mel. "Easy? Mel, if I have to hear my Mom quote Mr. Dewels RNR speech again..." Carter's eyes could be heard rolling as he said those words.

"You got ten minutes, Mel!" Mel's Mom's voice bellowed through the stairway to his room. "Carter, just tell me what happened, man. Get to it!" Mel demanded. "Ok, look, you already know that there wasn't any talking going on in there, but I do have this note that Gina told me to give to you – and it was good," Carter replied, with a justified smile creeping up. Mel's face turned, "Bro, how you gon' read a note that was for me?" Q, siding with his cousin, said "Yeah, man. That's fouler than a dead skunk." "Q, chill, I had to make sure that the letter wasn't on some crazy stuff. I was looking out," explained Carter. "Anyway, she was explaining that she really likes you and she dropped her phone number, so BAM!" Mel fought the smile that was beginning to form, maintaining his composure, saying "Aight, man. 'Preciate you for looking out. Next time, just run me my note. I'm grown and can handle it myself. So what's her number?" Mel asked. "Bro, you still on lockdown. I'll get you the note when we see each other in school. Chill. It's a done deal," advised Carter to his friend. "Messed up part is that I'm still in trouble at home and I turned in my test sheet, signed and everything."

Mel sat there confused, but excited to know that this actually might be a real opportunity to go with Regina. Hearing steps aggressively coming up the steps, Mel immediately blurted out "Ok, Q. So, Proverbs 18:24 and Romans 8:28, right? That's one from the Old *and* New Testament. And that's it right?" Q knew his cue to respond and said "Yup. That's all you have to know and you'll be cool." Mel angled the phone in a way for his Mom to hear the call, while Carter instinctively hung up, realizing what Mel was doing. "Quincy, Mel's gotta go. He has some chores to get to!" bellowed Mel's mother. "Ok Q, good looking out," Mel said as he hung up. Mel subdued his excitement of having a girlfriend, so it seemed. Oddly, he felt a bit of sympathy for the others who were served detention. As that feeling sat for a few seconds, he returned to the good news that Carter brought. Maybe there is some light at the end of the tunnel. Now he had to go and read those scriptures that he blurted out, to make the ruse seem real in the eyes of his Mom. Before he could reach for his Bible, he heard, however, "I'm not playing. Get that broom and that mop. The kitchen is waiting for you!" "Oh, well. Only a little ways to go until this punishment would be over and done with," thought an optimistic Mel, as he honored his mother's inevitable commands.

Chapter 7

A few of the children from the game night program had disappeared from the gymnasium. Contrary to what Mel thought, basketball and rampant running in the gym was not on the minds of all of the children in attendance. It was getting close to the "Halftime Huddle" where mentors and mentees gathered for a small message from the featured speaker. Rich, one of the mentors, approached Mel out of breath, "Hey, man, I don't know where some of these kids ran off too, but I've been all over the building and can't find not even one of 'em. You got any ideas?" Mel already knew the answer, and, without verbal response immediately walked towards the tool shed that sat on the opposite end of the parking lot, bordering the small field in close proximity to the church. The widened stretch of church property made it easy for the kids to be elusive, but Mel had been made privy to the frequent escape tactic. In fact, he was sure that he would know who he would see once he arrived.

"Lawrence! Come on, man! Every time, bro! Let's go, the Huddle's about to start!" exclaimed Mel. "Larry! Call me Larry! How many times do I have to tell you, man?" retorted Lawrence. Lawrence detested the full stretch of his given name. It was an unavoidable formality, being the son of Blessed Hope's senior pastor, Pastor Kingsley. The name carried prestige in the city for a number of reasons. Reasons including the incredible growth of the church under Pastor Kingsley's leadership, but countered by the many run-ins Lawrence, or Larry, as he preferred to be called, found himself in on a very frequent basis. The joke spread throughout the church was that LK, Lawrence's initials, proved to be the "typical" PK (preacher's kid). This moment was shaping up to bolster that unfavorable perception.

"And I'm not even the only one here. Look at everyone else. Always singling me out. Man!" Lawrence always appeared to have a chip on his shoulder. His short responses to even the mildest of inquiries always kept everyone on edge. The smell of a scented cigar emanated in the vicinity, with failed attempts to disguise coughs to try to cover up for the smoking that was taking place prior to Mel's expose'. "Everybody, get back to the gym. The Huddle's about to start. Lawrence, I'll let Pastor Chris know what happened and he'll deal with you later," Mel said in an authoritative fashion. "Rich, follow them in before they do something else crazy. Thanks, man."

As Mel began to follow the small group headed towards the Huddle, he felt a vibration on his thigh. "Oh, I forgot to respond to that text from Karina," Mel quickly remembered. He retrieved his phone from his pocket and saw the same unfamiliar number, but instead of a text message, it was now an incoming call. Mel debated on whether or not he should answer. Besides, he was the one in charge tonight and could not allow things to fall off of the rails again, like it just did. On the other hand, Mel could not shake the curiosity that he felt when he first saw the original message. And maybe, just maybe, it is something important that he needed to...*buzz...buzz*. Mel's cycle of thoughts was interrupted by the continued vibrating, forcing him to make a decision. Before he could answer, the vibrating stopped, and within a few seconds a voicemail symbol came up on the phone screen. Mel resolved that he would check the voicemail message after the game night.

Mel started towards the gym, in not too far distance from the group that started their march only moments ago. Mel's rampant thoughts started up again and he could not make sense of why Karina was reaching out to him and also if it really was the same girl who proved to be the bane of his existence during their elementary years. There was just no telling with Karina. While they did not remain the worst of enemies as they transitioned into high school, they did not instantly become the best of friends, either. To the best of his knowledge, Regina did not talk much with her or at all at around the same time, since the word was that she moved away to another city, ceasing communications with almost everybody. Rumors ran wild in the community, but even with the deepest depths of their relationship, Mel did his best to not feed into them or assume the worst of Karina. The activity of those rumors did fade away over the years, so it was concluded that the legend of Karina was finally dissipated.

Mel approached the gymnasium, seeing the group congregating at center court. By this time, Pastor Chris reappeared, walking from the administrative offices, with a serious look. He immediately transformed his face, remembering the many times he chided the church youth, especially Lawrence, about showing themselves friendly. Regina stood in the gym looking at her phone with a puzzled look on her face, stirring the confusion within Mel as he entered the rear entrance that was rarely used. "What's up, Gina? Look like something's wrong," asked Mel, trying to piece together the non-verbal cues he quickly observed. "I keep getting calls from this number that I don't recognize. I've had this number forever, so anybody calling me that *I* want to talk to – their number will show up 'cause it's saved," Regina responded with a cutting of her eye, regaining her assertiveness. Mel's curiosity pushed the investigative agenda, "Yeah, you have had that number for a minute. You know it's election time and these calls are coming in like crazy. Had to change up my number. Anyway, what number is it? It might be the same one that I couldn't shake."

Regina responded slyly, "Yeah, right. You probably only changed your number because them lil' girls you got calling you now. But, naw, here's the number." Mel peered over at the call log on Regina's phone. The screen showed a list of the ten most recent calls, with five of them having had come within the past two hours – all with the same number that Mel saw with the text attached with Karina's name from earlier. Was this a coincidence? Was this the same person – and was this really Karina? The questions echoed in Mel's brain at rapid-pace. "What – you recognize this number? Can't believe dude think he's winning this election, as bad as his reputation is," said Regina, referring to the election season call theory. Mel answered, tentatively, "Um...real talk, I got a call and a text from this same, exact number. Came through today, as a matter of fact." Regina's face returned to the puzzled state Mel saw when he reentered the gymnasium. Before the summit over the mysterious number could continue, Pastor Chris came over to Mel, seeking a quick recap of what he missed.

"So, uh...with the cigar smoke that came through the administrative offices window, I guess Larry was off in the back smoking again, huh," said Pastor Chris, with little to no surprise. "So you just call him Larry now, huh," Mel said with laughter. "I didn't *see* him with it in his hand or on his lips, but I'd be a fool if I didn't put two and two together, man. *Lawrence* was looking as suspect as he always does, attitude and all." "Ok, I got a handle on it. Thanks for holding things down for me. This dude..." Pastor Chris trailed off, shaking his head over the thought of having to report to his boss and spiritual father that his son had yet again been at the center of controversy. Sometimes he felt more like Lawrence's probation office than he was the role of the church's youth pastor. Pastor Kingsley depended on Chris heavily, as the demand placed on him of a growing ministry prevented him from dealing with his son as directly as he would have liked.

Pastor Chris collected himself and called all of the mentors and mentees in attendance, drawing them to the center court. "Alright, alright, y'all, let's get it together. We're about to get this thing going tonight. Let get it," exclaimed Pastor Chris, with a forced excitement. As the last of his unnatural call to action exited his mouth, the crowd began to file in, the bouncing balls began to lessen in volume, with Lawrence standing in the outer circle of the group, attempting to be out of the scope of Pastor Chris. As he maintained a tough exterior, the last thing Lawrence wanted was to have his name brought up to his father, who has repeatedly threatened sending him away to live with his grandmother in the countryside. Pastor Chris continued, “Tonight’s talk will be a little different. Believe it or not, my plans got changed after a meeting I just had. Really need for everyone to give me your attention. Tonight’s huddle is going to be as real as it’s ever been.” The message was aided with a serious tone that no one in attendance had ever heard from Pastor Chris before.

“Aw, man. I’m just trying to hoop before I gotta go home. Come on, ma…”, exclaimed Carrell, who was immediately given a serious look from Mel. Carrell immediately responded with abrupt silence, respecting the silent strike down from his mentor and quickly holding the basketball upon the last bounce from his dribble. Mel had gotten to know Pastor Chris very well and could tell that this talk was going in a much different direction from other Friday nights. Even as a mentor, he, too, was intrigued with what Pastor

Chris had on his agenda. The intrigue appeared to be shared by the rest of the others in the gymnasium at Blessed Hope, with a focus to a speech never given before on a Friday night. Pastor Chris took a brief sigh, which he hoped no one else could hear, before he reluctantly started on his impromptu speech before the now-captive audience.

Chapter 8

"Carter, you understand the new plays that Coach was talking about? Man, I missed *one* day of practice and it was like I missed everything," Mel said annoyed. Carter replied arrogantly, "Couldn't be talking to me. Ain't no Carter here. Now, U.C. – I can vouch for him. But, not Carter. No, sir! I have no doubt that *U.C.* would know the new plays!" Carter was still reveling in a show-stopping game against their school's rival, Barner High, where he had a statline that had the city buzzing, along with hitting the game-winning shot. 42 points, 12 rebounds, 5 assists, and 1 steal short of a triple-double feat – indeed, the crowd had seen something special that night. Sitting in the chairs of Memorial High's gymnasium, just days after the surreal moment, it felt like it had just happened.

"Here you go again," Mel shook his head, unsurprised by his superstar friend and teammate's response. "I just need to know if I need to set the pick closer to the elbow or nearer to the block. Remember, it's not an official nickname unless someone else gives it to you. 'U.C.' makes it sound like you thirsty to go to the University of Cincinnati or something. We got two years before college, bro. Chill." Carter responded with a smirk and shrug, "But, Mel, it's not my fault that the newspaper called me 'unstoppable'. I mean, you can't tell me that I didn't shut down the gym that night. Everybody's talkin'! Bet you I even got your girl Gina on my team. Matter of fact..." Carter playfully looked at his cell phone and widened his eyes. "I knew I missed some calls. She know good and well that I have to go to practice and I don't have but so many minutes to use with everybody calling me now after last Friday," Carter said, teasing his friend.

"Whoa, whoa – chill 'U.C.' or whatever you wanna call yourself," responded a now-offended Mel. "Yeah, you got off on Barner, no doubt, but leave my girl out of it. We already know you got everybody hollarin', thinkin' you the next big thing." "'Cause I am bro," said a laughing Carter. "But I ain't mean to make you feel some kind of way, man. I'm just playing, I got you on the new plays. And I definitely wasn't trying to diss your girl. Y'all cool?" "Yeah, man, it's all good," said a now-relaxed Mel. "I ain't trippin'. You need to help me focus on these plays, though. We still have the playoffs to worry about and with that game, you definitely like your boy out here – all eyes on me." Mel playfully hummed the melody of the song of the same name in a joking manner. Carter quickly responded in a serious tone, "All eyes on *us*, bro. I know I was hitting, but I'm not forgetting my team. Ride or die, homie!"

Carter, in all of his confidence had an innate ability to bring himself down to earth. This was something that was fed into him from his father, who even in his absence, knew his son would be great. Carter's father's encouragement was from a young age, as he had split from his mom, never meeting face-to-face, having only communicated with his son through letters. These letters were written from before his birth and were sent almost every other month, starting a month before Carter's birth. Carter's mom saved the letters and gave them to him to read at around the age of 7, per his father's request. Every letter he wrote to Carter gave nuggets of wisdom. "Son, no matter how great you get, keep God first," many of his ending lines would say. A few of his latter letters to Carter would have a sobering final request from his father, "And you're still too young to understand this, but have your mother show you these bible verses: 1 Chronicles 4:9-13, Jeremiah 29:11 and 1 Corinthians, chapters 6 and 7. That last one is one that I memorized and kept close to me. I hope you do, too. Maybe it'll keep you out of trouble better than it did me. I'll be there one day to visit you, though, to see if you know them. Until then, just know that I love you and I'm thinking of you. Love you, Carter." Unfortunately, his father never did return, with no true explanation given as to where he was and why he and Carter's mother went their separate ways. The letters remained keepsakes of a man who he would likely never get to know.

Carter was not without parental guidance, however, having his mother and stepfather who became the only tangible father figure to whom he was regularly accustomed. Mrs. Wilkins-Harris made it clear to Carter that no child of hers would be arrogant or too full of themselves, having countless conversations around the dinner table after many games where she saw her son standing out from his peers, starting from elementary years. While many were quick to celebrate Carter, seeing his athletic star begin to shine bright even in the early stages, his mother was quick to keep her aspiring basketball player away from becoming overconfident. Knowing where his talents came from, she knew all too well how high the attention could take someone and how hard the fall to the bottom could be when things did not work out as hoped for. As exciting as games like the one Carter just had against Barner were, he always knew that his biggest fan would also be his biggest dose of humble gravity, pulling him back down to earth. Still, Carter got his gloats in while out of her presence.

And just like that, Carter smirked and said, "And besides, the only play you need to have in *your* bag is 'U.C. G's Up'. You already know that whatever I can do at the King, I can do anywhere, anytime – off top! Coach, you, and the rest of the squad can fit on these shoulders, easy." Carter slowly and confidently looked at his developing shoulders, still sore from the consecutive sets of bench-presses done earlier in the morning. Mel shook his head, but chuckled in a reluctant mode of agreement. In fact, his best friend had the talent that was hard to deny. All eyes *were* on him, indeed. With the basketball queries all coming back to the confidence in the school's star player, Mel opted to change the course of the conversation to a new topic. "Hey man, you still taking Karina to the winter formal?" As abrupt as the question was, Carter sat hardly surprised, calmly responding, "Depends. You finally stop acting scary and ask Gina to get back with you?" Mel was unprepared to answer.

Stuttering, Mel said, "We...we...well, I mean, we – bruh, we good. We just need a lil' time, that's all. Don't know if I'd have the ends to pay for clothes and flowers for the formal, anyway. Might be a way out for me, real talk." Mel felt that he rebounded well from what he felt was an onslaught of inquisition. "Dude, you trippin'. You already know dudes been tryin' to get at her since they heard y'all stopped talking for a minute. Word is Ricky Mack is trying to take her to the formal. Don't worry about me and mine. Better watch out for your own – I'm good with mine!" "I'm straight, C. I just thought I'd ask since Karina's been M.I.A. the last few weeks. I know you said she was sick with something, but I was seeing if something was up, that's all." Suddenly, Carter found himself on the defensive, but did not want to be too generous with whatever information it was suspected that he knew. "She's cool, Mel. My fault for getting at you about Gina. I was just looking out," said Carter, with a retreated stance in the conversation.

Behind his subdued response, Carter was concerned about Karina. Despite the spotted reputation from prior years in elementary and middle school, they had gotten close, reuniting towards the end of their freshman year and starting to go out on dates at the beginning of sophomore year. Both went to different schools, but they made every attempt to see and talk with each other covering the gap that existed. Late night phone calls, the frequent texts – both were in a state of bliss neither could, or cared to, explain to themselves or anyone else. At first the new relationship did not sit well with Mel, who initially saw it as betrayal. However, it was Regina who convinced him that years had passed and he should give this all a chance. Regina's perspective was unique, considering that she, too, had become distanced from Karina over the course of time since their days at Southview. Mel had come to accept that his best friend in the whole wide world had potentially found his interests set upon his long-time rival. This was a life-lesson of biblical proportions.

Carter's concern was wrapped around the end of his conversation with Karina last Friday night. The last words she said were cryptic and left him with more questions than answers. In the alternating of tears and awkward silences, Karina said things like "might have to go" and "haven't been feeling good", which were nondescript and lacked any and all details. Carter asked again and again, trying to understand what could be wrong and how he could help, but it was to no avail. The feelings that he had for Karina had grown strong in a short amount of time, but he felt helpless and in the few minutes that this pattern stretched out, Karina finally composed herself to say after a deep breath, "I'm going to stay with my auntie down south, but I don't know when I'm leaving. All I know is that my mom is making plans and I can't stop her. I'll tell you when I know something. I love you, C."

Carter was not expecting those words, particularly the last four that entered into his hearing. Carter's immediate reaction was to respond with a similar response, but before he could utter the mid-syllable of “love”, he heard the line click, signaling that Karina had indeed hung up. The questions and confusion that ran through Carter’s head was rampant. While he did not know exactly everything he wanted to know, he also felt that he quite possibly could be part of the reason why Karina was going away. It was quite possible that the questions that he asked in succession internally already had answers to which he had parts in.

“Carter! You ready? We gotta go outside. My Mom’s here to scoop us!” Mel said, as he stood next to the gym exit, extending to the school parking lot. Carter snapped out of his momentary flashback, visibly shook his head, as if trying to wake himself up from a eyes-wide-open slumber, and gathered himself to leave with his friend. As he picked up his basketball and duffle bag, he peered in and saw a small glisten from a gold cross. The gold cross was the pendant given to him from his mother, who gifted the jewelry piece on the date of his graduation from eighth grade at Southview. The pendant was a gift with an inscription with a small quote – “If you can create problems, then you can create solutions”. This one time, as that inscription ran through his mind, looking at the cherished gift,

Carter suspected that he might not be able to fix *this* problem, this one time.

Chapter 9

"Pastor, this isn't good at all. Does Carter have any idea?" asked Pastor Chris, who still sat in the worn leather seat in Pastor Kingsley's office. "Son, keep your voice down. This news is still fresh off of the presses and is sure to create problems that I'm not sure how we're going to handle," responded Pastor Kingsley with an instructive tone. He pointed at his cell phone, "That phone call came through, showing restricted on the caller ID, and I knew – I just knew – that something crazy was coming to the surface. Chris, what do you think?" Pastor Chris pondered the given question and intently looked into the direction of a corner of the office, bordered by one of the heavily stocked bookcases of the Pastor's personal library. Indeed, this Friday went from the typical night with the kids to a potential catastrophe, unexpected to all.

"Ok, so, like you said – you got a phone call from a blocked number. The person is saying that they had a baby by...Carter?" asked a still-shocked Chris. "Yup," responded Pastor Kingsley, with a sigh and nestling of his forehead between his thumb and index finger. "And they're saying that the baby is almost 3 years old?" Chris' question increased with astonishment. He was merely repeating the details as they had been given to him, but could not fathom how it could actually be true. Carter simply could not be the father of this child. His athletic aspirations and reputation in the community just seemed to be too much to be put at risk. Yet, he was unsurprised at the possibility, as the youth with whom he was charged with serving as a mentor for had challenges no different from those outside of the church walls. Chris had become accustomed with the reality that his ministry's foundational scripture, John 17:15. He knew that although they were *in* the world, that it would be important to do all that they could to not be *of* it. This was an apparent test of this call to action.

"Don't know who the girl is or nothing. All we know is that she's calling us and says she wants Carter to step up. I told her to call Carter, but she cut me off before I could get the last words out. Something's up with this girl, Chris, I just know it," Pastor Kingsley reiterated his stance again, with a shaking, pointing finger. "No name, no phone number – before I could get anything out of her, she tells me that she'll be in touch and that we need to get a hold of Carter, immediately. Chris, do you know who this could be? You done seen Carter with his relationships before and as far as I know, this young man didn't take it this far with *anybody*, did he?" "Pastor, let me keep it real with you," responded Pastor Chris. "Carter was really no different than any of our other kids. Only difference was that he loved basketball more than anything else, so he kept his nose clean, if you know what I mean."

"No," Pastor Kingsley responded, inquisitively. "I don't know what you mean. Break it down for me, son." "Pastor – Carter, Melvin, all these kids are going to do what they're gonna do. The big advantage that our kids have is that they have us showing them who Christ is, giving them the blueprint. I know you, I, and all of the rest of the church don't want none of our kids cuttin' up and doing like these other kids out here, but facts are facts – they do what they do." Pastor Chris allowed for a brief pause to allow his spoken reality to soak in to Pastor's hearing. He knew that this truth was not ignorant to Pastor Kingsley, but with the reputation of himself and the church in the community and beyond, there was a small hope that somehow the youth of his church was different. True enough, some issues of premarital sexual activity had arisen or visible instances of teen or unexpected pregnancy had become a part of the church chatter, but, often due to the consistently full agenda that lay before him, Pastor Kingsley was not fully aware.

Before Pastor Chris could continue, Pastor Kinglsey interrupted, "Ok, Chris, but that's why we have these programs in place, why we built the addendum to the church, got ourselves more deeply involved in the community. As a matter of fact, that's why I put you into position to lead our youth ministry. This is the kind of thing that we were working to avoid. I know we all fall short, but come on, now, son." "And that's exactly my point, sir," Pastor Chris continued. "We *all* fall short. You gave me the ball and I ran with it. I prayed and prayed, not that I would exceed your expectations but that I would meet His. You saw through *my* shortcomings, having my first child when I was a young man in these streets and I had to go through I what went through to get here. All I'm saying, is that unfortunately the names change, but not the game." Chris spoke earnestly, having an embedded empathy for the ministry and the children in it, not being too far removed from his darker days. He was not speaking in defense, but more in an effort to bring awareness to the situation beyond spiritual parameters.

Pastor Kinglsey affixed his back to his chair, taking in what he heard, acknowledging the wisdom-filled response from Pastor Chris. He knew what Chris was like before he committed himself to a changed life. Seeing him that Sunday years ago in the second row of the balcony, with his hands holding his face and his eyes peering above his fingertips, despair and tear-filled, he knew that he had reached the end of his rope. As the service draw near to conclusion, Pastor Kingsley totally ignored his notes, deviated from the plotted sermon, and spoke with the conviction in his heart of what he felt at the moment. Calling for an altar call, the congregation unexpectedly sat in silence, appearing to be as immobile as feet planted in aged cement. As he continued to implore those in attendance, Pastor Kingsley began to wonder if he indeed was on the threshold of an unanswered altar call. Though he had seen it happen before, he just knew that this message was for somebody, even if it was just for one. Perhaps he should have just stuck to the script, done his benediction, and enjoyed the Sunday afternoon that remained.

As the slight sentiment of doubt began to gain momentum, Chris made his way from the balcony, moving with purpose towards the front of the church. He fought tears from flooding his face and lay in surrender at the foot of the stage, only feet away from Pastor Kingsley, who saw his faith seemingly rewarded before his very eyes. An elder of the church moved to minister Chris, but Pastor Kingsley gave instruction by way of a raised hand that he, himself, would minister to, who appeared to be, a tired and frustrated young man. Before he could start his prayer, one by one, the number at the altar began to increase, with a large majority being the youth of the church, doing similarly as Chris. It was at that moment that Pastor's spiritual discernment compelled him to share a revelation with Chris, speaking intently in his ear, "Son, whatever you are going through is not, and I repeat, *not* about you, nor is it in vain. It's for a season and reason bigger than you know." Chris did not look up, but remained in his vulnerable position, seeking relief from whatever burdened his young life. All he knew was that this was where he had to be.

Pastor Kingsley was aware that the youth of his community was hurting and that the church, as he had come to know it, probably would not be the most effective means. He had read books, visited conventions, brought in guest speakers, but nothing was making the impact that he wanted. It was at this moment, Pastor Kingsley realized that the answer to his prayers lay before him. The way that the youth of the church followed his lead to this altar call was symbolic of the calling that just had to be on his life. After a few minutes of prayer from Pastor and the elders of the church, Pastor Kingsley asked one of his armor bearers to have Chris meet with him after service. If his discernment was right, this was a divine moment that could set the youth ministry of this church and community off to another level never seen before. There was something different about Chris. Many times, he saw young men visit the church, hear, maybe even listen to, the message preached, but leave no different than how they came in. Repentance was heavy on this young man. As he had seen with the best of his members in their beginning stages, he appeared to be sick and tired of being sick and tired. Pastor Kingsley was drawn back to this beginning in the midst of this present-day crisis.

"Pastor, there's some things that you don't know. I wasn't trying to hide things from you, but as busy as you were, there just wasn't enough time to talk to you about every single instance. Being real, knowing what I know, it could definitely be a lot worse. God's been covering our kids in grace, more than you know. This may not be the best time, but let me get you up to speed on things," Pastor Chris said assuredly. "Mel is running the game night and can handle it for as long as necessary." Pastor Kingsley was not initially pleased, but wanted to give his young leader the opportunity to share his perspective and give clarity to what was going on at Blessed Hope, specifically with the youth. He wondered how had so much gone on without his knowledge, no hint of the issues that were unfolding within the church walls. To break down the tense environment that heightened, Chris began his impromptu presentation, "Ok, so Carter had a situation around the middle of his sophomore year, I think it was. He called me panicking, and..." Pastor Kingsley's phone rang, interrupting Chris in mid-sentence.

As unexpected as this call was as the last, this time, the number was not showing as "private", revealing a name and number on the caller ID. Looking at the phone vibrating on his desk, with a familiar name in clear view only to him, because of the privacy screen protector on his smartphone, Pastor Kingsley was intrigued. He picked up the phone, drawing it to his ear, saying to Chris before answering, "Son, you get back to the game night. I'd better take this call. We'll catch back up on this topic later on." Pastor Chris, slightly disappointed, but relieved and curious all at the same time, quickly got up from his seat and exited the office, "Yes, sir. Just let me know. Hope we can figure this thing out all the way." Chris closed the door wishing he could be a fly on the wall for the conversation about to ensue. In obedience, he quickly went back to resume his leadership of game night, in hopes that Mel did not lose control of the very active group of kids.

Chapter 10

"Maybe I shouldn't have bought these from the dollar store. This can't be right!", thought Karina, as her eyes widened at the small white stick in her hand. "Should I be looking for one line or two? Can't barely see the line on either one of these," she mumbled in a combination of confusion, disbelief, and anxiety. Small empty boxes sat on the bathroom floor, ripped open from the hurried opening upon Karina's entry back home. Karina frantically looked at the small white paper that was included identically in both boxes, seeking any hints on understanding what her eyes were seeing. The sole comfort in this moment was that she was alone, with her mother still at work. With her job recently asking her to work extra shifts, this made this Wednesday afternoon a little less tense.

Karina read the black and white print intently and frantically, "Likelihood of pregnancy is uncertain in the event of a faint line reading. Please take another test one week or later to be more certain of pregnancy status." "What...huh?" Karina stood frozen, with more questions running through her head than before. Tears began to fall from her eyes, navigating quickly over her cheeks. While uncertainty was the best she could gather from these tests that she just took, in her mind, all signs pointed to the answer she dreaded seeing up to this moment – she was pregnant. Standing in the bathroom, there was still a faint smell of the third episode of vomiting that took place that morning. As hard as she cleaned, even leaving the exhaust fan on while at school, the smell still lingered. Perhaps it was paranoia or just overthinking, but something just was not right.

Karina took herself to her bedroom and laid on her bed while her cries quieted, but still her thoughts ran rampant. "What do I do? Who do I talk to? Who can I tell?" Although she did not get a definitive answer from the tests that she just took, the presumption for her was clear enough. There was no way at all to prepare for this. Even worse, if her mother found out, it would be a catastrophe. She could remember the cautionary tales, using her own teenage pregnancy as the prime example of why she needed to wait. "Karina, Karina, Karina…if I don't do nothing right with you…don't get yourself caught up with these dirty lil' boys, actin' all fast!"

Karina could hear her mother's words with a hint of the southern drawl that her ancestry descended from. The words echoed in the walls of her mind, to no end.

She looked over at the mirror across the room and looked at a small picture printout from the photo booth in the video arcade at the mall. The three candid shots were boxed-in mementos of another Wednesday afternoon, only a few months ago. Looking at this piece of recent nostalgia, Karina took a deep breathe, realizing that a piece of the puzzle that she was in the midst of figuring out was likely in the shared space of those freeze frames. In the pictures were a mix of smiles and funny faces, shared between Karina and one other person. She was dressed in a royal blue t-shirt, but positioned herself in such a way that her torso was the only visible part. The picture poses to isolate her from the waist up was by grand design, as to keep her school uniform skirt out of view.

The moment that the pictures were taken was paralleled to this very day that she was in the midst of – Wednesday, after school, her mother working extra-shifts at work, giving her time to be left to her own devices. This was one of the times Karina would deviate from the direct instruction from her mother to go straight home and instead took the bus in the opposite direction to spend time at the mall. While she was not always able to be in the company of her friends, who appeared to have absolutely no restriction on their after-school ventures, she was determined to risk it all on this afternoon to go the popular hangout. Karina's priority to get to the mall was heightened due to the fact that she found herself in a new school. Left alone and separated from anyone with whom she had gone to school before, this was one of the prime opportunities to form new friendships, or at least have some fun since her mother appeared to become stricter since moving her away from Southview Academy.

On this particular day at the mall, as Karina sat at conjoined tables in the food court with 3 of her classmates, she looked over and saw a familiar face. The face brought a nostalgic relief for a moment, as she was still struggling to find a way to connect with the other girls there. Fashion tips were not the hot topic that she was hoping that it would be, as the discussion at the moment was centered around a popular television show that was only on cable tv – something that was not a fixture in her home. “Karina? Hey, what’s up?” the voice of the familiar face said. “Carter! Hey!”, Karina responded energetically, closing the 20-feet gap, leaving the table where she was sitting. Her previous company looked up to see to whom the fourth member of their troupe had darted off to. “How you been? I’m just chilling with my girls. I ain’t seen you in a minute.” It was more like a year. Carter remembered it clearly. Karina’s departure from Southview was abrupt and had everyone talking. The question remained unanswered – “where did Karina go?”

“That’s what’s up! You been alright? You the last person I thought I’d see today. I can’t get no hug, though?” Carter immediately asked, with his arms open, having placed his bag of sneakers immediately beside him on the ground for the proposed embrace. Karina laughed cynically, replying to the request, “Oh, I’m supposed to hug you now that I happen to see you one time? What would your boy Mel think of that? I’m sure he’d love that, huh?” Carter replied with a chuckle, “I see you ain’t forgot about Mel. Well, needless to say, I'm out here on a solo mission. Had to pick up some new shoes and, surprise, surprise – he decided to go straight home to get all on the phone with Gina. Guess you *and* me can catch a break today." Carter stood, still awaiting a response from Karina after giving her what he thought to be a compelling argument to comply with his request for a friendly embrace.

Karina gave a smirk and hugged her former classmate who had seemingly gotten taller since their last time seeing each other. "Dude, what you eating? I used to hug you and be right at your shoulder," Karina exclaimed. "You already know I'm a hooper, so I was gonna grow a little bit. God had to throw some inches on me so I could start dunking on everybody. If you'd come to my games you'd already know that, though," Carter said, slyly, with an air of confidence that had grown from his basketball exploits. "You still playing basketball, huh? It wasn't like you were any good," said Karina. She was well aware of how talented Carter was. Still, in this reintroduction, there was no way that she could allow her fondness of an old classmate lead anyone to believe that she had removed her guarded disposition. "Mel was even better than you, right?"

Carter laughed in response. This impromptu reunion had become comical to him. He found it to be pure coincidence and magic that he would run into Karina, of all people, on the one day that his best friend Mel would not be in his company. This was a good thing, too, as Mel still had a distrust and dislike for Karina, even to this day. Though he never admitted it, Carter had an inexplicable interest in Karina. Though he could never be completely outward with this forbidden fascination, Carter made his loyalty known to his friend and never allowed his intrigue to become known. Maybe – just maybe – this would be an opportunity to give a slow reveal and see what happens. "Girl, you were the lead cheerleader and watched me, Mel and the team go undefeated in seventh grade year. Stop playin' with me! MVP, remember?" Carter replied, feeling the need to give a brief resume of his middle-school resume.

"Still sensitive, I see," Karina replied, with a mischievous smile. Carter immediately realized he had been baited, which was par for the course for the Karina who he had known for years prior. "I mean, I wouldn't have to bring up the game you already know I have if you wasn't talking that nonsense. Anyway, what school you go to now?" asked Carter, forcing a transition of discomfort from himself back to Karina. The response came out slowly. "Well…I'm at Grace Academy, as you can see." Karina pointed at opened her arms modeling her school uniform that she was still wearing, the school emblem patch on the upper left side of her polo shirt. "Yo, I should've known. Your mom was super bougie and that skirt…that skirt, I knew it looked familiar. They came to Southview trying to recruit on High School Day…" Karina interrupted, "You and all the boys were trying to flirt with the ambassadors, lookin' thirsty and I clowned them saying that there was no way in the world I would be going to an all-girls school, way across town, away from all of my friends, but…here I am." She shook her head laughing in her own disbelief.

"Yeah, it's all good. The end of eighth grade was crazy, though. After we graduated a couple of teachers left at the same time, too. Even Mr. Dewels ended up bouncing. Me and Mel ended up at Memorial High. It ain't much, but it is what it is," Carter replied in a false humility. Karina, trying to appear unnerved by Carter's updates responded, "It is what it is? Boy, I already know you went there for the hoop program and that they're trying to get back to states. You're the first freshman to be playing varsity in like forever, right?" Carter was shocked, "Hol' up, you been doing your homework. Or you been stalking me. It's one of the two. Can't blame you either way, though." "Please, ain't nobody thinking about you," Karina regretted showing her hand a bit more than she should have. It was a fact that Carter's name carried through the city and his basketball stardom was becoming well known. Also, it did not hurt that she had actually become a fan of the sport while being a cheerleader. Sometimes, however, she had a hard time determining if she was a fan of the sport or of Carter.

"Well, are y'all any good?" Karina asked skeptically. "You did admit that I was on the team as a freshman, right? What you think?" responded Carter, still immersed in both confidence and a bit of surprise. "As a matter of fact, you should come to a game. We'll be on our old side of town pretty soon for the King Center Classic. Everybody'll be there." Karina subdued her excitement, "Um, I don't know. My mother might not let me go. She been on me tough lately." Carter responded, quickly interrupting, "All that trash you put on my name and my squad? You'd better be there. Come through! Don't worry about Mel, He'll probably have Gina there to keep him calm. Hold on, that's it – you still cool with Gina, right?" Karina's face gave an immediate response, "To be real, Carter, I haven't talked with anybody, even Gina. Ain't no problems, just...let's just say that my mom changed everything." Karina's façade of confidence began to transition to visible disappointment, reliving in her own mind the timeline of the past few years.

"Wow...I never would've thought that, as cool as you and Gina was. I remember back in seventh grade, Mr Dewels was zoomed in on y'all, when y'all would be talking in class. Y'all stayed in trouble," Carter laughed, in his brief moment of reminiscent. "Yeah, well, we don't talk, and yeah, those days seemed sweet, but, things probably weren't what they seemed," Karina abruptly responded, seeking to escape the conversation. "Look, I'll try to make it out. Maybe I'll get my mom to let me go with one of my girls over there," Karina quickly responded with a resolve to salvage a quickly sinking reunion. As unexpected as this meeting was, a new hope had ignited, drawing her from her current reality, bringing a piece of familiarity that appeared to have a different appeal than before.

"Alright, well, cool. But look – do me one favor. Mel and Gina will not believe that I saw you today, so I need proof, straight up," said Carter. "What kind of proof?" asked Karina, genuinely confused. "Hmm...I don't know. Maybe your phone number?" "Aha!" thought Karina, as she suspected that this friendly and unexpected meet-up was potentially take yet another interesting turn. Nonetheless, she gave a response that only fanned the flames on curiosity within the moment. "My mom is not letting me talk to any boys on the phone. She knows every call coming into my house and I don't have my own phone yet," Karina said with a bit of hidden disappointment. "But that doesn't mean you can't call *me*," replied Carter with an answer as quick as his reflexes on the basketball court. Looking at the entry of the arcade, he then said, "Yup, I already know what we're about to do. Come here with me real quick. I have an idea."

By this time, the girls at the table had become more intrigued as they saw Karina stretching the distance that once existed. “Karina, we’re about to leave. The next bus will be here in 15 minutes!” shouted Aleah, who herself was taking chances defying her own parents’ after-school protocol. “Hold on, I’m ready!” responded Karina. “Carter, where are we going?” Carter replied, reassuringly, “Look, you said that you can’t have boys calling you, I want proof that I saw you today, so – tadow!” Carter guided his hands towards a phone booth with a slightly tattered curtain shielding view from outside onlookers. The faux gold trim, burgundy accents, with a few burned out light bulbs did not come across as the “answer”, but Karina was willing to hear more. Carter proceeded, “I’m about to pay for some glamour shots that’ll be the evidence for today. I get what I want and, you’ll get what you need – my phone number on the back of the picture so you can hit me up.” Karina hated to admit that she loved the idea and chose to put on a veil of disinterest. “Ok, whatever. We gotta hurry, though. My girls are ready to go,” she said as she officially conceded to the impromptu idea.

In receiving the go-ahead from Karina, Carter reached in his pocket to retrieve the few dollars left from his sneaker purchase earlier. He hurriedly smoothed out the dollar bill on the corner of the photo booth to ensure a quick and smooth photo shoot as he promised. At the same time, Karina prepared herself to be photo-ready, turning away to apply a fresh layer of lip gloss and mentally detail what angles she could take to not let anything school related from being seen. Also, as much as this may be a fun, unexpected takeaway from today's escapade, she was not necessarily sure how she would be able to explain this one. The seconds ticked, with Carter already seated in the booth, holding back the curtain and waving her in, her questions and reluctance faded away. "Girl, we about to go!" reiterated Aleah. "Hold up, here I come!" responded Karina, as she prepared for the flashing lights.

Chapter 11

"Hey, Mel. This is Karina. From Southview. You busy?" The text message sat in the back of Mel's mind as he sat in the gymnasium. Pastor Chris had returned and taken command of the young group, continuing on the most serious Friday Night Huddle that the ministry had ever had since its inception. "You kids just don't understand how precious you all are in God's sight," Pastor Chris said, with an urgency in his voice. "When I tell you 'Jeremiah 29:11 – For I know the thoughts that I think towards you, says the Lord, thoughts of peace and not of evil, to give you a future and a hope' that's not me just spitting Bible talk – that's me telling you how much He loves you! He loves *you*!" The room was still eerily silent. Most of the kids in the group who usually thought that Pastor Chris was "doing too much" or trying to keep them from having fun, found themselves in a reflective state. Something was different about Pastor Chris this night. This whole night had become different.

"These streets – you already know that I know what it's like. No – I know what these streets *are*. I made a lot of decisions. Many of them I regret. And you don't know how bad I want to see all of you avoid 'em," Pastor Chris continued. "When I decided to show how 'cool' I was, selling drugs, running the streets, and out here having sex, that right there...that right there was the one that changed my life forever! Don't get it twisted – I was a boss! I had money, I had a couple of cars, some trap houses, I had the respect....nah, I had the *fear* of an entire community! Nobody could tell me nothing! So when I saw Christian's mom, I knew I had to have her." The audience of mostly teens listened intently, as part of this outpour was the allure Pastor Chris had, from his known reputation in the streets to his transformation to a Bible-carrying leader in the community and devoted father to his son, Christian. Questions started from back then to how genuine his transformation was, even from the most loyal members of Blessed Hope, to which Pastor Kinglsey always referred to Chris as the living testimony to what 1 Corinthians 1:27 is all about.

Pastor Chris found himself reliving the moments of the fateful moment that his words had led him to, pushing himself in the reality that his calling was embedded in moments such as these. "Veronica was, and still is, beautiful. I saw her, knowing that there was something special about her. What it was, was that she was a 'good girl'. I knew she had a church home, had both of her parents, just graduated from Grace Academy, on her way to her second year of college - all of that. She didn't have anything to do with cats like me. But there I was - flashing money, stunting harder than those dudes you see in the rap videos, using money stacks like phones, and eventually it caught her eye. Yeah, I got her. It was only a matter of time, but I got her," Pastor Chris nodded with a straight face, transitioned to one of visible regret. "I got who I wanted, or rather, *what* I wanted, and it felt...I felt great at first, you know. But then...that emptiness hit, y'all. Just straight up empty."

"My homeboys knew that I was trying to get at her and what did I look like not getting with her? I mean, I was the boss. I was the one people looked at and I had a rep to maintain. Didn't matter that that rep had nothing to do with what God wanted for my life. Didn't matter that the decisions that I was making, from selling drugs, to beating up people, and being promiscuous, that it was affecting more than just me. I was more concerned with what my hood *thought* about me than what God *knew* about me. Ain't that cold?" Pastor Chris ended with the rhetorical question to allow his audience to reflect. He himself was in need of no break, as the words flowed without pause in a steady flow he knew was being spiritually led.

"What I didn't tell you was that Veronica was the toughest one for me to get. I lost count of how many 'nos' and slaps to my hands that I got from her, and you know why – she knew who she was in God's eyes. She knew she was precious. She knew that sex before marriage was not cool with God, but then..." "Then she let you get it in, huh, Pastor C-Note", interrupted a laughing Lawrence, who added visible, mocking thrusts from his hips in the air, still stinging from being caught outside of the group activities earlier. Mel and a majority of the teens shook their head in annoyance, returning their attention to Pastor Chris. Looking over at Regina, Mel could see that she was likely warning her sisters to keep their distance from the troubled Pastor's son. Her facial expressions were demonstrative, to say the least, as her sisters' averted gazes appeared to have shown that the message was received.

"You know what, Lawrence, I sure did. I got it in! I got it in, and then...", Pastor Chris allowed a moment for increased effect. "And then, my life would never be the same ever again. As I was saying before Lawrence jumped in just now, Veronica knew sex before marriage was wrong...but just like how the devil kept getting at Eve in the garden...eventually, something changed. It wasn't that she said 'yes' as much as she questioned what she knew God *knew* about her. As soon as I got her to question if the whole 'saving herself before marriage' thing was all that serious, I knew I got her." Regret sat at the tail-end of Pastor Chris' words, but he mustered the fortitude to continue. "As much as you all see me being used by God...y'all don't understand – I was being used by the enemy, back then. And that's how he works. You may not give over and say 'yes' to something bad, off the top, but if he can get you to question God's plans for your lives – that's where the problem starts."

Bzzzz...Bzzzz...Bzzzz

Mel's phone began to vibrate again and he could not help but to think that he already knew who the caller was. Disguised with the "private number" labeling in the phone's external display, the anticipation was kindling. Instead of silencing his phone or sending it to his voicemail, he thought that it might be best to take this mystery call. Was it Karina – the same Karina who was his arch-nemesis at Southview Academy? If so, what in the world could she be calling him for now, after all of this time? To get the answers that he needed he knew he had to get away from the gymnasium and take this call. As discreetly as he could in the hushed group, Mel quickly rose and made his way to the hallway that connected to the main church building.

"Hello?" An air of silence quickly entered, lasting but a couple of seconds.

"Hel..." Before Mel could finish, a voice responded saying. "We have been trying to contact you about your car warranty. To hear more about this soon-to-be-expiring pro..." Mel pressed the red button on his phone in annoyance and shook his head. He thought, "If it's not the elections, it's the car warranty spots. Messed up part is I probably actually need a warranty for this beater that I got my mouth ripped open on."

Before Mel could regain his composure and place back in the gymnasium to hear more of Pastor Chris' message, a text message buzzed on his phone. The message was from Carter. "Hey, Mel. I gotta get at you, ASAP. I got a call from Karina. Yeah, man, and what she just dropped on me…we gotta talk. You at the house?" Mel could sense that it was serious. Carter was usually the cooler, more calculated of the two of them, so to see roles reversed was a bit odd. Mel took a deep breath and responded, hoping that auto-correct would not disrupt the communications as it often did. "I got you, C! I think we're almost done at the church with the game night. Can I get at you when it's done?"

Send.

As urgent as it sounded, Carter usually respected Mel's work at the church. Besides, whatever Pastor Chris was still saying to the group had peaked his interest still, even with the interruption. Mel tucked his phone away in his pocket, covering it with the bottom of his gray polo shirt, and moved quickly with a slight jog back to the group in the gymnasium.

"...and if any of you think you know what the consequences are for sex before marriage...bruh," exclaimed Pastor Chris, seemingly falling back to his former comfortable vernacular, often enlisted to close any remaining gap between himself and the youth. "I'm blessed to say that I have a beautiful little boy out of all of this, real talk. But the beef that I had with Veronica's family, risking her life a couple of times fighting my ex who wanted to have my baby, then...and then...and then," his voice stuttered leading up to the next issue. "Seeing Veronica almost die giving birth and her family making sure that I couldn't be in the delivery room to see my little boy come into this world. Man, y'all just don't know. When it came to her family, I was all kind of words that I didn't think that church people was supposed to be saying. But I was wrong. *Dead* wrong."

"My son was born on a Sunday. I was kicked out of the hospital by security. I was heated. I was done. I had no idea of what to do, where to go. But I figured, let me go to the church that these people call themselves going to and let whoever's there, especially the Pastor, have it - I was ready!" exclaimed Pastor Chris, almost seemingly reenacting his demeanor from that day. "So I jumped in the whip and then..."

Bzzzz...Bzzzz...Bzzzz

"I'm outside, Mel. Gotta talk, bro!" Reading the text, Mel knew that it had to be serious for Carter to actually make his way to the church, only minutes from his last text message. What could have Carter acting so urgently?

Chapter 12

"Man, if Berkshire had any idea of what I was going to do, they sho nuff wouldn't have let me get that 40-piece on them. That last dunk, when I went up..." Mel interrupted, "We know, we know - they should've fouled you, and you would've got an and-one anyway and made it 41, breaking the Classic scoring record set by Mr. Dewels as a freshman. Bro, we won the Classic! Me and Gina just trying to eat. You should, too!" Carter smirked, "Mel, you just mad because Coach took you out of the game for that trash 3-pointer you threw up that started the run from Berk Prep. Almost broke the backboard with that brick! Good thing I was in the game. You had the opportunity of a lifetime to follow my lead when they pulled you up from JV for the night, but you blew it, bro. You blew it!" Carter shook his head, while snickering, holding in mild laughter. "Even Mr. Dewels looked like he was laughing in the VIP section when he saw you!"

"Could we be done with the basketball talk for tonight, y'all. Y'all won, it was a good game..." Regina was interrupted by Carter. "A *great* game. A game for the ages for your boy. I gotta come up with a nickname or something. What y'all think about 'Half-Homeboy, Half-Amazing'?" Carter sought his closest friends' feedback. Mel laughed, offering his opinion, "Man, if you don't stop with these knock-off names, just because you share the name with a real pro legend…" The three friends shared a laugh in the booth at the local diner just blocks away from the King Rec Center. The diner was a popular hangout after activities at the King, but especially spiked after basketball games were played. This night had a different expectation attached for Carter, however.

"So, I guess the picture wasn't doctored after all. Had me thinking your photoshop skills had hit another level. Tripped me out seeing Karina at the game," said Mel, who still could not believe his eyes when he saw his former classmate just rows away from their bench at the gym. "Tripped me out, too. She looks the same and everything," Regina added. "Kinda messed up she didn't say nothing to me, though. You'd think after the way she dipped that she'd at least have something to say. We were girls, for real." Carter rushed to her defense, putting down the diner menu that he held momentarily, "Yeah, yeah...I know what y'all mean, but look, I'm trying to figure all of that out, too. That's why I invited her to the game. Good for old friends to catch up, you know?" Mel failed in his attempt of self-restraint and said, "Friends? Come on, man. You know good and well we never got along and she had the most enemies in the class. And Gina, I'm still trying to understand how y'all were so cool. She was the blocker of all blockers!"

"Now hold up, Mel. She was the one who played match maker and got you to stop being shy and got us to go together," Regina interrupted. "With my help, of course," Carter added, while stylistically pulling at either side of his t-shirt as if he had collars. "Exactly – the only good thing to come from *y'all's* 'old friend'", Mel pointed sarcastically at his friend and girlfriend, reiterating his stance. "Well either way, she's coming through to eat and kick it, so just chill and be cool. We in high school now – we grown!" proclaimed Carter, to both friends, but more so to Mel. "Speaking of which, I wonder where she at. It doesn't take any time to get here from the King." Carter's underlying romantic intent was becoming more and more obvious. While he did his best to quell his romantic interest in Karina, his anticipation of her arrival began to remove the layers of protection that he had built up, some of which included his self-enhanced recollection of his performance against Berkshire Prep.

"Well, I'll be cool, but she's going to have to be cool, too. If she start talking reckless again, man, I'm…", Mel was interrupted by Carter. "You going to do what, Mel? Bro, chill. Karina is different, I promise y'all. Look, y'all will see for y'all selves," said a now-defensive Carter. Regina, taking note of the abrupt response chimed in, in an effort to deescalate the rising situation and also uncover Carter's true intent. "Alright, y'all, chill. Like Carter said, it's just some old friends, or classmates, like you say Mel, meeting up and catching up. Or," Regina prepared her transition into her inquisition, "You and I, Mel, are here on a double-date with Carter and Karina. So, Carter, am I right or am I right?" Regina leaned in with her hands underneath her chin with widened eyes zoomed in on Carter from across the table. In jest, Mel joined in and performed the same mannerism, applying even more pressure on Carter, who realized that his plan may have been uncovered.

"If I don't admit then I know you won't quit, so whatever," said Carter with a sigh and a slight smile. "Look, even if it was that, can we just be cool when she gets here. I'm feeling a lot of heat off of this table and I want for Karina to be comfortable when she touches down." Regina sat back and smiled, with extra assurance, "See, spoken like a true boyfriend, taking up for his girl. Mel, you better be taking notes. Your boy's already ready to hold it down for his girl. Now, I really can't wait for her to get here." The side-eye that Mel gave Regina was sharp and direct, as cynicism now took the spot as his lead emotion. Somehow, he returned his focus to his friend, in an attempt to honor his request, regardless of how he felt about his potential new love interest. He understood that, despite his objection to such a relationship, that this was important to Carter and that, somehow, he would make the situation work on his end.

"Alright, C, I'll be cool. Anyway, I should've known something was up, how y'all were hugged up in those pictures you showed us. She got you sprung," said Mel, who immediately followed with laughter at the revelation of his best friend's infatuation. Instead of outward denial, Carter responded, "They're just pictures out of the little booth at the arcade, but whatever. Hey, isn't that, Mr. Dewels over there, walking in?" Carter pointed over in the direction of the diner entryway, as Mr. Dewels slowly walked in with a woman who they assumed was his wife or at least his girlfriend. "That man knows how to pull 'em, for real. How am I not even in his class and I'm still taking notes? Legend," proclaimed Carter. Before Mel could provide verbal agreement, Regina looked over at him with a look several times more menacing than the look Mel gave her for her comments earlier. Heeding the non-verbal warning, Mel withheld his comments, in hopes of not upsetting his girlfriend. "Hey, Mr. Dewels, what's up? Did you see me at the game coming for your scoring record?" yelled an excited Carter, as he also motioned for his former teacher to come over to their table.

As proper in his demeanor and speech, Mr. Dewels responded, "Of course, Carter. That was a great show you put on and your team pulled it out tonight. As far as the record, I think that you'll be chasing my ghost for a while, young man." Mr. Dewels had an immediate laugh, but fought hard to relent that his days as the top athlete in the history of the community were likely numbered with Carter's athletic ascent. He then added, "But, seriously, as two of my former students, I'm proud of what you and Mel are doing. I think you may have what it takes to take this team to the top while you're there. But remember – education first, Mr. Wilkins." Carter knowingly nodded, already anticipating such a message from his seventh-grade teacher. Mel nonverbally followed suit.

"So, I take it that these are your former students, David – the only ones that I never heard about. This is strange, since it seems like you have a couple of special talented ones here," chimed in Mr. Dewels' date, who appeared to be fighting for relevance in the interaction. Regina, feeling similarly, added, "Well, we were a special class. We had a little of everything – athletes, artists, and...and...I guess I'll just say me, too." Regina in her rush to include herself, could not determine her niche in the former semblance of students. Her satisfaction was in the fact that she was able to regain placement in the once male-exclusive conversation. To aid in the female representation within the conversation, a response confidently came through, “And I am sure, young lady, that you were and still are a rising star, in your own right! The talent pool is not reserved solely for the Y-chromosome pool, isn’t that right?” Regina, reinvigorated to find an ally in this male athlete-dominated dialogue, readily responded, “That’s right, gir- I mean, Miss…” Not having a name to go off of, an answer to the unasked question was supplied, “Miss Stewart, young lady. Since Mr. Dewels here will not introduce me, I’ll do the honors myself. My name is Angela. I am his fiancé.”

Fiance’? This would certainly be heartbreaking news to the community’s single (and married) women. Mr. Dewels’ embarrassment struck him and urged an explanation, “Yes, yes, my apologies, Miss Stewart. Yes, lady and gentlemen, I would like to introduce you to my fiancé. She and I plan to be married very soon. Of course, she is doing all of the planning. Sparing no expense, I might add,” Mr. Dewels felt emboldened to throw in the latter part of his statement, with a smirk and side-eye to Mel and Carter. “Oh, stop it, David. I would be perfectly fine with a simple wedding with a few close friends and relatives. You are the one who entertained the idea of having the wedding of the century," rebutted Miss Stewart, who gave her own look of solidarity with her sole female aid in the conversation, Regina. The unexpected, impromptu meet-and-greet was quickly spiraling into a debate of wedding plans, to which Mr. Dewels quickly noticed and attempted to redirect the escalating narrative.

Before he could create a way of transition to another, softer topic, the greeter approached Mr. Dewels and Miss Stewart. "Sir, your table is ready. If you would like to be seated," as they extended their hand to a small booth freshly-cleaned and set for their placement. "Just in time, I presume. Miss Stewart, let's continue our debate of wedding planning and décor and allow these young people to not be entirely bored on their Friday night. Great game again, gentlemen. Regina, it was a pleasure to see you, as well," said Mr. Dewels, who was hoping that Miss Stewart would relent in her stance within their witnessed exchange. Miss Stewart obliged, saying "Agreed. You kids have a great evening. It was a pleasure to meet you all, especially since you all appear to be part of the class that I am just now really learning about. Have a great night!" The three of them responded, thanking them and wishing them the same. There was a shared sentiment of confusion between the three.

"Bro, what did we just witness? That was nuts!" exclaimed Mel, who was mindful to keep his voice out of audible range from his former teacher and his fiancé. "Man, this was no different than when you and Gina argue over which movie to rent at the video store. They good," Carter nonchalantly responded. Interrupting the review of what just happened, the server came to the table to check on the party of three, with an empty placemat still vacant. "Are we still waiting on one more?" asked the young woman. "Yeah, just a few minutes and we should be ready. She's just running a little late," responded an anxious Carter, who checked his cell phone for any updates. Remembering that she did not have her own phone still, he replaced his phone on the table in disappointment. "Ok. Is there a name that we should listen out for? We can bring them right over once they come in," asked the server. "Yeah. Karina. Her name is Karina," Carter quickly responded. "Ok. Sure thing. I'll refill your water in the meantime. Be right back," said the server, who was writing Karina's name down on her notepad as she walked away.

"So, is somebody going to say it or are we gonna be quiet about it?" asked Regina, who quickly broke the silence created after the server's departure. "About what, Gina?" asked a confused Mel. "We haven't seen or heard from or about Mr. Dewels since he disappeared from the school right in the middle of our last year at Southview. We see him almost a year later, out of the blue, and no one thought to ask what happened?" exclaimed Regina. The two boys mumbled and shrugged their shoulders. "After they started going back and forth like a tennis match, I didn't think we had much to talk about with them, straight up," responded Carter, matter-of-factly. "Besides, it probably wasn't nothing, anyway. Real talk, he was the only male teacher at the school, so I'm sure he was just being pushed out." "I don't know, Carter. Dude was nominated for Teacher of the Year awards and all of the community loved him. I thought it was kind of odd, too. I don't know," said a comparably confused Mel. Carter was forced to consider his friend's quickly compiled evidence. Was there something more to Mr. Dewels' abrupt exit from Southview?

The server was already returning, however, she was without the promised refill of the beverages for the table. "Hey, you said her name was Katrina?" she asked. "No, Karina. Karina. No 't' in her name," replied Carter. "I'm sorry, but we got a small note that was left up at the greeter's station. It just popped up a few minutes ago. They probably forgot to get it to you while they were getting those two seated," the server explained as she pointed in the direction of Mr. Dewels and Miss Stewart. She handed the small yellow piece of paper to Carter, who, to her, seemed the most concerned. "I'm so sorry. I'll get those drinks for you now." The server quickly went to retrieve the beverages, while Carter silently read the note he was provided. "What does it say, man?" asked Mel. A visibly disappointed Carter slid the note to the middle of the table.

"Carter-

I am so sorry. I came up to the diner and realized that I had to get the chores done at home or my mom was going to trip. You played so good! The game ended up finishing a lot later than I thought and I had to get back. I'll make it up to you, I promise. I'll call you tomorrow, if I can. My Mom's been on me about being on the phone and I think she might be starting to suspect something. Tell Gina I said hi. And Mel, too.

Karina"

Regina and Mel both looked at each other and then at their friend who obviously did not anticipate being stood up. "Hey, Carter, if Karina's Mom is still anything like she was when we were at Southview, she was just trying to stay out of trouble, for real," Regina reassured Carter. "She'll get up with you soon. It's cool." Carter let out an undetectable sigh and responded, "I'm good. It's cool. I just was hoping to see her real quick and we could just chill. Now I'm playing third-wheel, as usual. Oh, well." Mel, feeling the awkwardness of the moment, interjected in an effort to salvage his friend's feelings, "Ok, bro, while we are waiting to order, tell us how you were able to split that double-team and spin that reverse layup before the half ended." He was sure that a review of the spectacular game against Berkshire would bring Carter's spirits up.

"Maybe another time, Mel. I'm about to bounce. I'll get up with y'all later," Carter grabbed his duffle bag and quickly exited the diner in a visibly dejected fashion. He made his way past the greeter who was on their way to the table. He approached the table and said, "I am so sorry about that, not getting you the note. It got crazy busy in here and I was just trying to get everybody together. My manager is taking your drinks off of your bill. Again, really sorry." "It's all good, man," said Mel. "Hey, let me ask you something. What all happened anyway? Did this girl really come here write this note and leave like that?" "Yeah, she walked in maybe a minute after those two at that table came in, the ones talking to you before I sat them. Crazy part is I'm positive that she looked right at your table. Anyway, she looked shaken, startled. I asked if she was ok, but she just asked for pen and paper and said that she had to go. She was out, quick fast. Really wish I could've gotten you that note quicker," said again apologetically by the greeter.

Regina and Mel were sad for their friend, but confused as to why Karina would look right at them and exit just as fast as she arrived. This was a confusing night that had no answers in supply for anyone.

Chapter 13

He hit the red button on his cell phone, and took a deep sigh of contemplation. In his reflective state, Pastor Kingsley looked at his office wall and focused in on his recent family portrait with his wife and three children, positioned close beside a slightly smaller picture of himself as a preteen with his family several years ago. As he looked at the faces of his bloodline, deep thoughts filled every space of his mind, reviewing the words of the conversation that he just concluded on his phone. As his eyes panned the paralleled portraits, he pondered the reality that a bad situation was potentially getting worse. Indeed, the scenario that he presented just moments ago to Pastor Chris was beginning to thicken and he feared that the reputation that his church had been building up for years, would be potentially put at risk. Pastor Kingsley took pride in having a church that had become a beacon for the community, but specifically for the youth. While he always had a heart for his community, it was in the youth that he grew excited, being proactive in subsequent generations of the church.

Having been raised as a son of a Pastor, he had seen firsthand what a church looked like that delayed their focus and attention on their youth. The congregation of his father's church was one of the biggest in the city. The charisma of his father, supplemented with the charm of his mother, drew in many people of influence to the church. The influence created a movement not seen before, as the mission was stated loudly and proudly in the benediction of every service. "Let us be like our Savior, Jesus Christ, and be about our Father's business! God bless, Family!" he would emphatically say, with a young Pastor Kingsley sitting beside his mother in the front row. Congregants would respond, matching the enthusiasm with "Amen!", some energized by the spiritual call to action, others because they were relieved to endure the often-elongated sermons preached.

Young Kinglsey would often look around the familiar setting. This building was as close to being home as the place where his actual bed was. He had sat, and at times, slept in, every pew in the sanctuary, having been stationed at the building with his father who poured into him relentlessly. Sunday was just another day for him, since he rarely saw consecutive days away from the church, being brought by his father, daily. His hope, as showcased often in his actions, was to see his son take up the mantle and lead the church. Young Kingsley loved his father, but was not quick to the idea of being the heir apparent. Many Sundays he would look over to the empty spot beside him on that front row. That spot laid empty many Sundays as was left vacant by none other than his brother, Wayman, who was the first set to follow in the footsteps of their father. "Wayside" Wayman, as he had been nicknamed by their father, had no problem in expressing his lack of desire to follow the predestined script of a preacher's kid. Once he graduated high school, he moved out and embarked upon a life away from the tight church upbringing that he had come to loathe.

Their father was at first disappointed, but that disappointment grew to a bitterness that became hard to keep confined to family boundaries. There would be Sundays where the spoken message of the day, as spiritually rooted as it was, would have a subliminal undertone speaking about his son. "The prodigal son, I would argue," he started, "was one who, once he came to himself, knew that it was time to get right with the father. I don't know about you, but I have seen this story right before my eyes. If you look carefully, I am sure you can relate, Praise God, with what I am telling you today. You can try, try, and try to show your child the way of God, but he'll turn his back, pack his bags, and move out to the parties, drinking, the women, and everything else he thinks is so good to him. Flesh taking over, have him out here carrying on like you didn't raise him right. My Lord! If you don't hold on to Proverbs 22:6 – 'Train up a child in the way he should go." He would conspicuously stop from reciting the rest of the verse and draw up the shouts and exclamations from the church. There, in the midst of the pregnant pause, was a justification, knowing that he was not alone in his parental trials.

"Amen, Doc!" "You betta preach!" "Lawd have mercy!" The church would join in and encourage the impassioned Pastor, who apparently struck a chord with many, drawing from a visibly personal experience.

It was at this point that the church had resigned themselves to not nurturing their youth. Silently, within himself, Young Kinglsey vowed to not go that way that his father had gone. The look in his father's eyes at that moment signaled that he had crossed a line that where he knew that he would be firm in his stance. He had witnessed arguments between his father and brother, sometimes leading to diminished hope for their family, but the look he would have in moments in the pulpit such as this held their own space in his memory. Young Kingsley knew that his love for God, family, and his faith would likely lead him to be a leader in position to supersede his father, but with that platform he would be the rebuilt bridge of reconciliation that his father had been the destroyer of, between the church and its youth. This determination would be foundational to his future and echoed in his mind through his early days of seminary and assuming the seat prepared for him by his father.

That phone call Pastor Kingsley received was unsettling. While he expected the call that interrupted his meeting with Pastor Chris to be a continuation from the same young lady with whom he spoke with, rather the voice was that of yet another individual who expressed concern. The call was not only a surprise to Pastor Kingsley, but it made an already tense and murky situation even more troublesome. With all of the wisdom that this revered man of faith wielded in every matter that came across his desk, this situation at first glance appeared to be the most problematic, with repercussions that could reverberate throughout the community, beyond the confines of the church walls. As he leaned back in his plush leather office chair, he had a slight chew on the right temple tip of his designer eyeglasses. While an audience had not yet formed regarding this matter, he knew that divine wisdom would be required.

“Should I call in the elders? Who else might know about this? How long will it be before the parents get involved?” The series of questions flashed at speeds faster than light in his mind. The most paramount component was how it could affect the work that he had been doing in the community with the youth. While most in his position would be mostly concentrated with the perception of the church, notably those who had rallied campaigns of criticism for many years, Pastor Kingsley always returned to how the kids would be affected. The small wireless speaker on his desk gently echoed the gospel jazz playlist that he used as his backdrop for most of his office work. It served as a great counter to the silent solitude that brewed from Pastor Chris' exit. As he channeled every bit of wisdom that he knew that he would need, he looked over at the original portrait of King Solomon that was gifted to him by the church's Performing Arts Ministry. It was an oil composition of the "Judgement of Solomon", showcasing the famed wise man standing in front of throne, presiding over the two women, each claiming to be the rightful mother of the sole living baby of the two presented to him. The reference scripture, 1 Kings 3:16-28, was scripted prominently across the bottom of the famous bible narrative.

Pastor Kingsley was torn. While he resolved himself to not be naïve, to gather as many facts as he possibly could, he felt the urgency to get the best possible result to a situation that, as he had become aware, was not fully understood. As the moment of reflective and nervous thought soldiered on in Pastor Kingsley's office, he looked down at his phone. "Lord have mercy! Again?" exclaimed Pastor

Kingsley, who quickly repented, feeling that he had violated the second commandment in a fit of frustration. “Forgive me Father!” Looking at the phone, somehow a call had not come through, instead it was a voicemail insignia. In a hybrid of anxiety and reluctance, he picked up the phone, accessing his voicemail box, which usually was at maximum capacity. Having recently cleared some of his voicemail inbox just a week ago from a myriad of calls from his wife, colleagues, corporate partners, and congregants, he knew that this new voicemail would be the first to be heard upon entry.

“Pastor. Pastor,” the voice said in between cries. “I am so sorry for earlier. Just so you know that was not me. That was my mother. Your phone didn’t ring so I just wanted to leave you this voicemail. I just got back in town and I just want to make things right.” Pastor Kingsley tried to place the voice, but was unsuccessful, as his congregation and community involvement made his voice match a more tiresome effort than for most. “I’m sure that you’re busy and I know that you can help. My number is...never mind. I will just call you back. This is...” the caller hesitated, stopping a short audible stretch, cleared of the initial cries. A pause ensued. Then finally, a conclusion came, “This is Karina Burke.”

Chapter 14

"You know I love you, right?" Mel rhetorically asked Regina, as they sat in the basement of their church. "Yeah, I know. That doesn't mean that we need to be out here doing anything. I'm not trying to be out here all loose like these girls out here", responded Regina, with crossed arms, and a look from her eyes that matched the cutting intensity of sharp knives. This Wednesday evening, like most Wednesday evenings, Mel and Regina sat together, away from the rest of their youth group. While their parents were faithful members to the church and used this as a vehicle to keep their kids involved in the ministry, the two teenagers took full advantage to use this as their own impersonal date night. While both families were aware of them being a couple, they were not as free in giving them room for frequent, traditional dates. The current topic of their discussion had been heightened in recent weeks.

"All I'm saying is that if I love you and you love me, then we're good. I mean, I ain't trying to be with anybody else. Are you?" asked Mel to his still-opposed girlfriend. In frustration, she responded with an audibly lower response, saying "Mel, I do love you, but if this is what our relationship has come to, we might as well just be done. What do I look like having sex with you, fresh out of our 'Promise to Wait' Ceremony? Even worse, it's not like we'd know what we were doing. We're both virgins and..." Regina paused, making effort to lower her voice even further, leaning in towards Mel. "I'm not going to be out here pregnant before my life even starts. Don't you even think about that?" The argument was almost similar, with little change in the arguments posed by both Mel and Regina. Points and counterpoints almost repeated verbatim from one exchange to the next. Still, the young couple stayed together and continued on in their relationship.

Both were feeling pressure from outside entities. For Mel, his pressures came from his classmates, who often joked that Regina was stringing him along and would never give in to his advances. For Regina, her friends were not as pressing, but she felt the burden from feeling as if she may not be meeting the call to be the best possible girlfriend to Mel. In addition, the added pressures of teen pop culture only made it a dire talk track for them both, fully aware that deep down, this was forbidden fruit that neither were prepared to partake in. Nonetheless, the inevitability of this conversation still ran its course and was beginning to weigh heavy on their relationship. Implicitly, they both knew that this was not going to happen.

Mel let out a sigh, perceived by Regina as one of frustration, however it was one of slight relief, as he had an understanding that as long as he could thwart the responsibility on Regina, he would never have to be the one who said "no". He bore the weight of being a teenage boy who was expected to have already become sexually active, but spoke not of his own fears. To Regina's point, he did not know what to do and did not feel that he had the knowledge gained from his sex education classes fully grasped, anyway. In addition, the words that Regina just spoke had permanent place in his mind more than she would ever realize. "What if I got her pregnant?" Mel often thought, when the thoughts of going to this unchartered territory came to his mind. He had seen a few of his friends travel this same path become parents in their teenage years. While he felt sympathy for them, he knew that it all came down to a decision that he himself would make. It was much easier thought of than done.

Mel looked down at the bracelet that sat on Regina's wrist, as the fluorescent lights of the church basement reflected dimly on the silver band and connecting links. It matched the necklace that was given to the girls of the church as a keepsake reminder of the commitment that was made on the "Promise to Wait" ceremony Regina alluded to. The boys, including Mel, received a small tungsten chain with a cross pendant of their commitment to celibacy. This program was in its infancy, with the youth of church that recently participated being the inaugural group. The younger girls wore their bracelets with excitement, while most of those of high-school years wore theirs primarily during any and all visits to church. As for the boys, they wore theirs more consistently, but often either tucked their chains away or were shrewd enough to be able to remove the cross pendant, affixing it only for their parents to not draw suspicion of their unauthorized modification. Unbeknownst to the children, these tokens of dedication to celibacy were an investment by the church inspired by none other than Mel's mother.

This, of course, only added to the hesitancy from either Mel or Regina to want to actually cross the line designated by both their faith and church community. It was Mrs. Gaines' idea to break the taboo conversation of teenage premarital sex, disrupting the traditional, unspoken cadence of refusing to speak on the topic, only categorizing it as a sin, without further discussion. As it had become prevalent in their community, more than any of them would have liked, Mrs. Gaines made the suggestion to the church leaders in a meeting. The idea was not initially received as well as she had hoped, but the senior pastor had been convinced when he saw his own niece become a mother in only her freshman year of high school. This instance compelled him to champion Mrs. Gaines' idea and the ceremony was planned as a culmination of a church program designed to discuss sex and reiterate where the church's stance was on saving themselves for marriage. This program, while controversial to some of the more seasoned members, proved to be a groundbreaking point in the timeline of the church. It was Mrs.

Gaines' hope that this would lead to helping the youth to know how important they were to the church, but especially to God.

"Alright, Gina. My fault. I *do* love you and I just...I just really want to make sure that I don't lose you. I'm trying to be with you, for real," explained a contrite Mel. Regina let out a relieved chuckle, "But that's the point, I ain't going nowhere. You got me. Stop trying to press me. Besides, we have plenty of time. I love you, too, Big Head." The two shared a small laugh of reconciliation and delicately held hands, serving as substitute for the small kiss that they would sneak from time to time at school or anywhere away from the church. "Hey, it looks like they are about to start back up again for the wrap-up," said Mel, as both he and Regina turned their attention to Terrance, their youth group leader who walked downstairs. Surprisingly, immediately behind by only a few steps was Mel's cousin, Q. Q, almost pushing Terrance out of the way, rushed towards Mel and Regina, with urgency.

"Yo, y'all would never believe what I just heard, for real," exclaimed Q. "What's the business, Q? You sound like something's up. You almost knocked down Terrance like something was on fire. " "Well, my boy's parents just got out of a school board meeting and apparently dude from your old school, Mr. Do..Do...Do-something, he's out, like, ASAP," explained Quincy. "Mr. Dewels? You mean, Mr. Dewels?" asked Regina, who was intrigued and confused at the same time. Mel shared these same feelings and followed up with the next comment to uncover more. "What? There's no way. I mean, he did dip out of Southview kind of quick, but still. What happened?" Q gathered his breath and responded, "Bro, I don't know. All I know is that at this meeting, there were some parents who came in and they wanted dude outta there! I think it might've hit the news, too." Mel and Regina still sat confused, wondering more about the details.

"Q, I hear all of that, but I'm saying, why? What would cause Mr. Dewels of all people to become public enemy number one all of a sudden. The man is a local hero who stayed and became a teacher. Who does that?" Mel asked, without expectation of any answer that would quench his curiosity. Regina nodded in agreement, adding to the query. “I don’t know, Mel. All I know is that your boy is out like three strikes. They told me that lawyers were there and everything. On top of that, I’m hearing that they might be taking down the trophies and medals they have down at the King. Whatever it is, your hero is going down,” Q replied, leaning back with his hands slightly open and lifted, reiterating his lack of further info.

Mel and Regina sat across from each other, exchanging bewildered looks. Neither could come up with an explanation that made sense. Mr. Dewels was a neighborhood legend to many, so to hear of such an abrupt exit was difficult to comprehend. The effort they both put forth in their own respective brains was becoming exhausting in the short span of time they were all currently rooted in.

Then the silence was broken.

"You know, call me random, weird, whatever, but...I have the strangest memory of Mr. Dewels. I remember..." Regina was interrupted by Mel. "Oh, yeah, when he did that reverse dunk at the Teachers versus Students game in eighth grade – that was craaaaazy! Q, you should've seen it - Dewels crossed up the entire team. Matter of fact, I think that he even had Carter's ankles DOA. He split the whole squad, rose up in the paint, had the ball at his own feet and then was like, BOOM! Had the whole school going nuts! If Carter was here tonight, he'd have to keep it real and tell you how long he had to wear ace bandages after that." As Mel continued laughing about this moment, Q took in the description of the nostalgia that his cousin had spontaneously narrated, compelling his own fanhood of the neighborhood figure, eclipsing the scrutinizing cloud of mystery that had begun to take shape. "And where were you at, Mel? Getting yammed on with everyone else?" asked Q, with piqued interest. "Look, it wasn't any point in all of us getting in on that poster. I went to halfcourt and waited for the next play to hit," responded Mel, with his hands raised, feigning a backing off from the situation, as if it were happening right then and there.

As the admiration of Mr. Dewels' sport exploits began to ascend between two of the three at the table, Regina corralled everyone back to her interrupted speech. Unfazed by the impromptu sports reporting, she regained her speech positioning. "Y'all...I was trying to say, for some reason, this memory is coming up, from all the way back in seventh grade. It was the day that I had to stay after school for not having that one assignment signed and returned. Remember that day, Mel?" Mel took a few seconds to file through his memories and then responded, "Yeah...yeah. That was the day when Karina was trying to hook us up and hate on me at the same time. It was just a day in detention. Could've been way worse, especially messing with Mr. Dewels. What about it?" Instead of a quick response, Regina mulled over how to explain her sudden trip back to a singular moment in her middle school years. She really did not know how to justify the immediate leap to that specific day.

"Mel, all I know is that something happened that day. I would ask Carter, but he got out early that day. I just have this sinking feeling that whatever it is that Mr. Dewels is catching heat over...I don't know. I just..." Before completing her sentence, Terrance, the youth group leader finally called everyone to order after returning from the bathroom. "Okay ladies and gents, it's almost time to start up the activities. Let's get it going!" Being interrupted for a second time in the short span of time, this time Regina had an internal sense of relief. She felt an alleviated pressure of having to know what memory was trying to resurface after having been repressed these few years. Try as she would, there was no getting around the sentiment of connection between that day and the controversy surrounding Mr. Dewels. Regina walked with the rest of the members of her group, shifting her focus to the activities set for that night's youth ministry. "What am I trying to remember?" She was embattled with guilt and confusion, all at once. Terrance, seeing the faces of some of the kids, more specifically the teenagers, quickly announced, "I know about Mr. Dewels, already. There are no specifics. Let's not waste time guessing about whatever's going on. Besides, we have plenty of stuff to get into here tonight. Let's go and make the most of our time." This would be easier said than done. The controversy had planted its roots deep, already, in the imaginations of the kids that night in that church basement.

Chapter 15

"Bro, I got a kid," Carter said in a still-shocked demeanor to his most trusted friend. "What?!?" exclaimed Mel. Standing in Blessed Hope's parking lot beside his car, his immediate response was accompanied by a confused face, not expecting such an announcement from Carter. Carter continued his narrative, "Mel, today's been crazy. After we bounced from the King, I got back to the crib and my Mom gave me a message and a phone number, but they didn't leave a name - no name. You already know that doesn't make any sense." Mel agreed, nodding as he listened to Carter's detail of his evening. "So, me, you already know I'm not falling for the okie-doke, so I called, but I hit it with the *67, blocking my number. After about like a half of a ring, I hear...I heard...man..." Mel stood mere feet away, trapped in suspense. Finally, he asked, "Carter, who was it, man? Did you recognize the voice? Was it someone you know? We know?" Looking at his eyes, Mel suspected that Carter knew who the mystery person was.

"Karina, man. It was Karina!" responded Carter. Mel's mind went into a mental whirlwind. Everything was beginning to connect as the words traveled from Carter's mouth to his own ears. Is that why he got the text message from earlier? There was just no way that it was a coincidence. That name was not common. Still, she has a kid – and Carter's the father? "No, no...just couldn't be," thought Mel, as these thoughts moved in his head at a rate of speed even he could not comprehend. "Little dude's name is Maxwell. You know, like dude that made the song about lifetime or something like that. That was me and Karina's song when we used to kick it. She sent me a picture and..." Mel interrupted the nostalgic referencing, "But is it yours, C? Sorry to say it like that, but let's keep it real. We haven't seen Karina in years. You haven't heard from her in years, since she bounced after that phone call you told me about. Now all of a sudden she pops up and you're the father. I don't think it'd take Maury to figure this one out, man. Just think!"

Carter responded, with conflicting emotions of confusion and an unfounded fatherly defense, "Hold up, Mel. Look – you got some points, but if you want to talk about keeping it real, I think little dude is mine. He has my smirk and...and..." Mel stood across from him, in his own air of confusion, "And what? What, man?" "The times line up," said Carter. "He's almost 3 years old and around the time Karina would've been pregnant, my Grandma was dreaming about fish. You know when she's talking about fish, it ain't about no filet-o-fish. She's predicted every pregnancy in my family from before I was born. And that's on my momma!" Carter's grandmother was known for her ability to forecast the new parents in the family. As unscientific as many perceived it, it would be like pulling teeth trying to convince him that Grandma hadn't pulled it off again, calling in advance yet another child in the Wilkins family.

"Grandma had this dream, bro, and I remember, she kept asking me 'Boy, you been out here tricking, messing with these fast girls, haven't ya?'" recalled Carter, while shaking his head about the allegation. "Of course, I got on the defense and tried to play like she was tripping. Besides, I knew that I only messed with Karina. I didn't think that there was any way that she got pregnant. But..." "That one time!" Mel completed Carter's thought. They both zoomed their memories to their sophomore year in high school, a few weeks before the winter formal. It was unforgettable to both, as the bookmark for this flashback was it being the only time ever that Carter missed a basketball practice. Carter never missed anything related to basketball. Pick-up games, watching it on tv, playing video games, and, yes, not even practice. A day like that one would be hard to forget.

"Hey, Mel. You still got me, though, right? One time!" Mel recalled the question asked by his best friend and teammate in the high school locker room. Instantly he was transported in his mind to that pivotal day. While Mel had covered for Carter before, this time actually felt like a lie – a big one! "Bro, we got the Invitational coming up this weekend. You sure you wanna risk it all like this? Coach might trip and 'poof' – there goes your dream of breaking that scoring record you keep dreaming about," asked Mel, who was trying to provide conscientious counsel to Carter. "First of all, you know that I get buckets. The record'll be mine, anyway. Second of all, it's not like I'm not going to play. I might have to come off of the bench, but there's no way Coach won't let me run. It's just one practice. And besides," Carter interrupted his explanation with a planted, forced cough into his two cupped hands. "I think I might be coming down with something and I need all of the rest that I can get." With flu season just beginning, Carter saw this as his opening to make a grand escape, even from his first love of basketball. The school and his Coach had become overly cautious to ensure that the student body was able to avoid the sickness.

Mel still felt conflicted, even in covering his best friend. Something did not feel right about doing this deed for Carter. Though he had to admit, since he knew that whatever it was he was escaping to, had to be a big enough deal. "Alright, C, if I'm going through with this, and I'm probably going to regret asking, what do you have shaking?" asked Mel. Carter, knowing that his response was not likely going to be met with a favorable reception, reluctantly gave his accomplice the response that he demanded. Following a hesitant sigh, with a lowered tone, as he leaned in to offer the reason for his exodus from their regularly-scheduled basketball practice. "Karina's mom is working an extra shift and I'm about to…", as Carter unfolded his plan, Mel interrupted. "You're doing this for…for Karina?!? Bro, come on! Are you for real?" responded

Mel, using a voice level that was several decibels above the one set by Carter with his initial attempt to provide detail. Carter threw a sharp look at Mel and pulled him to the corner of the gym, offset by the folded bleachers.

"Mel, chill, man! Coach is right off in his office and I gotta roll out to catch the next bus to her house," Carter responded, attempting to deescalate the expected objection from his girlfriend's arch-nemesis. Mel, already knowing what the likely plan of action was now that he was aware who else it involved, did his best to transition from adversary to advocate. Could it be that his friend was going to live out the fantasy that mostly every teenage boy within their school, community, and maybe the world thought about at that age? Behind his disdain for Karina, Mel could not deny the slight bit of envy of his friend's potential venture into forbidden territory. For months and months, Mel's suggestions of the like activity to Regina were denied. As their relationship continued, an innocent love flourished, but the pressures from their classmates, who themselves had never done the act, were persistent, especially in the ears of Mel.

Despite his overtures to Regina, Mel fought an internal battle, knowing that the very thing that he wanted was the last thing that he should be doing. His father, being a man of few words, had "the talk" with him, and kept his message simple – "I can give you all the bible verses in the world. Just stay out of grown folks' business." As vague as that was at first, his tone made it clear that he was not going to be tolerant of Mel having sex before the right time. He saw in Mel and Regina much as he saw himself and Mel's mother and had little difficulty in understanding what his son was up against in his male adolescent years. With that empathy, after his talk, he handed him a small box of condoms and said, "But if you can't keep it together, at least you have something to work with." He took out one of the condoms from the box, giving a verbal tutorial, with Mel trying to grasp every detail, while still slightly conflicted on where his father stood with it. The conversation was ended awkwardly with Mel's father, giving his son a nod for confirmation and walking out of his room.

Mel's mother's message was more direct, leaving no room for misinterpretation. In their kitchen, as she prepared dinner one day, she said, with no warning, "Mel, you know how your father and I raised you. Don't let me catch you messing around with Gina or any other girl until you are grown-grown and you got a ring on her. And don't think I don't know it's been on your mind. Remember..." Mel said, almost in unison with his mother, with an altered annoyance in his voice, "Don't start doubting my prophetic gift, now." With his eyes rolled and an accompanying silent sigh to avoid further repercussion, Mel knew that as much as the urges came, that sex at the time was not going to be worth the trouble. While both his parents had messages delivered in different ways, the sentiment was the same. It did not mean that it would not be a struggle, as it was for almost every young man in the stage of life. That it definitely was not.

"Alright, well...you got something to cover that, right? I mean, if you've gotta do it, at least be strapped up," advised Mel to Carter. Though he said it as some expert of sexual activity, he only repeated a combination of the words he heard from his father, some upperclassmen, and movie lines that became a part of his culture. His true knowledge base was lacking, as was Carter's. All that they knew was that they were supposed to "do it". The rite of passage, as unclear as it was, made all the sense in the world at the same time. Any questions of "why" that Mel, or any young man around their age, would quickly disappear in the wind, with the mutual understanding of the mandate placed on their teenage male lives. Besides, who would want to be the last one to cross the finish line on this achievement? Certainly not the competitive Carter, who validated his conquest with his sincere interest in Karina. "Yeah, I'm good, bro. I can't forget that," Carter reassured Mel. As simple as the response was, it appeared to be enough to dispel any concern that Mel had for his friend. To add another layer of surety, Carter reached in his pocket and showed tangible proof of his claims. The two friends nodded in a moment of solidarity intended to cover up the unspoken nerves. Mel, still conscientious of the talks on this subject matter with his parents, had some concern for his friend, hoping that he truly was not making a move that he may come to regret.

A brief, but awkward silence took place in the suddenly fast-moving moment. The gym door from the opposite end opened up slowly, causing the eyes of both Mel and Carter to dart over, wondering if there would be a witness to Carter's grand getaway. Both let out a slight sigh of relief when the figure walking in was none other than Regina, who was looking for Mel before basketball practice. Carter, feeling as if his luck was running out, as well as the time before the next bus was set to arrive, picked up his duffle bag and began to exit through the nearby door. "Hey, Mel, I gotta bounce. I'll get at you later. Don't forget to hold me down with Coach. Good looking out, for real, man. You know that I got you back whenever you need me." Carter hustled out of the gym, waving to Regina and throwing up the casual two fingers to his partner-in-crime. A conflicted Mel, responded, mirroring the familiar hand gesture often shared between he and his best friend. Something just did not feel right about what was about to happen.

By the time Regina approached the space where the two stood, the door that led to outside had almost closed, and she stood confused. "Don't y'all have basketball practice today? Where is Carter going?"

asked Regina. "Shhh," responded Mel, attempting to quiet his girlfriend, similarly to how he was just quieted by Carter not too long before. Mel explained, "*My* boy is about to go see *your* girl and..." Regina, just as Mel did, interrupted and said, "Are you for real?!?" Seeing that she had drawn what appeared to be the correct assumption, Mel nodded, with a side-eye of nervousness for his friend and disappointment of who it was that this experience would be shared. Mel quickly saw his opening, seizing what appeared to be a slight glimpse of interest from Regina. "So now that Karina and C about to go ahead and..." started Mel, who was quickly given a rejection stare with the feeling of a thousand knives. From the corner of his eye, he saw that his coach was walking out of his office into the gymnasium, preparing for practice. Seeing his opportunity for escape, Mel immediately jogged to evade the failed overture he had come under attack for. Within him was a slight sense of relief within the anticipated rejection. "Hey, Coach...Carter had to leave out. He had a sore throat, I think."

Chapter 16

"…and that's all that I'm saying, y'all. Think before you act. You have no idea how real it gets and how fast it happens. I love my son, but I can't lie. The 'what-ifs' play in my head, over and over. God can bless your mess, but why create a mess in the first place, you feel me?" asked Pastor Chris. Usually, he feared being too long-winded for the youth in the program, but this night, he felt emboldened to get this message across. The feeling that he had inside was a burning that he often felt when the calling he knew to be on his life went beyond being a babysitter on Friday evenings. Tonight was different – very different. As his spiritual covering often said, "If you can reach one – just one – your mission was not in vain."

Even Lawrence seemed to be resigned to a solemn state, at least subdued compared to his normal demeanor. "Say, Pastor Chris, you dropped some knowledge on us, I can't even lie," he admitted, as he sat with surprised, skeptical eyes taking notice. "I knew you were a hood legend, but, man…" "But, see, that's what I'm saying, Larry," interrupted Chris, who astounded Lawrence and the rest of the group when he chose to use the shortened version of his name. "That's the stuff you glorify. The rap music, the gangster stuff, all of that. At the end of the day, it has absolutely nothing to do with who you were made to be. Christ's plan is greater! I know most of you don't come here for the message, but believe me, y'all, you're in the right place at the right time." Pastor Chris continued his pace around the area of the gym they were all congregated, doing his best to capture eye contact with every person.

"As a matter of fact, I'm not simple enough to think that you would receive this message if it were just me. Look at Mel, look at Carter – they're not too far from where you are right now, either. They hoop, they kick it, they come from the same place as you, but they didn't get trapped. Don't get trapped! God's plan for you is bigger than having sex, getting money, and doing drugs." Chris could feel that his words, unlike most of the sessions, were actually sinking in the youth that night. This was shaping up to be the breakthrough moment that he awaited since the inception of the program. And to think, it all came by way of an unforeseen crisis. What came across as a small still Voice whispered, "Remember Romans 8:28.

Trust Me." Chris smiled and nodded to himself. "Thank you, Holy Ghost," Pastor Chris whispered back, away from the ears of his young audience.

As this moment took place, Regina continued to sit in the audience with her sisters. Taking in the moment as the rest of the group, she, too, became reflective of Pastor Chris' words. As he continued on in a renewed space of the continued talk, her phone vibrated. Hesitantly, she lifted it up to see what the caller ID said. "Restricted Call" prominently read on the screen. Usually, these calls received no attention from her, but given the events of the day, she figured that it was worth a gamble to answer this time. "I'll be right back. I have to take this call," she explained to her sisters, who were captivated enough by the words of Pastor Chris that their movement was likely to be minimal, if any at all.

As the kids sat in the gymnasium, still receiving the intentional message from Pastor Chris, Regina found herself more curious than ever about her unknown caller. She walked with quick pace towards the small hallway that stretched towards the parking lot from where she entered. Before making the final steps, in fear that the call would be routed to her voicemail inbox, she took a deep breath and pressed the button on the screen, answering the mystery call. "Hello," Regina said tentatively, still wondering what voice she would hear in response to her greeting. Could it be a call from her best friend from her middle school years? What appeared to be her number from her discussion with Mel was not showing up this time, but there was no telling who this was calling, especially the way this night was going. As the milliseconds of pause ensued, Karina thought, "This has gotta be, Kar...". "Regina? Is this Regina Vincent?" the caller responded. "Yes, may I ask who is calling?" asked Regina, even more confused as to who the caller was. "Absolutely. This is Detective Serena Price," responded the voice, with a direct and serious tone.

Detective? This was a call that Regina was not expecting, not prepared for. "I know that you do not know me, but I am reaching out to you, hoping that you could come down to the station to answer a few questions." "Questions?" thought Regina. What questions would they want to ask her and about what? Regina's record was spotless, even with her sometimes less-than-stellar driving, having only verbal warnings to show for the few times when she was pulled over. There was absolutely nothing that she could conceive that she would have to offer in terms of information to the police. "I realize that this call is sudden, but we are trying to gather facts regarding a former classmate of yours. A Miss...Miss," trailed off the Detective, as she fumbled through the papers on her desk. "Miss Karina Burke," continued Detective Price. "I understand you went to school with her, even close friends. Is that true?" "Well...yeah. I knew her," responded Regina. "But I haven't seen her in years. I don't think I could tell you much."

Regina, not comfortable in any protocol in talking with law enforcement, did all that she could to be an open book, not holding back in her responses. She thought it best, as she did not want Detective Price to have any suspicion that she had anything to hide. She wondered what situation could Karina be in that a Detective, of all people, is calling her, hoping to get information from her. "We just have a few questions to ask. It shouldn't be too long at all," affirmed Detective Price. "As a matter of fact, if it would make you more comfortable, I can come to where you are to get this done. Don't want to inconvenience you." The Detective's intent was backfiring, as Regina's nerves began to heighten. The questions about the questions in her own head were beginning to dominate her thoughts. "What does she want?" Regina asked herself, in addition to other related questions.

Knowing that any extended silence could incite suspicion, she felt the need to respond. "Well...well...I'm not at home. And, I have my sisters with me, so, so...I don't know," said Regina, with a slight stumbling of words. "I'll tell you what," said Detective Price, still aiming to keep a calm within the arrangement, "I will meet you at your home tomorrow morning, talk with you, and hopefully meet your parents, if that's ok." Regina felt a slight relief after hearing the suggested compromise. Having her parents in the midst would be a welcome accompaniment, especially as she knew that they had little to no doubt in her ability to stay away from anything that even remotely looked like trouble.

"Perfect. Let me leave you my phone number. I'll text it to you right now. Sorry about the blocked number when I called. The phones that they give us come that way. I'll be by around 11:00. Thank you, Regina," concluded Detective Price. "Ok. I saw the text. I'll see you tomorrow," confirmed Regina. Finally. The call was over. As confusing as it was, at least it was over. Regina's breathing was uneven, imbalanced between relief of knowing who was calling and the anxiety of what questions were going to be directed her way regarding Karina. As confusing as it all was, Regina resolved to leave the questions to the meeting of tomorrow and try not to give in to the curiosity bubbling within her. Looking up, as if it were perfect timing, she saw the custom-painted wall under bright lighting, prominently displaying the Bible verse, Matthew 6:34: "Give your entire attention to what God is doing right now, and don't get worked up about what may or may not happen tomorrow. God will help you deal with whatever hard things come up when the time comes." The painting was familiar to her as she remembered the Saturday afternoon she spent watching her sisters make faint contributions to the mural when it was being created.

Clutching her necklace from the "Promise to Wait" ceremony years ago that sat under her shirt, she took a deep breath, offering up a quick, but sincere prayer. "Lord, I trust you. Definitely need for those words that I just read to work for me now. I thank you, in Jesus' name." While concluding the prayer, her phone rang, yet again. Showing a restricted caller ID once again, Regina answered, with a divinely given boldness. "Hey, Detective Price. Is there something else that you needed?" The responding voice was different, yet familiar. This voice she did indeed know. Years removed, this voice still was as familiar as the day she first heard it. "Gina, this is Karina. Sorry I blocked my number, but you weren't answering. I'm in town and I really need your help." Regina stood in the hallway alone and speechless. Her newly-found boldness had subsided, drastically.

Chapter 17

"Karina...I just don't know what to say," said Ms. Burke, in a confounded tone. The gap of silence that followed was the loudest silence. The silence was as loud as an orchestra of clanging cymbals, performed by untrained toddler percussionists. While the words spoken were not a question, Karina sat on the couch knowing that a response from her was what she was demanding, but did not know what to say. The pressure in the room was high. The anxiety of the two members of the household skyrocketed in just mere moments after Karina shared news that she was never more reluctant to say out of her mouth.

The awkward quiet of the room continued.

Finally, realizing that someone had to reinvigorate the conversation, Ms. Burke followed up her statement, this time with actual questions, albeit with minimal words.

"Karina...how?"

"When?"

"Where?"

"With who?"

To the dismay of Ms. Burke, the silence again remained as it was before the rapid-fire series of questions. Karina sat, still speechless, feeling shrouded in disappointment, shame, and fear. The last of those emotions being the strongest because of the way in which she was raised. Karina, as bold as she was in school and everywhere else outside of her home, knew that she had little wiggle-room to deviate from the directives given from her mother. Consequences were both simultaneously clear and unclear in their home. The clarity was given during the rare times where Ms. Burke laid out to Karina what the consequences would be in the event she stepped out of the set guidelines. The lack of clarity usually held more weight with Karina, as the fear of the unknown left no room for her to deviate, or at least get caught. Karina's record was clean for the most part, at least far as Ms. Burke knew up to this point.

Ms. Burke, being a single-parent, refused to leave anything to chance, and never strayed from her strong-handed approach. With being apart from Karina's father and having to work five to six days per week to make ends meet, she did everything she could to create the best life for her daughter. Being a single-parent was not what she planned or wanted, but she was determined to make the best she could of her situation. As dire as things were at times, Ms. Burke remained determined to stay the course with Karina. If it could be at all possible, she wanted to keep Karina away from duplicating her path, making the same bad decisions that jumpstarted her adulthood earlier than it probably should have been initiated. Karina's consistent Merit Roll performances in school and aspirations to pursue a career in fashion drove her even more to help her along the way. Here in this moment, however, her fears that were once mere past imaginations, were potentially manifesting to a current-day scenario of life-changing proportions.

"Karina," said Ms. Burke in a slightly-elevated, now demanding voice. "I'm not gonna ask again!" The latter of her words were said with claps to accentuate almost every syllable. Karina, feeling the pressure of an avalanche of boulders on her chest, that had her heart increasing to a light-speed heart rate now that her response had now become seemingly overdue.

"I...Mom...I," Karina struggled to piece together a full statement. "Karina," said Ms. Burke, in an attempt to provide a final opportunity for her daughter to answer. Karina, knowing that her chances to have any semblance of a conversation was fleeting, took a deep breath, sat up, and pushed herself to speak as well as she could to her mother who sat in mixed concoction of inquiry and churning anger. "Momma, I just got the test and...and I just wanted you to know, because I don't know what to do. I just took the test yesterday – a couple of them to be sure. I think I took them right. I read the instructions. I read 'em a few times to make sure..." Karina was interrupted, sharply. "Make sure what? That you really are about to have a baby? It doesn't get much clearer than this. Even if it is a dollar store pregnancy test," retorted Ms. Burke. "So if it came up negative, what would've happened then. I swear, I don't know what to do with you! I have tried – Karina I have *tried*!" The frustration increased the intensity and volume of every word. The fever pitch that was previously set in the room had managed to go to an even higher level, almost inexplicably.

Karina sat with her head down, tears welling up in her eyes, but not dropping, forming what seemed to be an almost facial dam. She knew that there would be no sympathy to be gained from her mother in this situation and that any visible tears would only pour gasoline on a fire that continued to build with higher and higher flames. "I'm sorry, Mom!" cried out a mentally exhausted Karina. "First thing you've said to me that I have no question back to this whole time," said Ms. Burke with a cutting of eyes that were sharper than any knife in their kitchen. "So now that we've gotten this far, with you being 'sorry' and all, you still haven't answered any of my questions. What little boy did you get all tied up with?" And at once, the awkward silence returned. In this instance, Karina was more scared than ever, for reasons beyond what appeared to be obvious. "How much can I, should I tell her?" thought Karina. "If I tell her that Carter was over here that one ti…"

SMACK!

Before Karina could create her desperate stream of thoughts, Ms. Burke had closed the gap of space in one mere long step and back-handed Karina on her right cheek. SMACK! While the move surprised Karina, it surprised Ms. Burke even more, as she felt the reaction came from a place of deep frustration. While she often extended threats of discipline, it often remained just that – threats. This was a moment when her rationale had dwindled, compelling her to act with little to no thought. From her perspective, Karina was too slow to provide explanation as to what was going on, compelling her to think that she was still hiding details. How much still had yet to be known? When did it happen? And who was it with? These questions asked before still remained unanswered. This rash reaction would definitely not speed up the pressure-filled interrogation. While no bruise or markings were showing, Karina was in pain. The pain was more mental than physical, as she knew that she was in unchartered territory with her mother. This was a place that she worked to avoid, but had seemingly failed in all accounts in this situation.

"Girl, since you don't have nothing to say, clean yourself up and we're going to the doct-" "Carter! It was with Carter!" screamed a pained Karina. "Carter came over and...and...and that's how it happened. It was about a few weeks ago." "A few weeks ago, when? Karina, tell me more," said an unsatisfied Ms. Burke. "Around that time when you were working those extra shifts earlier in the middle of the month. He came by here and then -" An even more infuriated Ms. Burke interrupted, "So you're saying that little boy from your old school was in *my* house and y'all were in here like y'all grown or something, acting fast? Karina – what is wrong with you?!?" Emotions continued to rise for both Karina and Ms. Burke. While answers were coming forth, it did nothing to ease tensions, only heightening them.

"I took you out of that school to get you from out of that madness. You told me that you didn't even like your classmates, but somehow you find your way back to one of them and have sex with them? Then you mess around and let him get you pregnant? Karina, this does not make a lick of sense," said Ms. Burke. Her frustration came from the quick withdrawal she did with Karina from Southview. Karina complained that she did not like her school and wanted to leave, because she was being bullied. The school resolved that the allegations were unfounded and refused to pursue the matter any further. A frustrated Ms. Burke, who had no reservation in doing what she could to protect Karina, ultimately opted to remove her from Southview, even losing out on a refund of the tuition that she paid in full for the eighth-grade school year.

While she was not a fan of having to leave mid-year and scrambling to find another school to transfer to, she was not willing to compromise or put Karina at risk. She cared deeply for her only child and, from what she knew, she took her education seriously enough that she would not recklessly ask to switch schools. The only relief was that this would only be barely a semester, as she was on her way to becoming a high school freshman. She always had her eyes set on Grace Academy for Karina, with the rich tradition they had for helping the young women in the area get to the best colleges, with scholarships in tow. As expensive as tuition would be at the high school level, Ms. Burke would do whatever it took to get Karina in position to get to higher education and beyond. Seeing her daughter rising up from the couch, recovering from the physical discipline just received, holding her sore left cheek, she could not believe what this situation was shaping out to be. The possibility grew more and more that her daughter could become the next generation of a teen mother in their family. This a reality she feared and hoped would never come to pass.

As Karina walked away, her Mom yelled again, reiterating her frustration, "Karina, hurry your behind up! And you better hope that they can get you in at the office. Come on!" She had seen her mother angry, but the anger she was seeing was like none before that she had ever had to endure. Frantically, as she got to the top of the stairs to the second floor, she rushed to her room and went for her favorite sweatshirt that laid on her bed. Picking up her sweatshirt, a small business card with only a handwritten phone number on it. The blue ink reflecting 10 digits were a tempting call for Karina. She was given the card on that fateful day that she went to purchase the pregnancy tests by the cashier. The cashier, seeing the purchase Karina was making, reached into her pocket and slid the card into the plastic bag, with the receipt. Discreetly, she told Karina, "Girl, call that number, ASAP. The sooner you call, the cheaper it'll be. You're too young to be going through all of that." Karina, in her shame and fear, took the bag and walked out, thinking about the advice she was given by a complete stranger.

Could this be the solution? "I'm too young," thought Karina. This thought passed through her mind from the first day of what she knew to be morning sickness, which sometimes alternated as any-time-of-day sickness. The symptom that she had heard about from her mother was causing her to wonder why she had gone as far as she did and other regretful moments that she intended to keep a mystery from her mother or anyone else for that matter. Maybe this was the answer, after all. The responsibility that laid on the other side of about a seven-month journey was frightening to say the least. If she would choose to follow through on the unsolicited advice from her cashier advocate, maybe this whole problem would go away. Something had to be done, because life as she knew it was already beginning to change, as evidenced by her mother's reaction just moments ago. Maybe it would be best to know for sure, getting confirmation from the doctor on what the truth of the matter really was. “Yeah, might as well,” thought Karina to herself.

“Karina, they are about to close the office – LET’S GO!” Ms. Burke’ voice carried through the house like a natural megaphone, reiterating the assumed tone of a threat had quickly elevated to what could only be assessed as a promise – a promise of being “helped” into getting out of the house. In her best attempt to avoid that from taking shape, Karina responded, quickly, “I’m coming down.” She looked in the mirror, already preparing to clear up a cut or even a bruise, but somehow her face was clear of any marks, despite a resonating sting that still was felt around her cheekbone. She imagined that her once-visible dimple may had become an actual dent in her face. The force of her mother’s hand replayed in her mind several times since it actually occurred. Karina, not wanting to further anger her mother, put on the sweatshirt and placed the small card in her pocket. She moved with urgency out of her room and went downstairs.

Ms. Burke stood at the door, keys in hand, looked at Karina with her eyes speaking on her behalf, making it known that it was indeed time to go. No words we spoken as Karina put on her shoes at the door, walked outside to the car, as her mother used her key to lock the front door, and sat nervously in the passenger seat of the car.

SLAM!

Ms. Burke' door was closed so hard, the side-view mirror on both sides shook, while a small cloud of cold dust seemed to burst forth from the vents of the car. The air conditioner had stopped working for months and was still in need of repair. This was the most action that either of them had seen from the vents in months. The car started and not too soon after, Ms. Burke pulled out of their driveway, aggressively, racing to get to their doctor, in hopes of getting some impromptu aid. Looking down at the clock, Karina realized that the office had likely closed and the only options likely left were to go to the Emergency Room or to the Urgent Care. She let out a sigh of frustration, in hopes that her mother did not hear her. “Do you think we’ll still make it in time. They’re probably closed by now, right?”

“No, they’re still open, Karina. I called before we left and they’re expecting us. Besides, you’ve never been to this doctor before, so how would you know?” asked Ms. Burke. Karina looked confused. She had known of only one doctor for years and had no clue what her mother meant. “Come to think of it, I’m just as mad at myself for missing those appointments this past year. I probably would’ve caught on to how fast you were getting way before today,” Ms. Burke said regretfully. What started as shock, then transitioned briefly into disappointment, and now shifted into a fiery anger. Her anger now seemed to have a double portion, but still the majority of it being aimed at her daughter, as their drive to get to the office before they closed ensued.

Karina noticed that she was driving in what appeared to be the total opposite direction of the office that she thought that they were headed to, seeking an answer to this mystery. "Which doctor are we going to then, Mom?" Karina asked, mixed with concern and confusion. "You got real talkative all of a sudden, huh?" she responded. "Karina, I told you what I went through in having you. I was a kid. *You* are a kid. I know I've called you my 'mini-me', but this is one thing we can't have in common. I'm breaking this generational curse, if it's the last thing that I do." "Break this generational cur-" thought Karina, interrupting the initial playback. A proverbial, dark lightbulb lit in her mind.

"Mom...Mom...I can't do that. Please don't make me do that!" urged a scared Karina. What was once a possibility had now become a fast-approaching reality that she was not prepared for. The little white card option that she held in her pocket had now become her mother's plan of action. This was how she was going to "break this generational curse"? Karina became frantic and awaited a response, unsure even more what was going on in the head of her mother. "Karina, do you understand what having a baby does to you? Do you have *any* idea how your life changes? Are you ready to become a teenage mom? How are you going to pay for diapers?

Who's going to stay home to take care of the baby? You're going to have to drop out of school, I'm the only one working, bringing money into the house..." Ms. Burke continued, releasing a barrage of statements and rhetorical questions to Karina, who sat stunned, not knowing what to say, even if she was given the chance. This situation, somehow, had gone from bad to worse.

"...and on top of that, I am not ready to be a grandmother, Karina. I am not READY!" screamed Ms. Burke, as she finally took a breath after what seemed to be minutes of alternating interrogations and declarations. Speed limits were being broken, stop signs were barely being stopped at, and the anxiety of the moment kept increasing. Karina spoke, perceiving what appeared to be an opening to respond, "Mom...I don't know what to do, but I just feel...I feel like this isn't right." "Only people who pay bills have a say in this matter. What bill have you even put in on? We are going to fix *your* mistake. You will thank me later," she said as the car appeared to accelerate even faster, going towards the freeway exit.

35...40...50...60...75 mph. The needle on the speedometer was leaning intently towards the right side of the dial. Even buckled up, the concept of safety was beginning to dwindle as each second was taking them to a faster speed. Ms. Burke quieted herself and focused her eyes on the freeway ahead of her, while Karina's cries fell on her decidedly closed ears. Tears began to cascade down Karina's cheeks, overflowing from her tear ducts as if a dam had been blown up with unlimited explosives. This situation was becoming explosive indeed. Karina, as scared as she was, was beyond scared, riding as a passenger in a car that was taking her to place that she had come to the conclusion she did not want to go to. How would she take care of a baby? She had no idea. She just had a new found understanding that this would be a decision that she would live to regret. What had not come into discussion, not even once, was this was an innocent life. Unplanned, yes, but innocent, nonetheless. "If I am pregnant, what does this baby have to do with all of this?" wondered Karina.

As Ms. Burke had begun to cruise at a speed just north of 90mph, she looked to her right and saw someone standing on the side of the freeway, pointing something at her. "Aw, come on now! We don't have time for this!" she exclaimed. In her haste to get her and Karina to their destination, she became unaware of how fast she was actually driving, not realizing that with it being close to rush hour, police would likely be out to try to catch speeding drivers. Ms. Burke knew her fate, as a police cruiser that was a few hundred feet behind the officer immediately took off, turned on its sirens, flashed its lights, calling for them to pull the car over. Ms. Burke, not looking for even more trouble, slowed down and pulled her car over. Karina sat quiet, internally, relieved, as the remnant of tears trickled down in the trails set by their predecessors in the moments before.

Serving a direct threat, Ms. Burke cautioned, "Don't you say a word, little girl. As soon as we get done with this, we're still going to get this taken care of. Trust." Karina could not muster the energy or nerve to even give a compliant nod. An officer walked out of the cruiser and approached the car. She knocked on Karina's window, signaling for it to be rolled down. "Open the window, Karina," mumbled Ms. Burke. She rolled the window rolled down, ever so slowly, as the motor in the aged vehicle was beginning to wear and react slowly. “Is there a problem, Officer,” asked Ms. Burke, as she kept both of her hands on the steering wheel, adding a reassuring smile, insinuating that she would abide by anything asked of her. “My partner clocked you doing about 91mph back there. You do realize that this is a 65 zone, right?” inquired the Officer. “Officer, I do apologize. My daughter and I were in a hurry for an appointment. As a matter of fact, we were set to get off at the exit just ahead. It’s a doctor’s appointment that we’re trying to be on time for.” Ms. Burke did her best to get this interaction over with. She had not lost sight of her objective regarding Karina.

“Just over there? Well, uh, no doctor that I know of is open right now. As a matter of fact, the only offices open at that exit usually aren’t the kind I’d imagine you’d want to go to, ma’am,” advised the Officer. “Well, it’s a special appointment and we really have to get there. I take responsibility for the fast driving. If you could give us just a warning and let us get there, I’d really app-“ “License and registration, please,” the officer interrupted. Disappointed that her quick suggestion would not be accepted, Ms. Burke replied,

"Absolutely, Officer. Karina, please open the glove compartment and hand her the paperwork. I can give you my license in just a mom...ent." She looked around the car and realized that her purse was nowhere in sight.

"Is there a problem?" asked the officer. "No problem. Um...I can't seem to...I left my purse at the house. In my hurry to get to the doctor's office, I must've forgotten it. This is so unlike me. I usually always have my papers in order," assured Ms. Burke. "As you can see, Officer, there's a lot going on. If you could just give us a war-" The office noticed Karina's down disposition, as she received the car registration from her and immediately interrupted, and asked, "Young lady, are you ok?" Karina, not sure if she would be allowed by her mother to speak, looked over to her left, for what appeared to be a seeking of approval. Before she could connect a stern look to direct otherwise, the Officer reiterated the question, saying, "It's ok. You can talk to me. Is everything ok?"

Looking up at the officer through the open window, she noticed a small gold cross pendant that sat close to her neck, nestled right next to the collar of her uniform. Somehow a small comfort seemed to ease into her. She had not seen a small cross pendant like that since the one that sat on her grandmother's neck many years ago. There was always a feeling of safety she felt when she was with her and this feeling was eerily similar in this moment. "Yeah, um...I'm just not feeling too well, but I'll be ok." The officer sensed that the words just received were not accurate and that something was amiss in this car speeding towards a still yet undetermined location.

Sitting now as a spectator, with her nerves continuing to elevate as the seconds of the traffic stop continued to tick, Ms. Burke was concerned. Her concerns included getting Karina to the office before it closed and now potentially getting a speeding ticket while en route. Matters worsened with the possibility that the officer's impromptu interrogation would potentially uncover the private situation that had come to light only about an hour ago. "Officer," interrupted Ms. Burke with a polite, but nervous voice. "My daughter is just fine. I know that you have much more important things to do, as do we. If we could just be allowed to go…" The Officer responded, "Miss…" "Burke," she quickly completed the question inadvertently asked. "I am by no means trying to hold you up. I am at the end of my shift. You, like every one else on this expressway, have somewhere to go. Please give me a minute to run your info, make sure everything checks out, and we should be all good."

Two seconds of silence immediately followed. A frozen silence.

"Miss Burke, are we in agreement here?" she asked, as Karina sat in her seat, failing to maintain an eased demeanor that she was claiming to have. "Yes, Officer. We'll be right here. No worries, at all," said Ms. Burke, who felt the lie as it crept over the edge of the teeth of a feigned smile. The officer then walked away keeping an eye on Karina, knowing that she had a secret that in that moment she would not be given liberty to share. As she was about to enter her car, Karina began to cry, repeating the singular tear cadence from earlier. Seeing the silent expression, she was warned under mumbled speech, “Karina, if you don’t stop with all that crying…” Even with law enforcement just feet away, Karina felt that her mother had become a livewire and that it would be wise to not test the constraints of this newly-issued threat.

Chapter 18

The officer sat in the cruiser and took a deep breath. She had no intent on issuing a ticket or even checking information. The top priority was saving this scared young lady from what she knew would be the worst moment of her life. Having been a five-year veteran of the police force and native to the area, she was well aware of what the destination was going to be if she had not stopped them. Almost immediately offset from the next exit was an abortion clinic. This clinic was all too familiar, as she had been called to disband several protests and witnessed local teenage girls walking out of cars with faces looking just as petrified as that of Karina's. There was no doubt that this car was set to pull up to the parking lot of that office. The combination of women's and police intuition was in full effect, as it was clear that someone had to help this young girl. Making the situation even more peculiar was that she felt an inexplicable familiarity with the two women. All of the thinking that she did, nothing fully clicked.

She looked down at the tattered registration paper and thought deeply on how to set everything straight. As it was common for her to do, she placed her right index finger and thumb, lightly clutching the small cross pendant that sat on her neck and said a prayer. "Lord, You see I'm here dealing with another one," sighed the officer. "You already know. I just wanted to go home, get to my family and...and...here I am. I know I signed up for this, but at the same time, Lord, why me?" Though she always knew the answer to that often-repeated question, it always resurfaced, especially when she felt immense conviction to help beyond the constraints of her given duties. She followed with another sigh, already realizing the response she would have gotten, had she given it another second more, "Give me wisdom and please make sure this little girl is alright. Thank you, Father. Amen." Immediately after her "amen", was a sigh of determination intertwined with apprehension.

Immediately, as if divinely directed, she stepped out of the vehicle, determined to intervene if possible, changing the almost certainly deadly chain of events that were about to take place. Taking deep breaths, she reenacted her walk to the passenger side of the vehicle, preparing to do what she could. Knocking on the glass gently, the window slid down with the same squeaky slow descent as last time. The young girl had eyes that looked tired and desperate, while her mother had a serious look, almost as if she had just got done with a verbal chastisement before the officer's return to the vehicle. "Ok, um…looks like everything checked out, and…" "So we're good to go, huh? No problems, officer?" asked a seemingly excited Ms. Burke. "Not quite yet, Miss Burke. I will have to give you a citation for driving in excess of the speed limit. You and I both know that you were blazing through here," responded the officer. "But you know what, that's not even my biggest concern right now. If I could be honest. If *we* could be honest, I'm more concerned about where we both know you are headed." She then paused to allow what she hoped to be an admittance of guilt in this matter.

And she waited…

…a few more seconds longer.

It was a frozen moment in time. The officer served an authoritative look at Ms. Burke, while Ms. Burke feigned a look of confusion, and

Karina sat confused as to which end of this staring spectrum she would align with. "Ok, as I said, officer, we're headed to…" The Officer interrupted, with a stern voice, still managing to maintain her emotion and not allow her volume to amplify, "Ms. Burke, the only way we're going to get through this is if you're straight up with me. Looking at the face on this little girl, I can tell that this is not a routine visit to the doctor." Karina sat dejected, looking down at her hands sitting in her lap, now exhausted in honoring the demands of her mother during this traffic stop to appear as if there was nothing amiss to look into. She looked up briefly at the Officer, with what was a visual "thank you" or at least a glance that held out hope that this was a divine, or at least, law-enforcement intervention.

"Officer," Ms. Burke finally replied. "Are you a mother?" "Yes, I am, Ms. Burke. A proud mother of two young boys, 2 and 4," responded the officer, still hoping to find resolve. "So no teenagers and definitely no girls, huh?" retorted Ms. Burke. The officer, knowing that this was an effort to discredit her in this roadside debate, was determined to curtail what was emanating to become the opposite of what she determined her impromptu mission to be, asking "And your point, Miss Burke?" "My point," replied a reinvigorated Ms. Burke, "is that I am a mother, just like you, but I don't have boys. I have a teenage girl. A teenage girl who thinks she's grown. Grown enough to do things that, until she turns 18, I am held responsible for. You're asking me to be 'straight up' with you, then here it is – we are on a way to fix a problem that will save her future and her life, to be honest. And as 'straight up' as we're being with each other, this is *my* responsibility. I'll just take my ticket so we can go."

The officer, surprisingly, stood ready with a response, having listened to Ms. Burke' justification of her parental decision-making. Old memories that were packed away in the officer's past were quickly coming to remembrance and would serve as her supporting evidence as to why she felt compelled to intervene. She estimated that Karina was close to the age when she, too, was involuntarily led to an abortion clinic. Having been sexually assaulted by a friend of her family just months before her 16th birthday, she begun to exhibit signs of pregnancy. The shame of being pregnant before marriage was of more consequence than the fact that the pregnancy was the result of her mother's brother – a man whom she refused to ever acknowledge as her uncle. Reiterating the shame, she recalled no inquiry as to who the father was or for any related details. The answer given without any preceding questions was to “fix the problem”. Knowing that her family, who had deep ties in one of the biggest churches in the community, Blessed Hope Missionary Church, would be shunned for what they deemed was a shameful act in the sight of God. Her story, even if she got it out, would not, and did not, matter to anyone, including her own mother.

Without second thought, she was taken to a small, nondescript office building, where, unlike Karina, she was told in advance what the plan of action was going to be. The building had no windows, had a deserted parking lot with only one other car in sight, and looked as cold, cruel, and soul-scarring as the events that were about to transpire. The fear of this moment was becoming too much, confusing her as to if the churning in her stomach was the feeling of the forthcoming unknown or if the morning sickness that accompanied her pregnancy was making its presence felt once again. Despite her reluctance to go in, it was overridden by her devout obedience to her mother, who having just parked the car, unmuted her conversation by saying, “Come on, girl. Let’s go.” The direction was more blunt and direct than anything ever instructed of her. She would not dare to reply with anything short of compliance, lest she be disciplined harshly, as justified by Pastor Kingsley Sr and the culture of their home church.

The memory of everything that happened between her entry and exit of the building was a memory that still remained repressed. The physical pain lingered as she recalled the steps taken only a few feet behind her mother, who trekked from the small, cold building, hoping that no one would see their exit from a place that she saw as the best solution. As she walked out with her mother, she noticed that there sat an additional car in the parking lot that was not there when they first arrived. The door of this car opened up and a woman who looked to be in her late 40s to early 50s called out, “Excuse me. Can I pray with y’all?” While her mother tried to ignore the request to pray, she acknowledged the call with saddened eyes and altered her direction towards the mystery woman. The woman set herself with open hands to hold hands opposite of the young girl to pray, but instead she was met with a full embrace and a wailing that was seemingly held in from the trauma that just occurred. “It’s ok, baby. It’s ok,” she said while comforting the sobbing teenager.

Her mother, in her own apparent shame of being seen doing what she initially thought was the right thing to do, showed no resistance, and instead stood by her car. She contemplated if this was the right thing to do. She wondered if she allowed the pressure of reputation within a community to override her need to be there for her daughter. At least in this case, someone had stepped in to be, what she now realized was needed, a shoulder to cry on for her daughter. She prayed to herself, nonverbally, “Lord...help...please. I love my baby, but I just...I just don’t know, Lord!” As she prayed, the mystery woman whispered in the ear of this young girl, “Lord, you are a healer! Let your healing virtue cover her, in the name of Jesus! We believe that you hear her cries...” She stopped herself, discerning that the remedy to this situation was beyond spoken prayer, but laid in the reconciliation of a regretful mother and pained daughter. Immediately, over the shoulder of the still-sobbing young girl, she motioned for her mother to join their sacred space. She slowly obliged and knew to be attentive to the words soon to be delivered.

"Sister, I'm sure that you thought that you what you were doing what was right. This is probably all you know. I'm not here to judge at all. I don't know y'all from anybody else, but I do know this – Jesus loves you, both," she counseled. Tears slowly came down the cheeks of the woman who was full of resolve prior to this meeting, as the tears of her daughter slowly began to subside, now feeling the comfort of this loving stranger. "Look here, you are not the first, but definitely not the last that I've seen exit those doors. I know that I won't be able to stop everyone, but if I could just share the Father's love with y'all, maybe we can stop this with this generation," she added. Slowly moving back to confirm the words were heard and comforting appreciated, the teenager nodded, showing her understanding in this moment. "I'm not here to get to talkin', prayin', and all of that and you walk away still hurt. Here," the woman said as she began to remove her necklace from her neck.

The mother finally uttered, seeing what was happening, "No, no, please. We're going to be o…" "Sister, I've been called and sometimes my answer goes beyond a prayer or a hug. Romans 12:15 is my commission and sometimes I have to do a little more than expected. Take this young lady," she said as she presented her with a small gold necklace with gold pendant attached. "You wouldn't believe it, but my daughter almost walked through those same doors you just came out of. By the grace of God, I was able to convince her to not go through with it. Now I have a little granddaughter that is blessing my bones, daily. May this bless you and encourage you." She paused, allowing her shared testimony and heartfelt gift to take root. "God's not through with you! I'm believing that this is the start of your commission in your life – a Romans 12:15 commission! You watch," she said confidently has she hugged her one last time and slowly entered her car. As she returned to a bookmarked place in her Bible, she seemingly awaited the next person to comfort. The regretful mother and her daughter, looked upon each other and embraced, knowing that this divine moment was intentional and would change their lives, forever.

"Miss Burke," the Officer said. "Here's my offer – go home and we'll call it even. I know that this may not make a lot of sense to you, but I know how this goes and I would hate for you two to go through what...let me just say it - what I've gone through. It is a pain that no one should have to endure." Ms. Burke, hearing sincerity in the Officer's voice, still refused to back down in her determination. "Please give me my ticket so we can go, officer. Thank you," said a resolute Ms. Burke. The disheartened Officer, shook her head, and reached for her book of tickets to begin complying with the defiant mother's request.

Just then a message from her radio broke out "Signal 5. We have emerging activity at 211 Brown Street. Fights breaking out with protesters. A bomb threat was sent in. We need backup and the bomb squad, now!" The officer thought, "I don't think that I've ever been so glad to hear about a bomb threat in my life. Thank you, God". The strange prayer of thanks was from her deepest place of gratitude. She realized that the address mentioned was that of the building that Ms. Burke and Karina were headed. "Miss Burke, if you just heard my radio, that is the address you were headed to, right?" asked the Officer. Ms. Burke, now visibly slightly shaken, nodded and confirmed the question. "I don't know what more signals you need to see or hear to know that you and your daughter don't need to be going there. Me, stopping you the way it went down? This was no coincidence! Look, I don't have a teenager or a daughter your age, but you can get through this. I was blessed with a second chance. Based on what I was told, I wasn't supposed to be able to have kids after what I went through. Young lady, you have your whole life to look forward to. It'll be ok," assured the Officer.

Her focus went back solely on Ms. Burke. "Go home. Love on your daughter. She needs you. God's got you both!" Ms. Burke, finally absorbing the sobering evidence that it would be best to turn around, accepted, what she deemed to be, the hard truth. Seeing that her advice appeared to set Ms. Burke in the intended direction, she said before leaving, "I have to go. This is going to be a hot situation. Take care and have faith that it'll all be alright." The Officer ran to her car and drove off in the direction of the office building that was seemingly becoming a deadly battleground, flashing her lights and sirens. She looked in her rear-view mirror, hoping that she fulfilled the words spoken over her life by the previous owner of the gold cross that sat on her neck. She knew that as obvious as she tried to make it seem what the best move would be, there was no guarantee that Ms. Burke and Karina would execute a figurative and actual turnaround Ms. Burke, in her own reflection, sourced her own memory, returning to a time when she was driven to take herself down this same path, but was stopped by her own mother, whose words stuck with her, "Baby, God's going to do some awesome things through you and Karina. I don't know how to explain. All I know is that little girl blesses my bones, daily!"

Chapter 19

"So now I'm meeting up with a Detective tomorrow morning. Hey, y'all...I don't know – this is getting crazy," vented a mentally-drained Regina. Both Mel and Carter stood within feet of Regina, sharing in the confusion. The three former classmates were debriefing each other on what pieces of the puzzle they all shared for what was becoming a plotline rivaling a box-office drama. "And you're saying that her kid is yours, Carter? I'm saying..." exclaimed Regina. "Saying what, Gina? Trust me, it wasn't like I thought that just getting with her one time would come to this. I came ready – protected and everything," explained a now-defensive Carter. "But you just got done saying that it ended up coming off or taking it off or something. I hate to put it on blast, bruh, but you've gotta face facts, especially if this is your baby," said a sobering Mel.

"It's facts, man, but I'm still trippin' on all of this," replied Carter. "Truth is, if that baby is mine, why would she leave town, stop talking to me, and then just blow back down years later. I would've stepped up. Y'all know me! Karina had to know she could've let me know." The three still stood there wondering how to make sense of all that was going on. Karina was making her presence felt, even having not been in town for the past few years. Within a mere few hours, she had carved out real estate in the minds of Regina, Mel, and especially Carter, who stood in this moment not knowing how to make sense of all of what was going on. All they knew was that with every second that ticked away, they had more questions than answers.

"Does anybody even know where she went? I can't be the only one wondering where this girl's been. Y'all, believe me – if this is what is, I'll handle my business, off top. But you know I'm going to need that good paternity te..." "Carter, you'd better! I mean, she was my girl, but I'd think you'd be a fool if you don't get a test," interrupted an agreeable Regina. "She owes you that much and more, for real. But don't get it twisted, Carter, when she *was* here, she wasn't getting down with anybody. As strict as her mother was, I'm still surprised that you pulled off what you did – oh my fault. I wasn't trying to be funny." Mel and Carter both shook their heads, realizing poor choice of words that Regina used echoed the probable genesis of this matter. "But still, C, you need to find out, for sure. I'm sure if you go down the way to the clinic, you can find out. Better than going on that TV show, letting the whole world in on your business," advised Regina. "Yeah, we'd all be learning at the same if you went and did that. No telling how that could affect your hoop dreams if people saw you on that," added Mel.

"Yeah, but this is bigger than my dreams, Mel. If I've gotta kid...bruh, this changes everything," resolved a reflecting Carter. "Besides, there's a lot of dudes that had kids and ended up going to the league and it all worked out. Still a lot to think about, though." Mel had no doubt that Carter would stand up and take responsibility, if Karina's claims were indeed accurate. He knew that Carter's family would likely be shocked, as they did all that they could to protect Carter and his future. As his star rose early on in his high school basketball playing days, they felt the pressure to keep Carter shielded from people who they perceived to be vultures, looking to take advantage of one who many were predicting to be a basketball superstar headed to financial prosperity beyond that ever seen in their community.

This included intervening even when it came to his friendships. Carter's mother was adamant that the only person she felt comfortable around Carter was Mel. "Trust is a special thing, Carter, and not everyone should have access to yours. Remember that," she would often remind her aspiring star-athlete. Carter took her words to heart, despite the temptations to allow the bright lights of his streaks of success to distract him. Deep down he had an understanding that amongst his growing fan base and admirers, there were those lurking with less-than-good intentions. For Carter, while he felt that Karina fell nowhere near to that category, he knew that his mother would likely not be as endeared to the idea of her presence in his life. He knew it best to keep his relationship with her in a secret, sacred space. Carter's attraction to her, he knew, was authentic. Real. Nonetheless, he also knew that he would have an almost impossible time in trying to convince his mother that this connection should be as allowable as his to Mel.

As the three of them stood in the parking lot, still working to make sense of this growing narrative from their past, inside of the building Pastor Kingsley just missed a call on his cell phone. The call mysteriously never rang, but merely registered as an unheard voicemail message. "Maybe the network is cutting up, again. Might have to switch carriers or something, Doc. Can't afford to missing calls," he thought to himself. As busy as his phone often was, he still knew that this round of calls was in another category all in itself. Each call made and received was adding yet another layer to a complicated narrative that was still not as clear as he wanted it to be. Though he knew his strongest of his spiritual gifts to be that of discernment and wisdom, Pastor Kingsley was having a difficult time determining what should be done, much less how to assemble all of the involved pieces and parts. Rhythmically tapping his desk, he pondered all of the cast of characters who had been drawn to him this hectic evening. Outside of his inherent role in being the one everyone expected to have all of the answers and be able to bring peace to chaos, he had a desire to see the people involved, especially the younger ones, have a clearer path, beyond this night's revealed chain of events.

The most recent call only added gasoline to an already kindling fire of a situation. Complicating this matter beyond calls received from Karina Burke and her mother was hearing from yet another person who conveniently called shortly afterwards in the same evening. The call was not answered, as Pastor Kingsley had grown weary and wary of answering any more unidentified callers. The call was routed to his voicemail inbox, which was surprisingly cleared enough to receive the message from the mystery caller. Listening to the call, his curiosity peaked even more.

“Pastor…Pastor,” the voice repeated, almost seemingly still looking for the next words to continue the message with. The caller sounded as bewildered as the receiver would soon likely become. “I’m sorry to bother you. I know you’re busy, but…but…I have a situation that I need your help with. My marriage…” Pastor Kingsley let out a sigh of peculiar relief. Teen pregnancy and questioned paternity was the bulk of his matters for this evening. He never imagined that the emergence of a “typical” marital issue would be a welcome interruption. With this brief resurgence, he listened on. "...has been in a weird place for some time and I could never understand really. Over the past few years, since we got married, everything appeared to be fine, it really did, but..." the message was interrupted by what could be imagined to be a flood of tears. The audible crying lasted for what seemed to be several seconds. The caller, now recomposed, did their best to continue. "...but something was wrong. Something just wasn't right. And...and..." A few seconds of silence came into play, adding suspense to the message. Pastor Kingsley sat with an intent look at his cell phone sharing this moment via his speaker phone that usually filled the room at its max capacity, but was quieted substantially due to the potentially sensitive nature of this message.

The message continued.

"Pastor I thi...no – I *know* that my husband messed with...no, *raped* someone and...and..." The cries came back in past failed attempt to keep them from flooding back in the phone call. Pastor Kingsley's eyebrows raised, arched high, creating rows across his forehead from the astonishment. The message once thought to be "typical" had taken a quick and unexpected turn. He listened on to the voicemail message, trying to gather more details.

"...as much as I love him, I cannot, in good conscience, sit here and act like it didn't happen. I don't know how long or how many victims there are, all I know is that this has got to be made right. I'm so glad that we don't have kids of our own to explain this to. That would've made this even harder to do." The caller paused, taking, what sounded like, a deep breath, before continuing on. Pastor Kingsley could feel the lifting of burden from the caller, though, the weight of the moment still registered through the voicemail. Still with no way of knowing who the caller was, he already assumed the responsibility of helping in whatever way that he could. It was a brave, unspoken call to action that Pastor Kingsley felt prepared to answer, as a part of the call on his life to help the people of his community.

As the call continued, he listened intently for more information, more detail on this new case he committed himself to, even in the midst of the prior unexpected drama his evening had opened with. "I know an allegation like this can't be made without some proof, some evidence. I'm not a cop, but I know I'd have to have something, and believe me, I do. Since I've already put myself out there, I'll go a step further and say that..." The caller's voice trailed off again to silence, with light cries in the background. The reservoir of courage used to get out the prior words had seemingly become depleted. Pastor Kingsley resolved that any words past this point would be out of extended grace from up high. Having worked with victims of sexual assault, he had gotten acquainted to allowing those who confided in him the opportunity to share at their own pace. While he received formal training and education to hone his certification as an advocate, he had an innate ability to know the best cadence for revelations such as this. Though this was a voicemail message he was listening to, he would not allow himself to be overanxious or become impatient with its delivery.

The speaker continued.

"I think the victim that I know of had a child. I don't know if it's a boy or girl. From what I can tell...from what I can tell...Pastor, my husband had a kid with a little girl and here I am stuck here, childless. We've tried for years and he does this and a child came out of it? What did I do wrong? How and why do I deserve this?" The question was asked with an elevated tone with rhetorical backing. Hearing this detail provided some insight as to who this might be. Pastor Kingsley counseled many couples who struggled to have children, so this likely could narrow down who this could be, assuming that they were actual members of his church. "They have to be members," he thought. "I would hope that my number isn't just floating around out here for people to call me with their problems. Then again, there I go limiting the call. God's mission fields – always something to tend to."

The message picked up immediately, as Pastor Kingsley's inner dialogue subsided. "I know it's selfish, but after all of this time of trying...my husband's got a whole child out here that either doesn't know he's the father or they have someone else thinking they're the father or...or...or...or who knows? All I know is that I do have proof of everything that I am talking about. I called hoping to talk with you, but I'm sure you're busy. If you could give me a call back at..." As the number was about the be shared, Pastor Chris walked in the office. Pastor Kingsley immediately scrambled and hit the red button on his phone to end the call, hoping that the privacy of the voicemail was call was still contained.

"Son, you know you can't barge in my office like that," chastised Pastor Kingsley to his protégé. "Especially a night like tonight when..." Chris responded quickly, apologetically interrupting, "Sir, I know, I know. I came up here as soon as I wrapped up the event. I got the kids waiting on their rides in the gymnasium right now and thought I'd come right back to see what was going on." Pastor Kingsley extended grace and responded with a report, "Not much changed, son. Still trying to make sense of what's going on. How about you? How did the rest of the night go with the kids?" He was seeking some positive news for the night. Anything would be a welcome escape from the night's torrential events so far. Anything with the youth usually brought a joyful hope to his soul. On this night, it would be a much-needed bright spot in a sea of storylines that brought forth seeming darkness.

"Well...it was definitely a sobering one. I went in to P.K. preacher mode," said Chris, with a forced chuckle. "I just started talking, keeping it real with them. Dropped a testimony on 'em, making it known that there's so much more than just getting into whatever they can get into at this age." Pastor Kingsley had a puzzled look, "What made you go that route? You usually keep things light, staying away from being too serious and lecturing the kids. You know even *I* stay away from that." Chris responded, in a transparent tone to his mentor, "Sir, after all that's going on with Carter, it just weighed heavy on my spirit. I did what I thought was necessary. I think the kids got a lot out of it. I wasn't just sitting there lecturing, but I did make it known that I had something to talk about." Pastor Kingsley accepted Chris' response, as he knew that his discernment was a gift that he had that continued to sharpen. He did respond, however, with a cautionary inquiry, leaning forward in his chair, with his elbows on his desk.

"Ok, but did you bring up anything about the situation? I trust you Chris, but..." "Sir, absolutely not. I kept the talk about *my* experiences. No mention of Carter at all," he interrupted, as respectfully as he could. Pastor Kingsley felt a bit of relief and nodded his head in approval to the words he had just heard. He leaned back in his chair and took a moment to relax, as he knew that the evening left little to no room to do so, before or in the remainder left to come. "So," Chris continued. "What can I do? I'm in it with you, Pastor. Wanna help where I can?" As the question finalized, Pastor Kingsley's phone once again vibrated, signaling a text message this time. His palms immediately covered his face in mental fatigue, as Chris sighed and looked on in sympathy for his spiritual father. This night would be a lot for anyone and was proving to be a lot even for this spiritual powerhouse.

After removing his hands from his face, Pastor Kingsley slowly, but, out of a call to duty, picked up the phone to see what message had come through. The message that shown through the slightly tinted privacy screen read: “Pastor, I just left you that voicemail and realized that something as serious as this can’t be done through blocked numbers and calls. Here is my number. In case you don’t have my number saved, this is Mrs. Dewels.” Pastor’s eyes opened wide. “Wow…” he remarked, as Chris sat perplexed, waiting for clarity. The weight of the night, in one moment, had increased, exponentially.

Chapter 20

The kids filed out of the gymnasium, some with faces of disappointment, but many of them with sobered faces, as if they had received as dose of reality. While one complained, "I was just trying to hoop tonight, man", another contemplated, "I can't even lie. Pastor Chris is the realest." The majority definitely favored the result that Pastor Chris had hoped for. It was apparent that the message that he spontaneously gave to this group resonated with them. As Regina, Carter, and Mel still debated the newly discovered details, they took note of the faces of the crowd as they were making their way to the parking lot, many into the waiting cars of their parents.

Mel, felt a tap on his shoulder and turned around to see who was trying to get his attention. "Hey, Mel. Can I talk to you real quick?" asked a serious-sounding Carrell. Mel could tell that this was not the same Carrell that he had mentored up to this point and responded affirmatively with a nod, assuring his friends that he would be back to resume their discussion of the night's events. They walked away and restationed themselves by Mel's car, a few spaces away from their initial meet. Mel thought he had Carrell figured out and could not even begin to imagine what this was about. He had given him advice here and there about life, ranging from the integrity to not cheat on school work to how to approach girls. He never felt that his words really stuck with him, but he took relief in knowing that there was not much that he would not share with him. That level of trust was something that Mel did not take for granted, since he knew that it was not something available to everyone.

"So, look, I've been dealing with a problem for a minute now, and, um...I just wanted to know what you thought," started Carrell. "Problem?" thought Carrell. "What problem could a 12-year-old have that was so deep beyond being put on punishment or losing a pickup basketball game on the playground?" He did not want to jump to conclusions, so he regained his focus and listened intently to his young mentee. Mel did not want this instance to be a step backwards in the relationship that he had been building. "Ok, 'Rell, what's good? I'm here. Talk to me. What's going on?" asked Mel.

Carrell hesitated. He began to reconsider this impromptu outpour. A brief interruption of silence ensued, as he looked around to make sure that this conversation was as private as it could be within the invisible walls of the space they stood in. Perhaps Mel had pushed a bit with the quick, reactive response. Nonetheless, he chose to wait and allow Carrell to regain his thoughts. Carrell, having surveyed the area, determined that he could brave the continuation of the conversation. "Aight, look…Pastor Chris, he, um…he was in there talking about his life and everything, you know?" "Yeah," responded Mel to the rhetorical question posed by Carrell. "And, uh…I mean…I know I'm just a kid, but I feel like…I feel…" Mel refused to make a repeated mistake and stood patiently, offering a look of sincere empathy, leaving room for Carrell to be open in what seemed to be coming of age expression. What Mel would have given to have had this same opportunity to share with someone when he was Carrell's age. He wanted to be the mentor that he wished he could have had growing up.

Carrell continued his incomplete thought, "I feel like…I know that I want to be saved, man." "Saved? You wanna be saved? Whoa…" Mel internally exclaimed in his own mind. With no spoken words, Carrell could tell that his admittance was being met with surprise. He continued on, apparently in an attempt to prove how genuine he was. "Mel, I'm for real. Before we came out here, Pastor Chris was chopping it up with us, telling us how he came up. He wasn't preaching or nothin', but he was keeping it real with us. Dude was an OG and for him to change his life like that…" "I know, right," interrupted a still-surprised Mel. "Trips me out, too, for real. But I guess when you find that there's more to life than money, cars, and girls…my fault, little bro. Go ahead." Mel realized that he was interrupting the special moment.

"Yeah. Well, uh, right before he wrapped up, he asked if anybody wanted to give their life to Christ. You know, that same speech he give every time we come through. Well…you know," Carrell trailed off again. Mel, determined to maintain his stance as a listener, resolved to allow Carrell to carry the conversation. His patience was rewarded with Carrell picking up where he left off. "Nobody was standing, raising their hands or nothing. I didn't either. Being real, though, I felt some kind of way. I felt different. It was like I was hearing the same message, but it was hitting different. I...I can't explain it." Mel read this as a cue to finally intercede. "Ok, so do you want to answer the call, little bro? If you do, I got you," chimed a hopeful Mel. This was a moment that Mel knew Pastor Chris would have loved to have seen happen. On a night like this, this was the type of encouragement that would make it all worth it, in his sight.

Carrell, again, looked around, surveying the parking lot, taking note of anyone who was witnessing this true confession of a twelve-year-old suddenly interested in being saved. Mel, noticing the infrequent hesitance said in a firm, but friendly tone, "'Rell, this is a big step you're taking, but believe me, it's the best. I know that you may not have a lot of friends out here talking about being 'saved' or even caring to do the right thing, but this is a goo- no, *great* thing that you're doing. Like you were saying, it had to be something big for someone like Pastor Chris to give up all of what had to be where he is now. I know I haven't told you everything, but I got to a point where I made a decision. I wasn't perfect and I'm still not. I just need you to know that if you know, then you know." Mel let the supportive words sink in to Carrell's ears. He did not allow too many seconds to pass before he returned with the question for confirmation, "Ok, so you're ready?" Carrell, feeling the pull from the words of Pastor Chris, and now the push of his mentor's words took a deep breath and responded, "Ok. So what I gotta do?"

Mel placed his hands on Carrell's shoulders and began to pray. As confident as he was showing himself, he, too, was nervous, as he had not been asked to lead any of the participants in prayer for salvation since he started helping out. The nerves struck so much, the words that Mel had internalized from his mentor training, led by Pastor Chris had evaded him in the moment. He reflected to the week-long training, where Pastor Chris took the volunteer team to task, giving them a curriculum mostly heart-laden, with some seminary aspects provided by the books he was studying at the time. While Pastor Chris did his best to honor Pastor's Kingsley's request for the formality of the training, he felt led to make it as relative as he could for his young staff. While reviewing the section of repentance, he thought it best to shed the brightest light on the spirit behind it, more than just the commonly attributed words within the prayer. With all that they were being asked to commit to and remember, Mel and the team were relieved that they did not have to memorize the prayer fashioned by the leadership of Blessed Hope. "Thank you, Father!" he whispered under his breath in the training held in the sanctuary, looking up in gratitude.

Pastor Chris took time to articulate the need to encourage his young staffers to pray from their own hearts. "I'd be crazy to think that you're going to remember every single word of the 'Sinner's Prayer', especially since, true story, we're probably not going to get a lot of kids jumping up and down, asking for Christ to be Lord over their lives," confessed Pastor Chris. If I kept it all the way real, there's no telling how many of these kids will make that decision, but please believe, when that time comes, we've gotta be ready. We can't miss on that opportunity and your ability to memorize a prayer is not going to be a stumbling block. All you've gotta do, when that time comes – let the Spirit lead you. The Holy Spirit will send you in the right direction and He will *never* fail you." The people in the room moved past relief into a reinvigorate understanding of why they were there, seeing that it was bigger than watching kids on a Friday night.

That moment resonated within Mel, as he began to pray with Carrell and he began his impromptu prayer for salvation. Regina and Carter continued their own internal investigation, trying to understand what to make of the return of Karina. As they talked, Regina's sisters walked up to her, seemingly ready to go home, disappointed that their escape from their punishment at home was almost on par with the serious-toned evening they just experienced. "We're done. We can go home now," said one of the disappointed sisters, with the other nodding with rolled eyes in agreement. Regina smirked, but deep down hoped that something said in the event stuck with her younger siblings. If anything good were come out of tonight, it would at least be that. She responded, "Ok. Well y'all not gonna rush me up out of here. I could've let you sit at home like you were supposed to. Just go and stand over there by the car. We'll leave in a few minutes." Walking away, they both added sighs of frustrations to their already-rolled eyes, going in the direction of Regina's car.

"Yo, I know I've got my own situation pumping, but Mel is over there looking like he's about to start a prayer meeting with little man, over there. I guess he might be transferring to seminary for real this fall," chuckled Carter. Regina, knowing it was Carter's slight attempt at a joke, defended Mel, "Leave him alone. The way things are looking right now, especially for you, you going to be the one standing in the need of prayer." She sang the latter part of her defense, clapping rhythmically and in jest, mimicking the lyric of the familiar church hymn. "You got jokes, huh?" retorted Carter. "Welp...you might be right. I mean, I know this isn't the end of the world, but still..." He shook his head still contemplating how this enigmatic situation could potentially work out. "I mean, ol' girl didn't even let me know the business. If I really am the father, don't you think it's messed up that she wouldn't even hit me up," he said, reiterating his stance from earlier in this conversation. "Well, 'ol' girl', as you call her, might be your BM, so get ready for that. Remember, we were all friends, so I hope at the least y'all two can lead with that," advised Regina.

“Friends or not, Gina, this is still foul,” replied a defensive Carter. “I’m not trying to be selfish, but I think I’ve got some say in this, too, right? I’m not saying that I got this all figured out, but explain to me how it's cool to not say nothing?” Carter placed emphasis on the rhetorical question, not expecting a real answer from Regina. His frustration was alternating with anger and trying to come to terms with the reality of possibly being a father. Underneath it all, he understood that the possibility was high enough that, given the circumstances, this was a life-changing moment. The thoughts ran through his head on how he would he tell his family, how could he continue his pursuit of a basketball career, or if he could even continue going to college. The plans that Carter had laid out for himself were on a collision course with a new reality that he would have to embrace. On the other hand, he always knew, or at least felt, that he would be a great dad. The sentiment was backed by his desire to be a present father to his child, being there the way that his biological father was not and the way his stepfather was.

Meanwhile, Mel had just wrapped up his prayer with Carrell, finishing up his own Spirit-led rendition of the “Sinner’s Prayer”.

After encouraging Carrell to take lead and make his confession known, Mel ended the prayer, "…and Lord, I come into agreement with Carrell. Let this moment be the forever change that you had predestined for him from before time. In Jesus' name. Amen." Both opened their eyes after the Amen was submitted as proof of closure of the prayer. A couple of seconds of silence immediately followed, as they both stood across from each other. Mel broke the sealed silence with a question, backed with inquisitive excitement. "So…how do you feel, little bro?" he asked Carrell. With no hesitation, Carrell responded, with his own question, "So where are my super powers or whatever Pastor Chris be talking about?" Mel laughed, shaking his head, knowing that his young mentee was referring to the gifts of the Holy Spirit. It was a popular topic in this church, as the Pastor Kingsley had given exhaustive teachings on it, charging his staff to have the same understanding in their delivery to their respective ministries.

"Naw, for real, man. When do I get those powers? I'm trying to know what people be thinking and knowing everything going on. When Pastor Chris told us about that, I thought that was the coldest," exclaimed Carrell. Mel, not wanting to totally ruin the special moment, thought it best to give a thorough response. "Ok, Carrell, check it – what we just did, what *you* just did, in praying that prayer and asking for salvation was the biggest thing you have ever done. The 'super powers' that you're asking about are gifts that we get as we go along. They are cool, no doubt, but there is more to it than just being able to say you can read minds or know the right words to say. You feel me, 'Rell?" asked Mel. Carrell responded with a confused look, which would turn this special moment into an impromptu Q&A session.

As Carrell's questions began to take rapid-fire delivery and Mel did his best to keep up with his newly-saved mentee, Carter stood across from Regina still in deep discussion. "I am not looking forward to tomorrow morning, at the same time, I wanna know what's going on. Am I tripping in saying that?" Regina asked Carter, who she could see had a rising anxiety within him as the moment continued. Letting out a sigh, he began to respond, "Naw, Gina, considering that I might be..." Before he could complete a full response, Carter felt his phone vibrating in his pocket. Quickly, he reached in his pocket to see who was calling. The caller ID read "Pastor Chris calling". If there was a time when he needed to talk to Pastor Chris, this was definitely it.

Carter answered the call, "Hey, Pastor Chris, what's good? You got some great timing, for real." Pastor Chris responded, "Good to hear you, man. I know it's been a minute and you're probably out kicking it on a Friday night, but I wanted to check in." Carter, less fazed by the call, replied quickly, "I would say it's slow motion on a Friday, but, believe it or not, this has been the most action I've seen on a Friday since my senior year at Memorial." Realizing that he was the one called and not the one calling, he immediately brought himself back to ask for the reason for the call. "I know you couldn't have just called just to chop it up, though. If it's about those Js, I don't have the plug on those like I used to," said Carter. Pastor Chris let out a small sigh as he pondered on the next words he was going to bring into the conversation. While he pondered and the silence from both speakers set in for a couple of seconds, Chris could hear familiar voices in the background. These voices were more than familiar.

Quickly, he recognized the voices were those of the very children that he just released from the Friday night event. “Hold on, C – where are you at right now? Are you outside somewhere?” he asked to see if his summation was right. Before he could answer, Pastor Kingsley, discerning that one of the central pieces of tonight’s mystery might be right there at the church, he immediately asked, “Wait a minute – Carter’s here? Son, have him come on up. We need to get to the bottom of this tonight.” Chris did his best to respectfully try to calm his mentor, putting up his free hand mildly as to say “I’ve got it”, as he did agree that this would be an opportune time to be able to talk with Carter. “I’m actually right outside of the church right now. Sorry I couldn’t make it tonight to support…” started Carter, but he was quickly interrupted by Pastor Chris. “C, C…it’s all good. Don’t even worry about it. Look, I know this is all a rush, but you think you could come up to Pastor Kingsley’s office? Wanted to talk to you, real quick.”

Carter had a solid relationship with Pastor Chris, so there was not much that he would ask of him that he would not do. However, he did find it odd – all of it. The timing of the call, how he just happened to be in the church parking lot, and the drama of Karina, all combining for one cluster of drama that he never saw coming. Weighing all of these components, he thought to himself that this would likely be the least of all of his concerns, taking a moment to talk with Pastor Chris, and Pastor Kingsley, too, more than likely. At the very least, it would give him an opportunity to share with them the anxiety he was experiencing with the imminent return of his girlfriend from years' past. As good as Mel and Regina were as his friends, this was deep. Besides, Regina had her sisters to worry about and Mel was still trying to convince Carrell that salvation was not going to be the superhero manifestation that he expected. After all of the internal reasoning, he responded, "Yeah, I can come up. I got time. Here I come. See you in a minute." He hung up the call as he began to enter the building.

Regina, noticing Carter's initial steps in the direction of the church while trying to calm her impatient sisters, called out to him, asking,

"Where you going, C?" Carter responded, turning around in his delivery, "I'm about to holla at Pastor Chris, real quick. He just hit me. I guess he wanted to ask me about something." He added a shrug, which was a departure from his tense disposition that he just had up until receiving the phone call. "I'll be back out in a minute, if you and Mel and can hold up." Carter, still feet away with Carrell, took note of the interaction, but resolved to still be there to continue his on-the-spot counsel. Coincidentally, his own words just spoken to Carrell just ran across his own mind, regarding the gifts of the Spirit. "The time'll come, Rell. The gifts – there's seven of 'em. You got counsel, understanding...I can't remember all of them, but the one that I got is word of knowledge. Sometimes I end up knowing things from God's vantage point about some people and situations – I can't explain how, Rell, for real."

Mel's spiritual gift was in action and was leading him to believe that pieces of the puzzle were going to come together for his friend, as he watched him walk into the church. He did not know how for sure, but he just knew it. He nodded to himself and silently mouthed "wow", in awe of the chain of events so far that night. Carrell, still loaded with inquisition, hit the arm of a dazed Mel and asked, "I hear all that. So am I gonna get test scores and start killing it in school? As a matter of fact, I got a math test that I gotta pass or I'll be on punishment. That's what's up, huh?" Mel managed to muster a much-needed laugh at the simultaneous boldness and wonder of Rell. The laugh was certainly a comic relief from a night weighed down with unexpected drama and uncertainty.

Chapter 21

"Man, this sucks," Carter whispered under his breath, out of frustration. The four walls of the vacant classroom used for detention felt as if they were slowly closing in on him and his three other classmates found guilty of not having their completed tests signed and returned. The room was eerily empty in population, compared to most days, with the only people in today's group being all from Mr. Dewels' class. The four detainees, Carter, Karina, Regina, and Darryl sat at their own workspaces, tables slightly larger than the standard size desks that they were accustomed. Karina sat close to the corner furthest from the door, with Gina no more than 10 feet away to her right. Darryl and Carter were similarly seated towards the front of the classroom, with Carter closest to the door. The room was spaced out with the afternoon sunlight breaking through the classroom. Mr. Dewels, having heard Carter's remark clearly in the almost silent classroom, chided him from his position in the front of the classroom, behind the desk, now standing, "Mr. Wilkins. You know there is no talking in detention. Quiet, please." Carter responded at an audibly elevated level to ensure that is compliance was acknowledged, "Yes, sir."

The other three students shared similar discontent being held after school for detention. Regina sat before an open notebook, giving the appearance that she was hard at work on her math homework, but instead scripting a note. The note was Regina's attempt to salvage the destroyed rendezvous set for her and Mel. As the wrote her note, she plotted on how she was going to get her note to Mel and how soon it could get to him. Left with little to no options, she resolved that the most probable solution would be to send it by way of his best friend. After surveying the classroom, she took note of everybody's current activity. At the front of the classroom, Mr. Dewels, sat back in his chair, reading a novel. Darryl still strongly intent on another of his comic illustrations, set his eyes firmly on his soon-to-be masterpiece. Sitting furthest from her was Carter, who was leaning on one of hands in bored frustration. Finally, was Karina, who appeared to be somewhat mirroring Mr. Dewels, opting to spend the remainder of her time by reading the book assigned to the class at the time.

Karina opened her book, looking to pick up where she left off in her reading. While she earned high grades, reading was not one of her favorite learning activities. Nonetheless, the book assigned to the class had begun to be more interesting than she anticipated. It was so interesting that she knew immediately wherever she would leave off, not needing the aid of a bookmark as she usually would. This is what made it even more odd, as she saw a small piece of paper in the book. As she began to unfold the paper, the classroom door opened up and it was Regina's mother. "Gina," she said. "Come on. Let's go." Waving her hand, she gave a stern look in parental fashion, not immediately giving any greeting to Mr. Dewels, who appeared surprised to see an early retrieval of any of the children.

Before Mr. Dewels could stand and offer even a greeting, to Regina's mother, almost immediately behind her came Mrs. Wilkins-Harris, setting her laser-focus on Carter as he sat pondering how much trouble he was really in for. Carter hoped that he would get even a slight reprieve, seeing as how he did show the test paper to his mother and got it signed. "Boy, come on. You lucky I saw that you left that test I signed on the kitchen table. That grade was bad enough, but you forgetting it and me having to use my lunch break to come and get you," scolded Carter's mom, as she flashed the signed test that subjected him to confinement in detention walls. Mr. Dewels was finally able to verbalize a greeting to the two mothers, saying, "Good afternoon, ladies. Before you go, I just need for you to sign this document for early detention dismissal. Everyone else is gone in the office for the day, so this actually will save you a trip." Both mothers approached the desk where the sheet was placed, with a pen to fill out the sign out sheet for the students in detention.

Like most women, even with the frustration they held within themselves for their children, they found it hard to not take a moment to cast their eyes on and engage in conversation with their children's desirable teacher. Almost instantly, their countenance changed, taking in the most-sought after man in the community. "Hi, Mr. Dewels. I got the message from the school while I was work and came by to get this taken care of as soon as I could. I hope that Carter wasn't too much trouble. I certainly do not ever want to inconvenience you," said Mrs. Wilkins-Harris. Ms. Vincent added, immediately afterwards, "Yeah. I got the call, too, and as hard as you work with these kids, last thing you need to have happen is to be stuck here, doing overtime. Just so you know, I really appreciate all that you do here at the school, especially for the kids. Um...is there anything else you need for me to get on for you?" A look of awkwardness came upon the face of Mr. Dewels and Regina, who immediately stopped the gathering of her belongings, embarrassed by the flirtatious statement. Carter was suffering some embarrassment of his own, but thankfully not to the extent of what Regina was experiencing, as he did not think that the level of flirting was any higher than what was being shown by Regina's mom. "To get on Gina about, I mean, Gina. I'm so sorry," stuttered Ms. Vincent, who realized how her words more than likely came across. She took some solace in at least being an unmarried woman, unlike many of the women who overtly threw themselves in Mr. Dewels' way.

"I totally understand, Ms. Vincent," chuckled Mr. Dewels, in response to the strange communication he was given. "No worries. I understood your intent. No need to explain further." He was not aloof to the flirts thrown his way, often responding kindly, respectfully rebuffing the overtures. His refusals did nothing to slow down the desire or intrigue that was held for him. The mystery from the rejections continued to run rampant through the community, as the eligible bachelor seemed to be in no hurry to attach himself to any woman, despite a line of admirers that were hardly in short supply. Even Mr. Dewels' students were wondering if their teacher had any aspirations to find himself attached to one of the many women who had him in their crosshairs. It was a controversy that did not seem to be stopping short any time soon.

In an attempt to disrupt the embarrassing conversation and ill-perceived gestures, both children, Regina and Carter were anxious to get out of the room and school, with their moms in tow. Regina interjected, saying, "Mom, I'm ready." She hoped that she could be the final aid needed to stop the not-so-subtle overtures that her mother was seemingly making. As she trekked her way from the furthest end of the classroom, she was still mindful of an opportunity to get her note delivered. If there was anybody who could get her message to Mel, it would be his best friend, Carter.

Carter, still seated at the desk, not moving quite as quick, saw Regina's hand with a folded piece of paper being subtly handed to him. Having an idea of what the note could be, he almost felt emboldened to demand compensation from either Mel or Regina for all of the courier work that he had carried out through the day, continuing even now in a detention setting. He definitely earned his "best friend" title today, brokering what he was sure was a real possible love connection.

Carter discreetly took the note and placed it in his pocket, as Regina walked towards the door. He followed Regina's move, striving for the same hope that he could allure his mother from the entrapment of the undeniable essence of one Mr. Dewels. As all of the interactions were taking place, both Darryl and Karina were still in their seats, trying to pass the time the best way that they could. When she first saw her friend's mother arrive, she dreaded being down to having no ally to remain with her, burdened with an eerie feeling she could not explain. She returned her attention to the small piece of folded paper in the book that she was preparing to resume her reading. Upon unfolding the paper, she immediately recognized the handwriting as that of her mother.

Intrigued, Karina hurried to read the contents of the note:

"Karina-

I thought long and hard about signing that test you wanted me to sign, up to this morning. I really thought it'd be better for you to suffer the consequences, whatever they were. Since I know this was your first bad grade, I'll bring it to the school signed today. I left it at work in my locker, so I'll drop it off at my lunch break. Do better and you'll be better, baby.

Love you,

Mom"

Karina's eyes lit up. Could the test have gotten here to the school today? Surely, her mother would not make a promise, especially a written one, and not keep it. Her mom was huge on being a woman of her word. It was a principle impressed upon her in their household that Karina would be reminded of as a participant of one-sided conversations. Karina's mother would often unknowingly go from lecturing her about a misdeed, then transitioning into a tumultuous relationship experience with one of her "friends". Karina, being a first-hand witness, unbeknownst to her mother, became determined to not fall into the category of the men her mother would reference, doing all she could to be an ally rather than another cited enemy in her timeline. Though only cresting into her teenage years, she was forming her own understanding of how hurt her mother was. This gave even further reason to do all she could to lighten the load that she saw her carrying. The C- that she earned on this particular test was certainly not at the bottom of the class' performance, but was comparably a lowlight of her own educational results.

Looking at the clock, while simultaneously looking at the combination of her classmates escape from detention and their mothers' visibly apparent flirts with Mr. Dewels, Karina held out hope that she may be able to get out before the full hour of detention had completed. Like most kids, to her this was prison, even if it was limited to a finite 60-minute sphere in the afternoon. Before she could even raise her hand and enact the urge to approach and ask Mr. Dewels if he received the signed test, no less than mere seconds, with just over 20 minutes left in the detention period, in walked a woman, who appeared to be a bit older than Carter and Regina's mothers. Her hair had very slight streaks of gray, but they were not dominating. She wore a dress that Karina would have thought appropriate for one of the teachers in her school. This was a sentiment that would prove to make sense in the conversation to follow.

"Good afternoon, Atman. How are you?" asked the woman, in the direction of Mr. Dewels. Mr. Dewels responded, without hesitance, but appeared subdued in his normal confident manner, "Hel...hello, Mrs. Murdoch. It is good to see you." "At...At...At-what?" wondered Karina, as did Darryl, the only other witness in the classroom, stopped his drawing for a moment to take note, but seemed unfazed by what appeared to be their teacher's name. As far as they knew, his name was David. At least that is what they heard spoken in casual conversations between teachers of the school and sometimes with parents. "I wish that I could say the same, Atman," responded the woman, who politely placed what appeared to be a signed test before Mr. Dewels, on the desktop. "Come on Darryl, let's go. And if I have to tell you even one more time about drawing that demonic-looking mess...give me those, now." She saw the drawings that Darryl had been intently been working on since earlier that day and immediately confiscated them, with Darryl having almost no verbal response. His look seemed to be one of sad acceptance.

Mr. Dewels, still appearing flustered by the entrance and greeting of this woman, was slow to interact as he just had with the previous parents who came in. "I spoke with the principal earlier and they know that I am here to pick up Darryl. He'll pick his grades up and this'll be the last detention that you will see him in. Isn't that right, Darryl?" she said, directing a serious gaze towards the young illustrator. "Yes, ma'am," he responded, with almost no hesitation, as he immediately then gathered his backpack and jacket to leave. "Maybe that's his grandmother," Karina thought. What confused Karina further was the deflation of the usual confident swagger she was used to seeing from her teacher. What was it about this woman that caused such a swift change in his demeanor? Regardless, once Darryl was gone and it was just her, she knew she would be able to plead her case for her own release. Her mother just had to have dropped off the test. There was no way that she would not have lived up to her word, no matter how disappointed she might have been about the result.

"Have a good night, Atman. Come on, Darryl. I still have to get some groceries to cook for dinner, before we go to church tonight. I have a meeting to be in attendance for," said the woman, who stood with a firm expression, standing resolute. Darryl put up no objection or resistance, as was the same with Mr. Dewels. It was clear that this woman had an air of influence that superseded even the heralded teacher of Southview Academy, who never seemed likely to be rattled in any situation. As she and Darryl proceeded out of the classroom, Karina knew that this was finally her opening. As Mr. Dewels was capturing his own breath, getting himself back to his once composed state, Karina raised her hand. She waited to be acknowledged, lest another reason of talking without permission would stack against her, prolonging her detention stay.

"Yes, Ms. Burke," responded Mr. Dewels, sitting back down relieved, with his open briefcase at the desk. Karina took a quick breath and replied, with a prepared defense in tow, "Mr. Dewels, I think that my test was brought in today, by my mom. She dropped it off at the school today, I'm sure of it." Mr. Dewels brandished a confused look. Indulging Karina, he then responded, adding subsequent instruction, "I cannot attest to receiving your test today with your mother's signature, however, if you would like to discuss further, it might more appropriate for you to come up here to my desk, as you are the lone student who remains in detention, with the early exits of your classmates." Determined to prove her case, she stood up, approaching the desk at the front of the room, with the book and letter in hand, scribed by her mother and serving as evidence that should verifiably exonerate her. The fairness of her teacher, she was confident, would ring truer than ever in this circumstance.

Approaching his desk, Mr. Dewels sat back, prepared to further understand Karina's inquiry. "See, here's the letter that my mom gave me today. She said that she was going to drop off the test today, signed and everything," she said, as she handed the letter to her teacher. Mr. Dewels took the letter and read the message just paraphrased by Karina. He nodded his head in what seemed to be an agreement of its authenticity. Karina's hope elevated further as she hoped that this would be enough. "Thank you for this letter, Ms. Burke," said Mr. Dewels. He reached into his briefcase and retrieved a stapled couple of papers, with Karina's name at the top of it and her mother's signature nestled off to the upper-right corner. This was the test sheet that caused her detention to take place today. Karina's hope transitioned to relief, assured that she would be able to make an exit, similar to that of her three classmates, and get home in her newfound freedom.

"Do you know what this is, Ms. Burke?" asked Mr. Dewels, holding the papers in his left hand, just slightly half of the distance between himself and his student. "Yeah…that's my test! The test that you wanted signed and returned to you today. Now that you have it, I can go now, right?" "Ms. Burke, this is not a test that I wanted signed and returned. This is a disappointing effort that I am still confused as to how you earned this grade. Yes – *earned*," said Mr. Dewels, with concluding emphasis. "I look to you as a leader in this class and this performance – it was lackluster at best. You see, I can use such words with you, as you are one of my more mature students. I really think you are capable of so much more, Ms. Burke." Karina stood confused. At the root of all of this, she simply wondered in her mind, "Ok, so um…can I go now?" She hoped that the lecture that she was receiving was the benediction leading to her eventual release.

Out of her mouth, she spilled her preceding thought, "Ok, Mr. Dewels. I understand and I will do better, but now that you have my test signed and everything, can I go now? It's getting to be less than less than 15 minutes anyway. Please." "Ms. Burke," said Mr. Dewels, as he casually stood up and went to the classroom door, turning the lock and pulling down the installed shade. "You earned a C- and I think that your maturity would tell you that you are capable of so much more. I say, as your teacher, that your road to redemption could start right here, right now. What do you think?" Karina began to lose hope, and rather than disappointed, she grew in confusion in the changing tenor of this conversation. Mr. Dewels...sir...I just want to go home. You...you...you have the test that you wanted, and....I mean what else do you want?" asked Karina.

"You're a very smart young lady, Ms. Burke. A mature young lady. Look, let's sit here for a little while longer and figure out some ways that you could get back into top scholar form. Allow me to ask you, would you be willing to do anything to get your grades up to where you and I know you're capable?" asked a now-peering Mr. Dewels, whose eyes began to wander over Karina in ways that sat uncomfortably with her. She did her best to try to stand strong in this unchartered territory of a conversation, "Yeah, I guess...I guess I would do what I had to." She started to stutter in her normally confident speech, as her feeling of confidence and security began to dwindle as each second ticked away within that moment. She looked at the clock which did not seem to move anymore and now had a trapped feeling, with seeing the lock on the door turned, the shade drawn, and no one else in the room with her. She quickly remembered that there was no one else in the school. Indeed, she was there alone with Mr. Dewels, who, by the second, was taking on a darker and darker figure than she had ever seen before.

Mr. Dewels, proceeding in his dark directives, then said, "Ms. Burke, I know you are able to do some great things. Here, here...have a seat on this desk and let's...let's..." His words faded in her hearing as things were happening that she could not understand and appeared to not have any control over. Darkness appeared to cast over the room, despite open windows giving full view to a sunny, afternoon day. The eerie solitude of the room and building in whole made for this to be even more of a nightmarish moment. As Mr. Dewels continued, his flowery, proper, teacher-specific rhetoric lessened, transitioning into a sly, predatory tone that had never fully surfaced before. His demeanor had taken on a persona to which Karina was incredibly uncomfortable and had never experienced, and she was sure that anyone else would say similar if asked. Karina's hearing had faded, as did most of her senses, having tensed up, as something was about to happen that would definitely change her life, forever. "...let me show you, Karina," assured the teacher, who had instantly become monster before Karina's very eyes.

Chapter 22

Pastor Kingsley sat back, as he entrusted Pastor Chris to take lead and leverage his relationship with Carter in gaining the best insight into this situation. Wisdom encouraged this line of thinking, being aware of the sensitivity of this situation, needing as much finesse as possible. "So, you're saying that it's possible. Well...I can't lie. That changes things a bit, C," conceded Chris. "And she just left town, not telling you *anything* about her being pregnant?" "Not a word, Pastor C, not a word," Carter quickly replied. "She bounced after a phone call and I didn't hear anything from her. You can ask Mel and Gina. They'll tell you." He felt the need to defend himself, all while expressing his confusion over the matter to the two men who just called him up to apparently clear up their own confusion. So far, it appeared that they had not gotten to far in knowing much more than they did prior to the phone call that initiated this meeting.

Still pondering, Pastor Kingsley saw that the time had come for him to interject and see what he could extract from this growing, confusing scenario. He sat up slowly in his leather desk chair, removing his glasses with his right hand, preparing to take lead in the conversation. He knew that for this to be effective, the conversation had to stay in that vein and not turn into a church-led interrogation. At the forefront of his mind was keeping himself as far as he could from his father's traditional pastoral way of doing things. "Carter...I know that this is a lot to take in. My Lord, it's tough for us to take in. So, shoot it to me straight...are you ready to deal with this responsibility, son? I mean, what it all boils down to is you might have a little kid to tend to and..." said Pastor Kingsley, before a brief pause, considering how he would complete his introductory words. "...just know that we will support you, give you and that young lady counsel, and do what we have to do. But first thing's first, son – your life as you know it is going to change. You understand?"

The room was quiet, filled only by one voice at a time, with the silence adding to the pensive nature of the situation being discussed. The paternity of a child by an athletic prodigy was not a foreign topic of discussion in this neighborhood, unfortunately, as many dreams that flirted with stardom on courts and fields across the area were often given a 180-degree redirection. At first glance, it appeared that Carter was soon to follow in that dream-spiraled tradition. While he continued to plead to those aware of the situation that the uncertainty was strong enough to stave off the closing of his own hoop dreams, he could not help but to contemplate a series "what-ifs". What if Karina *did* have a child and the paternity pointed towards him? What if the college journey that his mother always placed a high premium on would have to make a sharp stop? What if all of the time spent playing a game he loved and had a natural God-given talent for would have to instantaneously take a backseat? These questions ran through Carter's mind, before simply responding to Pastor Kinglsey, "Yes, sir. I know."

The words, while few in quantity, rang strong in quality to Pastor Kingsley, who could feel Carter's contrite heart. He resolved it to be best to not look at the choices that were made to get to this point, but to see how to best move forward. He felt justified, knowing that Carter was different than most, not only in his athletic prowess, but in the way that he carried himself as a regular young man from the neighborhood, staying relatively humble. Discernment rang through Pastor Kingsley, compelling him to follow up, after a few seconds of added silence, "Son, you may have done something that wasn't right, but just know that God's got you and we do, too. We still have to get to the bottom of all of this. Do you know where she's a..." He was interrupted by the vibration of his phone on his desk. "Excuse me for a moment." "Do you need us to leave, Pastor," asked Pastor Chris, having gotten accustomed to being asked to exit the room in times prior. "With all of this going on, might as well stay. No telling who this might be," replied Pastor Kingsley, having not looked at his caller ID.

Before pressing the button to answer, he saw that it was a familiar name showing on the caller ID – "Lil' Larry – Son". Normally, a phone call from his son would incite a shaking of his head and wrinkles on his forehead, especially on a Friday night, but tonight, it was a welcome interruption from the chaos of the night. The craziness that came from his son, who was stereotypically as rebellious as most children of leaders of the church were often thought to be, never left a dull moment. He tried hard in his fatherhood to not venture too close to the parenting methods of his own father, who unforgettably built taller and taller walls between himself and his brother, Wayman. The manual on what not to do was written in full, in Pastor Kingsley's eyes, by his own father. As challenging as it was at times and he anticipated it would be, in Lawrence's teenage years, he prayed and prayed that the scripture he often heard from his father in the pulpit would hold true and reiterated so often in his family counseling would hold true for him also. At times, during moments of frustration, in an attempt to show restraint, he would recite Proverbs 22:6 as a form of meditation. Better, Pastor Kingsley thought, to do that, than to react, or overreact, as his father did, widening the gap between Wayman and the entire family and church.

"Larry," said Pastor Kingsley, in an attempt to start the conversation in a light manner. "What's going on, son?" "Hey, Pops, look, can I roll out with my dudes? I stayed here the whole time, and didn't start no trouble, neither. Is it cool?" asked a hopeful Lawrence. Pastor Kingsley took a few seconds to formulate a response, almost confused by the question. Regaining, immediately, the proper stance on his name, "Lawrence, you must think I'm a fool. I already know you've been smoking tonight. What you can do is go hang out in the gym until we're ready to go home. Can't believe me you interrupted me to ask that. Must be out yo…". Lawrence sighed and sucked his teeth, heard loudly through the phone, even for Chris and Carter to hear. "I shoulda known you were gonna trip. You didn't even take the time to ask if it was me smoking, huh? Always take Chris' side. Treat him more like your son than even me. Ok, *Pastor*!" answered an upset Lawrence. "I'll see you shortly Lawrence. Stay your behind in that gym," warned the comparably-upset father.

As the father and son argument continued over the phone, Pastor Chris, distanced from Pastor Kingsley's desk with Carter, took this as an opportunity to further his discovery with Carter. "So…what's the move, C? As heavy as this is, I'd love to hear what you think. I can only imagine what you're feeling right now," said Pastor Chris. Carter ran this question through his own head for most of the night, not fully knowing what the "move" would actually be. Being a father was the last thing that he thought would be on his mind in this stage of his life. The fact that he was surprised by a possibility that came from his high school years made this all the more tough to take in. "Pastor C...I don't know, I really don't. I mean, Imma do the right thing, but I can't help but to wonder if that baby is mine. I can't get the fact that Karina came out of left field, calling everybody, blowing back in town. I'm not trying to fall for the okie-doke," responded Carter. "I'm not trying to talk crazy or anything, but, real talk, I'm going to the league. Last thing I need is someone trying to cash in on me before I even get the bag."

Pastor Chris had a hard time not empathizing with Carter, as he himself had been in situations before his salvation experience where several women he had sexual relations with would allege his paternity. Having been the recipient and requestor of several paternity tests in multiple scenarios, the results all would return similarly, declaring him to not be the father of the child in question. His empathy kept him from being too overbearing in this matter, understanding how Carter was feeling. Letting out a quick sigh, Pastor Chris followed, "I hear you, man. I hear you. Well, look, before we walk out of this office tonight, we gotta have something set. I'm backing up what Pastor just said, as far as us having your back. That's without question, off top. First thing's first, though – we gotta figure out where you stand in all of this." He solidified this supportive statement with nods, but followed right behind with another. "But don't get it twisted, we're gonna look out for that young lady, too. Don't think that we're all just Team Carter on this. As a matter of fact, no matter what way this goes, let this be a wakeup call, little bro."

Carter, nodded reluctantly, understanding that with the support that he was seemingly getting, he did indeed have to wake up. It became incredibly difficult to get past the fact that one bad decision left open the possibility that he might be a father. If only he could go back and do it all over, he was thoroughly convinced that he should have stayed at school for practice that day. The slight attempts by Mel to convince him to stay were obviously not enough to override his determined hormones that day from skipping practice, rendezvousing on the bus to get to Karina. "I understand, Pastor C. Believe it or not, I'm mad at her, but at the same time I'm thinking that it had to be something crazy for her not to let me know she had a kid. That's the part that I can't get over," said Carter, in a seemingly sympathetic voice. Pastor Chris quickly responded, "Yeah, but through it all, C, you have no idea what she was up against. Mom was probably tripping, she was scared – who knows? All we know now is that we have chance to make it right, here on out. When the opportunity to make something right comes, don't miss it. This right here – this is it. One-hundred." Pastor Chris' impromptu counsel was apparently sinking in, just in time as it appears that Pastor Kingsley's exchange with Lawrence was at its tail end.

"...and don't let me catch you out here with not one cigar, cigarette, or nothing! Tired of having people run up on me telling me that my son is out here blowing more smoke than a chimney in the warehouse district. Don't make no sense. Stay...in...that...gym! And don't go *nowhere*," Pastor Kingsley concluded, before ending the call. Having almost forgotten that he was not along in his office, he looked up and apologized for the interrupting call. "Gentlemen, sorry about that. Where were we?" As the apology and question left his mouth, a voicemail alert emitted from his phone, just seconds after placing it back on his desk. Pastor Kinglsey let out a frustrated sigh and apologized again, excusing himself to check to see who the voicemail was from. Carter and Pastor Chris both nodded, showing understanding of the pressure that was being felt by Pastor Kingsley, who already worked with a full plate. They returned to their ongoing conversation, working on the next steps, in the temporary absence of Pastor Kingsley.

"Pastor, this is Elder Murdoch. I just received a call from a young lady complaining about her husband allegedly messing with some young girls. I won't go into great detail, Pastor, but I will say that I think that she's telling the truth. And I don't think that it's a coincidence that I happened to work with him before I retired. As a matter of fact, I knew from back then that that he was trouble. It took a while, but the truth is finally coming to the light. I know you're probably busy, so I'll leave you her name. I will get the intercessors together and lift their names up in prayer. Her name is Angela and her husband's name is Atman. Atman Dewels. I'll wait to hear back from you, sir. Good night."

"Well," Pastor Kingsley thought to himself, "at least I got one mystery solved for tonight. What's next, Lord?"

Chapter 23

"Dear Diary,

Yesterday was a HUGE surprise. I thought it would be a regular old day, but ended up seeing an old friend.

I went to school and, of course, I had another pop quiz in Algebra and then the big test in History class. These people must not know about me. I took those tests and I know I aced them. Honors track or not, this work is so easy. I think it might even be easier than what I had back at Southview. It's not like I had a choice, though. I had to pick up quick after I left out of there. Plus, Mom would tear my behind up if I didn't keep my honor roll streak going.

Well, anyway, after school, I knew Mom would be working OT at work, so I went to the mall to go chill with my girls. Well, I don't know if we're girls yet. I mean, they cool and I've had a hard enough time trying to make friends since Southview, so it is what it is. Rachel and Aleah seem cool, but Jenny looks like she's kind of shady. I don't know about her.

I had a little money to spend, like $20, so I was going to get some food and just chill. I was just trying to make friends like Mom is always pushing me to do. It's funny how she wants me to make all kind of friends, but she's so overprotective and won't let me do nothing. Then what's really messed up is that if she catches me, then I'll still be in trouble, even if I was with the perfect kids. She doesn't trust nobody. I'll have to keep this whole day and any other time I do this on the hush.

We were in the food court eating and talking. I'm not gonna lie – I was bored. I couldn't wait to get up out of there and go home. These girls just have their own kind of fun, on some other type of stuff. I'm just there, but then I looked over and saw Carter. He looked cuter than how he was when we were at Southview. I always wondered how he was. I was too shy to try to go with him. Plus, Mel wouldn't let that happen, with his hating self. I finally got bold and talked to him. I could tell he liked me – I think. I did my best to not let him know that I like him. He probably could tell, though.

He's still hooping and now he's at Memorial. I tried to act like I didn't know how he was, but I've been seeing his name popping up everywhere, so he probably knew that I was just acting like I didn't know nothing. Before I left, he asked for a hug. Trying to be all slick. I hugged him, though. Then he tried to be all cute and took pictures with me in the photo booth. I was a little nervous, because I didn't know what he wanted, if he was going to try to do something, but all he wanted was to take a picture, for real. The few guys that I've been with, I usually already know what they want as soon as we start talking. After what happened with Mr. Dewels, I won't ever lose control again. But I think Carter is different.

So, we split the pictures that came out and..."

"Karina," shouted Ms. Burke from downstairs. "It's about time for you to get to bed. I just got in from work and you still have some cleaning up to do down here before you go to sleep. I'm tired, girl. You need to hurry up!" Interrupted in her diary entry, Karina knew not to keep her mother waiting, especially after coming from work. She placed her pen as a bookmark in her life narrative and placed it within one of her pillowcases as a temporary hiding space. As much as Karina did not want to march downstairs to conclude her chores, she was still running off of the euphoria of her impromptu meet-up with Carter. It was just over a day since reuniting with her former classmate and it kept a smile on her face ever since.

As she began to wash the few dishes that were in the sink, she began to regain her mental footing as to what happened yesterday afternoon. While being rushed to leave by Aleah, she knew that the photo booth suggestion was something that she wanted to do, even at the risk of missing the bus. After assuring her that she would make it out in time, Karina entered the photo booth and took the quick snapshots with Carter. As she rushed to meet with her classmates who were rushing to get outside to the bus stop, Carter stopped her. "Hey, I still have to run you my phone number. You can't just run game on me and dip on me like that. Did you think I was playing when I told you what I was going to do?" His attempt to hide his interest in Karina was failing with each passing moment during this afternoon at the mall. He felt that running into her was destiny, especially after the way that they separated suddenly before. Starting to fade in her attempt to hide her own interest, Karina went into her backpack and pulled out a pen for Carter to use. The smirk that comfortably rested on her face gave Carter reassurance that the attraction was mutual.

"So, look, don't be waiting to call me a week later trying to play cool, either," said Carter as he wrote his number on the back of the set of photos he just sponsored. "Got me out here sounding like *I'm* the girl or something. You know it's not supposed to work like this right?" He laughed at what he perceived to be a reversal of assigned gender roles, but was willing to overlook it for the opportunity to continue his conversation with Karina, whenever she would be able to call. He knew that as much as she would want to call him, that it could be hit or miss with how strict her mother could be. Karina responded, while reminding herself of the urgency to get to the bus stop, "I'll get at you. You don't need to be intimidated by a girl getting the number. It's not like I've ever been afraid. You know me, don't you?" Carter could not deny that statement, remembering Karina to be one of the most confident girls in their class. The more he thought about it, it probably could not have happened any other way.

Karina gathered herself to rush and catch up to her fellow passengers, already probably having reached the bus stop. As risky as it was, she was willing to do what she could to connect with

Carter. In trying to find her way in her new environment, it was refreshing not only to see a familiar face, but one who she had a strong liking for. She did a light jog to get to the bus stop, as Carter looked on, with heightened wonder as to when he would hear from Karina. He took in the latter moments of their encounter as she departed from him, picking up his shopping bag, intending to begin what he hoped would not be too long of a wait in hearing from her. Both teenagers were fond of each other, hoping that this chance encounter would not be their last. While the feeling was mutual, they did their best to not let on to other how they felt. They failed, miserably.

Karina was almost done with the cleaning activities that she was commissioned to do. The time needed to get the chores completed appeared to go quickly, as most of the time was spent thinking back to what at the time appeared to be a chance meeting with Carter at the mall. She wiped the last part of the kitchen counter surface, and yelled upstairs, "Mom, I got it all clean. I'm going to bed now." She heard nothing back at first, but then as a few seconds passed, she could hear the faint, familiar snores of her tired mother. There was no question that she worked hard, spending more time at her job than she did in her own home. As overbearing as she felt she as a times, Karina knew that she was taking care of a lot, being a single parent and not getting help from anyone. She wished she could have more time and more of a relationship with her mother. Karina was sure that if they spent more time together and their connection went beyond seeing each other for an average of an hour a day that some of the struggles that she faced in growing up probably would not be. As much as she loved her mom, Karina needed and wanted more from her. She just did not know if and when it would ever happen.

Walking up the stairs, Karina chose to return to her room, rather than the bathroom to get herself ready for bed. Seeing as how her mother was fast asleep, this would leave time to finish her diary entry. There was more she wanted to say and, if nothing else, she had no one to talk with, so the pen and notebook that she used was as close as a confidante as she would have for herself. She closed her door and retrieved the notebook from her pillowcase, laying on the bed to continue her narrative.

"...I took mine with his number on it. I had to admit, I felt kind of fly. Usually, it's dudes who get the number. I walked away like I was in control. I like it that way."

Karina paused for a moment and smiled. The smile was less about the chance encounter and more about the measure of control that she felt. It was a feeling that she had not felt in a very long time. She immediately returned to the notebook.

"It was so hard, but I had to catch up with the girls. Last thing I could have happen was to miss the bus. Thank God I got there right before it got there. We got on and of course, Jenny was already talking about some drama she got herself in from earlier that day. Something about liking some boy from Memorial High. I hope that it wasn't Carter she was talking about. Anyway, I acted like I was listening, but I was gone. I mean, all I could think about was how I was going to be able to call Carter. It probably won't be too hard. Mom's at work almost all of the time, so how could she tell, anyway? I took a look at the pictures that I took with Carter and I was cheesing. I mean, I really like him. Like, for real. Too bad I don't have Gina to call. She's probably still mad at me for leaving Southview like I did. I don't have anyone to talk to.

I think if I had someone to talk to, I wouldn't be so messed up like I am. I mean, I haven't been happy in so long. And then when Mr. Dewels started messing with me, it made it worse, but I guess I let it happen because no one really was talking to me anyway, other than Gina. Mom is always working, I don't even know my dad all like that, so it's like, what am I supposed to do?

It's cool, though. Maybe I can start to have a real relationship, with someone my age. Maybe Carter and I could start talking and – well, who knows? I was hoping to be able to call him tonight, but the phone wasn't working. Momma probably forgot to pay the bill or something. It's cool, though. I'm going to make him my man and I know just what to do. Carter probably had some girls, but now I know exactly what he would want and I'd make him forget about all of them. I know he wouldn't be scared.

Well, Diary, I'm about to go to bed. I'm almost done writing in here. I have to get ready to put this in the time capsule that Grace Academy is making us do at the end of the year. I figured it would be a good way to stash this away. Last thing I want is for anyone to know what my life's really like. I've been living with some secrets for a while now, but as long as they don't know, how it could it hurt them?

Good night, Diary."

Chapter 24

"I saw what I saw, Detective," exclaimed Grace Academy's school counselor. "I thought that I was just protecting some old teenage mementos. You know, some clothes, old concert tickets, pictures – but...but not this." While the counselor was sharing an eye-witness account, there was still an air of shock that sat within, still in unbelief of the recent discovery. "So, just so I fully understand – you opened the time capsule and you saw a notebook, open with..." started Detective Price. "Let me make myself clear – I didn't open *anything*, but the time capsule itself was popped open when it fell. When it popped open, a notebook fell out, right here on the floor," interrupted the counselor. "Pictures and other miscellaneous items fell out, but what stood out to me was the ultrasound. I can't shake the feeling that this was *somebody's* baby!" The shock of the visual evidence still stood at the front of the witness' mind. They continued, "Grace Academy has strict rules for the young ladies in how they conduct themselves in and out of these school halls. I mean, these were things packed in from high school *girls*. *Young* girls. It broke my heart to see this." "Well, I hate to break it to you, but I still do not understand why you felt the need to call us in.

Teenage pregnancy isn't necessarily a crime, I hate to say," said Detective Price. "I really think that there is more to it than that, Detective. I really do," replied the counselor, in concern.

Detective Price sympathized with the counselor, hoping that there was indeed more than what she initially saw. She had affinity for helping anyone she could, but this situation was confusing, not truly revealing what she would be needed for. However, because it potentially involved children, especially young women, she wanted to see what she could do. After her promotion to detective, she felt it to be a calling to continue to be an advocate for young women wherever she could. Answering the urgent call to the department from Grace Academy, she knew that this moment was inevitable. Doing her best to compartmentalize her feelings, she proceeded to ask the sole witness more questions. "Where is the time capsule and these items that you're talking about? I'd like to take a look at them. I have gloves and will determine if I need to take or leave any items here, since they'll likely be deemed as evidence – that is, if there is anything attached to them that we may have to investigate." The counselor, motioned their fingers, inviting her to walk into what appeared to be their office.

The office was clean, but otherwise there was a cluttered pile on the floor, with a few canister-like objects and various articles on the floor. The canisters had very slight rust marks, with light traces of mud on them, but at first glance did not appear to have been buried for too long. The odd appearance led to subsequent questions that Detective Price would not hesitate to direct for understanding. "How long were these canisters buried for? I can't imagine that it was for very long. Most time capsules are in the ground for years. 10, maybe 20 or more in some cases." The counselor nodded, having calmed with regained composure, and explained, "Yes. These canisters were dug up way before their set time. It's part of a tradition of all of our sophomore classes. Like I said before, they put in a treasured item, something that they hold dear and we...we lock it away. We bury it by our track area and we get it out for their ten-year reunion."

"So, let me guess – this is a little soon for these to be ready to be popped for a ten-year celebration, right?" asked the detective, confident that there was more to the story. "Not even by a little bit," replied the counselor. "As a matter of fact, these were the most recent capsules that we buried, coming from the last 5 classes. The reason that they're here in my office is because of the crazy rain that we got that was beginning to make parts of our field, where these were buried, an absolute swamp. We thought it best to retrieve the capsules, to protect them from being potentially damaged. Our groundskeepers were able to get them out, thankfully." Detective Price was still confused as to why any of them would be opened, with her eyes glaring as portals of confusion. The counselor, sensing that more questions were on the way, continued the narrative. "To my surprise these capsules held up really well, even with the incredible amount of water and mud that they were submerged in. It looks as if our school board really invested well in these capsules. They appeared to be sealed, protecting all of the contents inside. However, like I explained before, when one of our groundskeepers was bringing them in, one dropped and fell just right and that's how it opened. We had no intention of opening any of them, whatsoever. We were just going to re-bury them, maybe in a different spot, since there's no telling when the original spot will ever dry up or if it even makes sense to use the same area."

The additional explanation temporarily satisfied Detective Price's curiosity for the moment. Still, she perused the sole, open canister with the spilled items, focusing in on the small notebook that was most likely the one that incited the call to the police station. She looked at the counselor's desk and saw the ultrasound picture that she mentioned. Obviously, there had to be a name or some other identifier to gain some clarity. As she approached, the detective was enlightened, and thought to see what name or other data would be on the perimeter of the picture. Almost interrupting the perusal of the ultrasound, the counselor expounded on what triggered the call to the police department. "And, yes, that notebook is at the center of it all. Detective, it went against all that I stand by as ethical, but after seeing that ultrasound, I thought it best to be read by somebody, especially the page that it fell out of," they further explained in a morally-upright tone, initially pointing at the item at hand. Her explanation transitioned into a confession of sorts, "And looking onto that one page led to an entry that I thought to be most concerning. Turns out this is a diary of a former student. Looking into her records was not easy. She did not graduate from Grace and transferred out at the close of her sophomore year."

While the counselor articulated all that they could, Detective Price noticed the conspicuous absence of the ultrasound identifiers. It appeared to be intentionally cut, likely with a pair of scissors. The motive for doing that could have been a multitude of possibilities. She pondered to herself. Could it have been a baby being born from the typical ill-fated teenage relationship? Was the picture of a sibling that was still unborn, awaiting its entry into the world? Did this baby even get a chance to be born at all? Perhaps this baby fell to the terrible fate of the abortion clinic that she warded young women from for years. The likelihoods continued to stack and mount, as the seconds of the moment continued to tick away. The remaining information on the black and white article that was not cut off, was blacked out with a permanent marker, leaving it to be nothing more than a black and white snapshot of a baby still within an expectant mother's womb. The questions continued to run rampant in the detective's mind, only to be disrupted by the counselor, who pointed out a specific space in the notebook.

Without words, she was handed the notebook, peeled open to what was an obvious diary entry. While both of the individuals who stood in the office were not enthused with the prospect of reading the private edition of a life story that was likely never intended to be shared to foreign eyes. The counselor stepped back as Detective Price read the words scripted in pink ink, on pages with surprisingly minimal signs of any damage from being in the buried, submerged time capsule.

"Dear Diary,

Well, I guess I know the truth now. I am pregnant. I'm pregnant with a baby. A whole baby. And I don't know what to do. I ended up telling my mom that I was pregnant. It was not good at all. I was scared in just trying to tell her and now I'm even more scared, now that she knows. For as long as I could remember, she would always threaten me and tell me that she would slap the taste out of my mouth, if I ever got out of line. I never thought that I would know what that felt like until today. She popped me so hard. I mean, REAL hard. I didn't have any more words. All I know is that when she asked me who the father was, I froze up. Well, maybe I didn't freeze up. I just knew that in this case, the truth wouldn't set me free. If she knew who it could be, she would've really lost it.

So I told her it was Carter's baby. She didn't hesitate to let me have it. I've seen my Mom mad, but never this mad. If I would've told her that it might be Mr. Dewels' baby, I don't know if I would've lived beyond that. How do I tell her that my seventh-grade tea..."

Detective Price stopped reading, with a heart-rate catapulted beyond normal pace. Was this admission of a possible statutory rape? If so, that was what she likely was her calling to this quickly-evolving situation. The words that her eyes just read were leading her to believe that this may go beyond the commonality of a teenage pregnancy had heightened in its issue, with the diary documenting the alleged possibility that a baby was fathered by this young author's teacher. To disrupt the internal dialogue taking place and to determine how much more the counselor may know, she lowered the notebook and asked, as calmly as possible, "By chance, did you read this entire diary entry? I just want to know how much you know. It might save me some time." Detective Price did not want to alarm the counselor any further, especially if for some reason they had not seen the full entry and the illicit details of suspected sexual assault. The counselor quickly replied, "No. Like I said before, I had a tough time reconciling with the idea of reading this private reflection. I know as a school administrator, this may fall under a gray area, but...as a counselor, I just did not think it would be right to read this young lady's notebook. The only reading that I did was of the inside cover of the notebook, where I looked for the student's name – Karina Burke. After that...that's when I called you. She had an impressive record, too. A promising student. She left right before I came to Grace, right before the close of her sophomore year. Abruptly, I might add." In hopes that the detective believed the given response, a question followed, in curiosity, "How bad is this, Detective?"

Detective Price took a sigh and did her best to reply. "Well…I respect your stance on not reading this and, to be honest, this is probably one of the toughest things that you would have ever laid your eyes on. I will say this – what I just read hints a possible situation at hand, much bigger than we could have ever imagined." The counselor's head nodded, in a mixed emotion of acceptance and concern. The suspicion that a potential problem was coincidentally stumbled upon this Thursday afternoon had become more of what she would believe to be divine appointment. As she spoke, she laid two gloved fingers, discreetly on the cross pendant that she still wore around her neck, silently praying for discernment on how to proceed next. What seemed to be her law enforcement fundamentals kicked in next, as she went further in saying, "I am going to take this notebook and ultrasound with me to the station and file a report. In the meantime, let me get some information from you to get things rolling. I apologize, in all of this, I never got your name. This is so not like me. Could I have your name please?"

The counselor responded, "Oh, sure. Absolutely. My name is Angela. Angela Dewels." As unique as that name was, Detective

Price stood as subdued as she could, realizing that this was likely a relative to the name mentioned in the diary. She immediately began a follow-up question, for clarity. "Miss Dewels..." The counselor interrupted, quickly, regaining a measure of energy not as prevalent during the interaction up to this point, "That is *Mrs.* Dewels. I am married to David Dewels. I'm sure you know who he is from his basketball glory days, from way, way back. Detective Price nodded, attempting to be unfazed, and replied, "Oh, yeah. Definitely hard to forget. I have a feeling that his impression will go a bit deeper in the very near future. Mrs. Dewels, before I leave, I think it'll be best to go over what we have here. Please have a seat." She sat down with a reinvigorated air of concern, not sure where this conversation would go next. The rain that was calming down outside appeared to intensify, as the two women moved towards a serious dialogue mirroring the weather scenery outside of Mrs. Dewels' office window.

Chapter 25

Regina's nerves were still resetting after the meeting she had earlier that morning. She still tried to process the revelations that she had just learned. Meeting Mel at the bench in front of the King rec center was a therapy session she was in dire need of. Mel walked up from the parking lot and approached Regina, who sat, appearing shaken. "Gina, you good? How did the meeting with that detective go?" asked Mel. Gina responded slowly, "Well...it went ok, I guess, but...well...what would you say if I told you that we...we had a pedo as a teacher when we were at school together?" Mel sat up and back, showing immediate shock in response to the question just asked. "Pedo? As in pedophile?" asked Mel in response. "But the detective came to ask you about Karina. You can't be serious."

"Yes, Mel. You know what a pedo is and, yes – we had a teacher who was a straight up pedo. Allegedly, he did something with Karina. My mind is still processing all of this, for real, and I'm surprised I'm not throwing up now," said Regina, whose haziness was now transitioning into visible disgust. "Detective Price came to my house today and made it clear as day that Mr. Dewels was doing some crazy stuff at Southview. Karina somehow got touch...let me say this – if what Detective Price said is true, it was *more* than just 'touched'." Regina, after sharing her words, stopped with a concerned look focused at Mel. Mel's face was frozen, with a stare that resounded a mix of confusion and disappointment. There was no way that this could be true. Mr. Dewels was their teacher. Mr. Dewels was the guy everybody looked up to. He was a hooper, a community legend, he was...he was *the* man. How could this man, the envy of every boy, girl, some aspiring athletes, and almost every woman in the community at the time, single and married, be a pedophile? This just could not be. Mel refused to accept this shocking revelation from Regina, who he also knew would not have any reason to make up such an incredible statement without proof.

"Ok, Gina, that, um...that's some heavy stuff. You know you can't say something like that without having some proof, some receipts or something. I'm not about to assassinate this man's character and it's based off some he-say, she-say mess," said a now-defensive Mel. His shock quickly transitioned to defiance, as he could think of no way that any allegation of the communication standard-setter could be true, or even hold up with any actual facts. "I mean, we see celebrities all of the time get caught up like this and half of the time, it's just talk. And you saying that he was messing with Karina – I mean, this is the same girl that was trying to act all grown and be up in everybody's mix back when we were kids. Mr. Dewels wouldn't be some old perv and touch on her, though. I'm saying, did you even get real proof? He's probably with that lady we s..." Regina interrupted abruptly, "Look Mel, why would I lie? I mean, I liked this dude, too, but..." She paused herself, knowing that Mel would not entertain any more of this revelation if he could not get something that would substantiate their claims.

"Well, what else is there to know? You seem to have the inside scoop right now," asked an inquisitive, daring Mel, who felt justified in his stance. He doubted that Regina would intentionally stir the pot in such a way that it could potentially take down a man of integrity – so he thought, anyway. And with the possibility that this involved Karina, too – this moment in front of the King rec center was becoming mind-blowing, to say the least. This was their teacher

– the *best* teacher, ever! He was most of the time, anyway. He would be serious in the classroom, but had charisma to captivate his students, hail the respect of the other teachers on staff, and the support of the parents. While other teachers struggled to get parents to attend parent-teacher conferences, with empty classrooms and a stack of report cards and graded assignments, Mr. Dewels' classroom would sometimes have a logjam of parents waiting to meet with him. There was a combination of admiring women and other men who regarded him for his athletic exploits. Reflecting on his time at Southview, there was nothing that signaled that their teacher could even be remotely close to what Regina is saying in this conversation.

On the other side was Karina. While there was no question that Mel was not Karina's most staunch supporter, he certainly would not wish something so vile, so painful, so hurtful, on even her. It was beyond understanding that she would have been a victim of such a terrible crime and have said nothing – absolutely nothing. The vocal, outspoken girl that he had come to know, and often despise, would be the absolute last person he would ever suspect would have something like this happen to her and no words would be said to make things right. Mel's sympathy was rising up. While they almost never saw eye to eye, this is something that he would not have wished on her or the next highest-ranking enemy. Mel began to piece together moments from his time at Southview, as classmates with Karina, and started to develop perceptions from why she may have acted how she did at times. Karina was defensive, often the most heard in the class, and had no reservations on expressing herself. These were defining characteristics that she carried for the majority of their time together.

While reassessing their history, Mel realized that there was a time when some of those blunt actions that she had come to be known for had subsided. As a matter of fact, Mel began to pinpoint that during the latter times of being classmates at Southview that Karina oddly became more reserved, withdrawn. While their relationship as arch-enemies did not lose its steam, hindsight made it clear that something had indeed changed within her. In hearing the narrative of this morning's events from Regina, it had to be considered that if Mr. Dewels did do something to Karina, that it would make the most sense that that was the root cause. Maybe for all that he knew, *this* was the reason why she left before the end of their highly-anticipated eighth-grade year, when they would be the royalty of Southview Academy. It could also be considered that this would serve as the explanation as to why Mr. Dewels abruptly left Southview in the time following. The many thoughts that ran through Mel's head begun to overwhelm him. He did his best to reset himself and allow for Regina to respond.

Mel waited for her response, but did not have to wait long, disappointed that his challenge had actually been taken on. How legit must this situation be if there was going to be follow up on the accusation? "Mel, I was sweating bullets when that detective came over today," exclaimed Regina. "But let me tell you...based on what they were asking me about, I started piecing the puzzle pieces together and things started making sense." "Like what? I mean...if he did do this, was it just with Karina? Was it with anyone else? It couldn't have been any one in..." Mel froze and instantly zoomed in on Regina and transitioned in to his own quick, immediate interrogation, "Wait…he didn't mess with you, did he?" His anger sprang up with the possibility that the love of his life had been a victim at the hands of Mr. Dewels. All of the efforts to defend his former teacher had been thrown away, as a result.

"No, no, no, no, no, no, no, no…." replied Regina, immediately, in an effort to calm the seemingly ascending angst of Mel, quickly and calmly placing her hands on his for added assurance. "It definitely didn't include me. I'm good and please believe that I would've said something. No way it would be six, seven years passed and I wouldn't have done *something* about it." Mel exhaled a sigh of relief. His suspicion, to him, was not unfounded, but he felt comfort in knowing, not only that Regina was not victimized, that Regina would likely have made enough noise in the event of such a traumatic event. Regina appeared to regain composure, having escalated in hers, matching that of Mel in the moment. "Ok, ok…I was about to say. Man…" replied Mel, still doing his best to calm himself down. It appeared that with this exchange alone that there was something inside of him now starting to take what he assessed as mere allegations as a more than likely scenario. After the official crossing off of Regina from the possible list of victims in this alleged crime, his mind immediately cycled through a list of any other classmates that it could have possibly involved. While Regina was held in the closest regard, he still shuddered at the thought of it being any of their classmates.

The moment became a roller coaster of emotions, quickly taking both Mel and Regina through a slew of memories, which were now tainted with sick suspicions surrounding their once-beloved teacher and former classmate. To even imagine that such activity was going on in the midst of their preadolescence was alarming and cast a dark shadow over what they once fondly adored in their time spent at Southview. Though details were unraveling at an accelerated pace in the past 24 hours, it felt like there were still more skeletal revelations to come forth. The calm climate of the day, devoid of the stormy weather that consumed the weather forecast the past few days, was the only peace that could be felt in the midst of unfolding chaotic tragedy being unfolded. As more answers were revealed, they would be overridden by more questions. The moral dilemma of being unaware of something that had happened right in their midst. "How?" "When?" "Where?" The array of questions ran through both of their minds and did not appear to have an end or any answers in immediate sight. Finally, a new question came into the discussion, creating a new branch in the evolving, disturbing narrative.

"So...uh...I know for them to ask you, there's gotta be a case coming, right? Are they going after Dewels?" asked Mel, now attempting to put his finite legal knowledge into action. The extent of what he knew about court and cases was limited to what he heard, usually from second-hand accounts given by his friends who had relatives facing often petty legal matters or infrequently watching court television shows. Even Mel knew that those instances did not carry the serious weight that this situation could hold potentially. Regina responded, faintly and confused, with all she knew, saying, "Mel...I don't know. I mean...look, all I know is that for this to get dug up the way that it did and to have this all happen at the same time with Karina coming back into the picture with a kid no one knew about..." "Hold up, Gina – we forgot all about that! Yo, this girl's life is...it was all over the place," interrupted Mel. "Think about it – Mr. Dewels was messing with her *and* she got pregnant, then bounced out of town. Wow…"

Both Mel and Regina took inventory of this quick reminder of the other connected elements to this volatile situation. "Hey, Carter's going to trip when he hears about this, for real," declared Mel. "I'm not sure how he's going to handle all of this. I know he hasn't messed with Karina for a minute, but…" Karina immediately interjected, "And we need to keep him out of the loop on this, Mel, because we don't know if…maybe he still has feelings for her?" Mel's face turned again, mirroring any other time when his best friend and Karina were romantically suggested as a pairing. "Is that a question or are you just talking reckless again? Look, my dude might have a baby by this girl, so there's going to be some kind of attachment – legally. Other than that, he's spectator in the stands on this whole thing, like we are," declared Mel, resolute in justifying letting Carter know about the recent discoveries just uncovered. "Besides, I know if the shoe was on the other foot that he'd do the same for me. That's real. As a matter of fact…"

Bzzzzz…

Bzzzzz…

The statement that was proceeding from Mel explaining his blood-laced loyalty to his best friend was interrupted by a vibrating phone. He looked up at Regina, who replied, "Don't look at me. I turned my ringer on today. I was hoping that it would've interrupted the grilling that I got this morning." Mel reactively reached into his pocket to retrieve the phone, which he apparently did not feel the vibration strong enough to realize that the alert indeed belonged to him. Mel and Regina shared a look of awkwardness, not knowing what twist this sordid narrative could take now. Seeing who it was that was calling him, the same unfamiliar number that had taken residence in his call log since yesterday, he answered hesitantly, audibly unprepared. "Hey, Karina. What's good?"

Chapter 26

"So that's why I'm here. I've been dealing with this pain on my own...well, I guess my mom, too. I don't know what to do, but I'm feeling like I've gotta make things right," explained a burdened, but resolved, Karina. The therapist sat up, increasing their showing of attentiveness, and asked, "So do you think that it's entirely up to you to make it right? How does your mother feel about this?" Karina responded, "Well, you know...let me put it like this – you see my son is here with me. She refused to watch him, since I told her that I was coming up here. She always said that black people don't talk to therapists and she was on my case when I said I wanted help." Though seemingly annoyed in having to provide this response, she continued. "When I said that my mom is dealing with this pain, too, I more mean that she's helped with my son now and then, but, really, in a way she added to it."

The therapist listened intently, pondering for a few seconds more all that Karina just shared, while tapping her pen on her small notepad. The quiet of the room filled the gap between responses of the two in the room, at an almost piercing rate. Finally, a response emitted, with tentative, but thoughtful sentiment. "Well, Karina, I'm glad that you're here. Truth is, what your mother told you is one of the worst stereotypes that people of color continue to often perpetuate and..." The therapist paused, making sure that the right words were spoken. "...it's something that keeps pain and hurt bottled up, way longer than it ever should. This was brave of you, Karina. Very brave." Karina, still a bit unsure if she had made the right move in venturing to see someone who was easily a perfect stranger, but highly recommended as someone who could help in one way or another.

Looking at her son who somehow managed to fall asleep upon arrival to the office on the couch, that she as the patient would normally occupy, on the opposite end of the room, Karina knew that she had reached a breaking point. There was a guilt and long-standing shame that built up to a level that had become a weight on her conscience like no other. Karina loved Kerwin. It was the name that she came up with almost instantly when she finally got her mother to relent and allow her to continue the unexpected pregnancy, recalling it from a soap opera she used to watch while under the care of her grandmother as a child. She liked the name because it was only a few letters in difference to her own name. Even in choosing the name, she was not confident in declaring who his father was, using it as a way to further avoid the sensitive topic. When she realized she was pregnant, knowing that there was a possibility that Carter could also be the father, Karina gave her son the middle name of Maxwell, which was a callback to one of their favorite songs while they were dating in high school. Karina knew, however, that all of this was only a delay of the inevitable and that one day Kerwin Maxwell would want to know who his father was.

Wanting to continue to dialogue after the words of reassurance, the therapist continued, saying, “Now that you have made the bold step that you did to be here, what do you want to talk about? I am here for you and want to help as much as I can. We’ll do this together.” Karina sat not knowing how to answer. Her mouth sat slightly closed, lacking response. It had been longer than she could remember since she had someone genuinely extend a listening ear of any sort. Karina was wise enough to understand that this scenario was constructed as that of a doctor-patient relationship, but was hopeful that it could at least spark in action what she should do next. For years Karina had felt as if she was in an inexplicable haze, one that was made worse by her mother. She sought comfort from her mother, but often felt non-verbal disdain, having seemingly followed a similar path of teenage motherhood. This strain on their relationship further prevented her revelation of the sexual assault she suffered at the hands of Mr. Dewels.

After careful thought of the posed question, however, Karina offered up a response to pierce the pregnant silence of the room. "I have a lot to get off of my chest and...and the only reason I think I wanna do it now is because I'm tired. I wish I could say that I was courageous and tough and whatever else you said about me, but I'm just tired. I have secrets that I don't know if I can keep in any longer and Kerwin...I can tell that he's wondering if this is really supposed to be it. He's in a house of only women, but that little boy is so smart. He knows that there's more to this whole thing." The burden that sat on Karina upon her arrival was beginning to lessen. It was still heavy, but slight remnants of peace started to emanate within her, without explanation. Maybe this moment was the right time and place for whatever was needed to come to pass. Her therapist offered up a slight smile, in hopes of preemptive encouragement, readying a response. This appeared to be a point where they could establish an objective, or a starting point, on what needed to happen for Karina to begin her path to becoming whole. In the anxiousness of getting the wheels turning, there was also an established balance of caution, not moving too fast, potentially undoing the foundation that was being laid. The sensitivity of the yet-to-be-known maintained its presence in the room.

"Karina, you sound like you are ready. If you're comfortable, we can start your journey today, to wherever it is you want to go. A lot of my patients who start on a path like this sound like you – reaching a point where things just have to change. I won't say that I know how you feel, but, rather, that I want *you* to know how *you* feel and for you to decide how bad you want that to change. How does that sound, Karina?" The question was asked with an inherent sincerity that compelled Karina to reply with relent, compounded with surrender, "It sounds like what I need, Doctor. I'll do whatever I have to. I just…" Tears began to create almost paralleled paths from both eyes, mimicking the bursting of water dams, as shown in the sudden nature of the silenced cries coming from Karina. As the seconds within this introductory session continued, she became more and more hopeful that, as the therapist said, she could start a new path. Almost immediately, Karina was offered a box of tissues, to which she took with no hesitation.

Karina, slightly embarrassed by the sudden outpour of emotion, took the tissue offering, pulling 3 sheets from the box extended to her. She gave a light chuckle, as she tried to regain her composure, trying to get back to the quieted setting that allowed for Kerwin to sleep through the hour-long therapy session. "You know," Karina started, through a resolved demeanor. "For you to say how *I* feel and the choice that *I* want to make – I couldn't tell you the last time that I've had that. Especially a choice. I feel like I haven't had that…for who knows how long." Seeing the resolve from Karina showed, her therapist immediately continued, not wanting to risk what seemed to be momentum in this initial visit. In an attempt to gain further trust, the notepad that remained in firm grasp for note-taking since the onset of the session, was placed on the small table. It was hoped that the gesture would be symbolic of an attempt to take down any defenses that may have still remained, making room for a more unfiltered dialogue. At first glance, it appeared to be reaping immediate reward.

Karina sat up, took a deep breath, and attempted to formulate a response. Her mind, filled with details (many of which, buried) would likely be the first steps to whatever journey she and her therapist would now embark upon. With the discomfort levels beginning to subside, it still would not be an immediate disclosure of information. Trust was still going to have to be earned. It was a long time since Karina truly embraced that word – trust. This was something that she had lost true feeling for, having it totally removed on the day she was assaulted by Mr. Dewels. "So, um...I guess...I don't know where to start," said a once-hopeful, now seemingly re-dejected Karina. The therapist responded with a reaffirming tone, "And that's the best part, Karina. We'll go at your pace and start wherever you want to. We're at ground level and we'll go up as high as you'd like." "But you say 'ground level'. I'm saying I'm at rock bottom. I don't know what you can do with that," responded a lightly-skeptical Karina. With a readied response, the therapist said, "Hitting rock bottom just means that you are in a place to start a new foundation. Let's build together – starting today, Karina."

Reassurance once again began to set on Karina, who had become aware of the time ticking away on the scheduled therapy session. Looking at the traditional clock on the hand, seeing the hands move in what seemed to be faster than normal, she wanted to act as fast as she could to not waste any more time. "Ok, so, um...let me start with saying this. Back in my seventh grade year...my...my." She stuttered and was stuck in what was forming to be mid-sentence. Karina stopped herself, as her therapist sat looking on, with folded hands, exuding a continued patient disposition and choosing to stay in a listener's role. Karina, starting to feel unrushed, took a deep breath and tried again to begin her narrative. "My teacher...my teacher, Mr. Dewels, he...he...well, you know." The therapist, not wanting to lose the established position as Karina's listening advocate, replied by saying, "Well, Karina, I only know whatever you choose to tell me, but just know that whatever you say, I'm here to listen. And take your time. I saw you looking at the clock a minute ago. You're good."

Something in the way those words were administered gave Karina enough courage to continue in what she felt led to share. "He touched me. As a matter of fact…it was more than just touching. He…he…I lost my virginity to him," said Karina, who felt the need to stop her words, in an effort to balance herself and use her remaining energy to keep from crying, again. Within a few more seconds, she picked up where she left off, "It was afterschool. I got put in detention and I was the last one there and…and…and he…he touched on me and…hold on, let me set this straight. When I say I lost my virginity, it didn't happen that day, you know. But that day he did stuff to me that no kid should ever have had to go through, you know?" The therapist, listening intently to Karina, gave a slight, encouraging nod and leaned in closer, in hopes that it would confirm that the words had not fallen on deaf ears and that more detail would be welcomed. "Sure, Karina. So, it sounds like your teacher, he made you feel uncomfortable, which I am sorry to hear that that happened. Did you tell anyone? Anyone who could be an advocate for you, like your m-"

Karina interrupted, still mindful of her son sleeping, so she kept her tone relatively as low as she could. "My mom wasn't trying to hear that. I mean, she would've probably thought that I was making it up or something because I got in trouble for whatever it was that got me in detention that day. Plus, my mom loved my teacher. He couldn't do any wrong. It was going to be my word against his and my mom would've thought I was lying, anyway." The therapist once again nodded in response. Karina continued, "So, all I did was try to act like it didn't happen, which was stupid of me, but what could I do? I just kept going to school and acted like nothing happened. Only thing was..." Karina paused again. The next stretch of her story forecasted in her mind was not going to be easy to say. Her throat tightened up and her eyes wandered as her son started to move around in his sleep, almost teasing that he may be preparing to end his afternoon slumber. The reality had set in that this was the first and only time that she had shared any of this with anything or anybody that was not her diary.

“Doctor,” asked Karina. “Can I stop there? I don’t know if I could do this.” “Sure, Karina. Again, this is all about you. This is our first session and you’ve shared way more than I would have imagined, so no worries. We have plenty of time left, but this is your time. So, what do you want to do next?” Karina, starting to feel an air of embarrassment setting in, elected for a brief escape. “Um...I really need to use the bathroom, actually. Is it ok if I do that? And could you watch Kerwin for me. He’s knocked out and I don’t want to move him and get him all awake and running around. You have no idea.” The therapist laughed at a low enough volume to ensure that the boy would not be prematurely awakened and responded, “Sure, Karina. The bathroom is just outside of the office door that you first walked in. I’ll watch Kerwin while you go. Go ahead.” Karina said “thank you” and went to the restroom that was located as described. This first visit to the therapist had gone from a plunge into the unknown, with her son in tow, to a purging of her soul, uncovering memories buried beneath her deepest depths.

Chapter 27

As the door slowly swung shut after entry, Karina went to the sink countertop and faced the mirror, looking at herself. The painful memories, as traumatic as they were, were indeed buried. They were buried so deep, that the revelations that were beginning surface almost seemed as if this was the first time that they had ever been admitted to as being the truth. Karina had come to realize that for the most part, these painful points in her past had become, in part, repressed. She stopped herself in the office, not out of discomfort, but more so because details of what happened and how it made her feel had become a challenge to unpack for her new therapist, much less for her own self. While she expected that more tears would fall from her eyes, once she got to the safe haven of the office restroom, they did not. A combination of shock and discovery was more dominant of Karina's emotions. Walking into the small space, seeing that no one else was in there, she felt as if she had bought herself a small bit of time to regroup and reassess herself before going back to speak with her therapist. She also felt that this was a much better alternative than choosing to smoke a cigarette from the pack that she still had, despite a swearing off of the habit.

This was a stronghold that plagued her since about six months after giving birth to Kerwin.

Karina ran the water from the faucet that sat before her, cupped cool water between her two hands, and splashed it on her face, in an effort to reinvigorate herself. While doing so, some of the troubling memories flashed before her. She remembered the initial encounter in that day of detention, being left alone with Mr. Dewels, who had proceeded to inappropriately touch her. Immediately after the act, he advised Karina, saying, "Ms. Burke, let's keep what happened to day between us. I know you to be a mature young lady and this is something that we could keep to ourselves. Understood?" The scared and shaken seventh-grader that she was, Karina nodded and immediately looked down. She did not know what to feel, especially since this was her beloved teacher. One moment shame had set in, then it was combined with confusion, but then finally both were displaced by a heavy weight of fear. Fear had taken full residence within Karina, looking at the teacher, now-turned-monster. The deep brown eyes that were one of the key attributes that the young girls and adult women alike had adored of Mr. Dewels, had now become dark, soulless portals - portals that extracted Karina's innocence.

As Karina's memories began to unpack, she remembered that the dark moment that had sadly become more lucid, would not be the last. Days followed in the weeks and months ahead, being sometimes forced to stay after school for unearned detention periods and even being detained inside during recess. The touches that she knew was not right had become expected, and, in likely her only defense mechanism within reach, she did not fight back, kept quiet about the improprieties, and even went as far as to block them out in her memory. Eventually, the touches evolved to even worse, taking the initial assessment of the bold robbery of her innocence and elevating it, minimally, to grand theft larceny. Karina had resolved a few things in her mind, justifying not reaching out for help. One of her reasons was to avoid burdening her mother, who already bore the stress of taking care of her and their household as a single parent. Karina believed that, as she was often left to her own devices to be responsible, even at such a young age, that this would be the best course of action. Secondly, the reputation of Mr. Dewels was a force of nature within itself. There was no way in the world that a story like hers would be believed. No, it was settled that it would be best to remain quiet.

Karina stood alone in the restroom, staring in the mirror for what seemed to be for several minutes, but only seconds had passed, as confirmed by her cell phone that she brought with her. She had no intention of leaving the therapist with Kerwin for too long of a time. The exit was just a means to regroup and regain order of her senses, trying to reassemble herself after the flooding and reemergence of her traumatic, closeted encounters. As she gathered herself, it become clear to her that the pain that was unlocked was likely not going to go back to being filed away in a secreted file cabinet within her mind. Whether it was today with this therapist, down the line in another session, or by some other means, something had to change. The reasoning mentioned to cement the identity of Kerwin's father was of legitimate concern and was justified in its mystery, as it was tied to these cerebral resurgences.

Making her way back to the office, exiting through the restroom door, Karina's mind recalled her rendezvous to the mall during her time at Grace Academy. Her bright, fond memory of her reunion with Carter would sadly be counteracted with an experience of direct opposite sentiment. Having not immediately hearing back from Carter following their impromptu encounter, Karina planned an immediate return visit to the mall the day after next with her friends, in hopes that she would somehow again run into him. Positioning herself in the food court as she did a couple days prior, time was passing and the hoped-for reunion sequel had become less and less of a likelihood. Disappointed, she wanted to leave, returning home before her mother, who was again working a double-shift and would likely not arrive until later in the evening. Waving to Aleah, Rachel, and Jenny, she cut short her mall adventure early and set out to the bus stop that was just on the outer perimeter of the mall parking lot, catching a different bus than the last visit. Little did Karina know that the let-down of the day's events would plunge to an even deeper descent.

A black car slowly drove beside Karina, with a familiar voice emitting from the driver's side window. "Ms. Burke. What are you doing here? Shouldn't you be at home. I always knew you to be a responsible, mature young lady." The voice was cold, unmistakably familiar, freezing her in her movement. Karina knew who it was, feeling a sinking nausea within herself that she never thought she would experience again. Today had sadly become proof that she was wrong. "Ms. Burke," the driver repeated. "It's been a while since I've seen you. I hope that you haven't forgotten me since you left Southview. How have you been?" Karina mustered what strength she had left and resumed her walking, using quick, fast strides to shorten the remaining distance to the bus stop that still stood in the distance. "If it's ok, I can give you a ride, Ms. Burke," suggested the driver. "Public transportation for a young lady such as yourself? Please, allow me." "Mr. Dewels, please leave me alone. I don't want a ride. Please," responded a desperate and agitated Karina. The distinguished and proper speech of her former teacher and thief of her innocence had not changed in his approach, still unassuming to most, but the same monster she remembered and feared.

"Let me guess – your mother is working extended hours and you thought it best to venture to the mall with your friends. Tsk, tsk...I am shocked, Ms. Burke. As mature as I thought you to be, as I've *known* you to be, I would never expect such behavior from you," said a cynical Mr. Dewels. Seeing Karina, his predatory instincts had taken a retroactive turn, having sighted a victim who complied with her silence, prolonging the hidden crimes. Seeing his young prey, his strange fire had reignited, by a chance sighting in this mall parking lot on this very afternoon. He knew what to say, how to manipulate, how to ultimately get his way when it came to Karina. His eyes locked in with a sadistic focus, seemingly surpassing his shrewd predaceous deeds in recent year past. A plot was unfolding in his mind and would be verbalized in mere moments.

"Ms. Burke, allow me to give you a ride home. I'll get you home in no time and your teenage escapade will remain a secret with me. Come," Mr. Dewels said, as he gestured a wave to Karina. Karina, doing all she could to ignore her past assailant, kept walking and saw the bus that she was intending to ride to get home emerge from the corner. A sight of relief came from her, as she was not too far from the bus stop and this unforeseen ordeal would be over as fast as it started. Karina's heart sunk however, when the bus marquee which usually had the route to which it was assigned prominently showcased began to transition to now show "Not In Service". Mr. Dewels, having seen the same thing, quickly interpreted what was occurring and followed up his offer with the impending threat. "Well, Ms. Burke, if that bus was your way home, it appears that you might just need a ride after all, especially if you hope to make it home before your mother arrives. On second thought, I could always reach out to her myself and let her know…" His words faded away in volume and dredged up even more anxiety within Karina. In this scenario there was no lesser of two evils – it was just evil.

Karina feared Mr. Dewels, having endured encounter after encounter of soul-scarring pain that was fresh in her memory. There was no way that she wanted that to happen again to her. On the other hand, Karina also feared the many repercussions that came from her mother, whose iron fist was likely to be as heavy as it had ever been, especially if it were discovered that she had snuck off to the mall, in direct disobedience. “Seriously, Ms. Burke, the last thing that I would want is for you to get in trouble over something so small. The bus you need is no longer running and desperate times often call for desperate measures, right?” reasoned the sly-speaking Mr. Dewels. While fear was a competing weight on both scales of decision for Karina, her body was slowly agreeing that this may be the best option to go with, while her mind was still in staunch disagreement. As the Mr. Dewels’ door opened, she inexplicably, albeit slowly, took a seat in the car of her attacker, who still was purporting himself to be her rescuer on this day. Deep down, Karina hoped that this decision, forged in desperation, would not be one that she would live to regret.

Mr. Dewels, now confident that words would no longer be necessary, bore a smug look of reassurance, eyeing Karina as she entered the car. Upon her closing the door, he slowly drove off. Karina sat nervous, refusing to even put on her seat belt, still unsure if she had made the right decision. As she heard the doors of the vehicle lock, she jumped, feeling her liberty being stripped away by yet another layer, now due in part to her own added collusion. Driving to increased speeds, matching the posted speed limit, he continued his charade, by asking, "Ms. Burke, on which side of town do you reside, again? Is it still in the same neighborhood from your time at Southview?" Karina, now knowing that nothing could be worse than Mr. Dewels actually knowing where she now lived, resolved that she would rather be dropped off in proximity, than to give the exact location. "Um...its close. If you could, just...just drop me off at the corner." Surprisingly, the response was one of compliance, as he replied, "That will be no problem at all, Ms. Burke. It is probably not best that someone know your exact place of residence. There's the mature student that I remember." He said this, while tapping on the side of his forehead, signaling intelligence.

Karina had slight relief, hoping that this ride would be over with soon, and that perhaps Mr. Dewels actually did have intention of performing a good deed. Though this would fall incredibly short of holistic redemption in the evil that he had done to her, at the very least she could say that she bravely stared her enemy in his face and finally corralled a victory, albeit of desperate proportions. She controlled her breathing as best as she could, remained watchful, doing her best to keep herself together, especially while still in the presence of Mr. Dewels. Then, her small semblance of forged calm would be ripped away in one fell swoop, with a few troubling words. "Oh…" said Mr. Dewels, feigning a troubled sentiment. "I just realized that I forgot that I have to pick up something important. Will it be ok if I stop to make a quick pick up? It will only be a quick detour, Ms. Burke." Knowing that the question was more of a formal announcement than a request for her permission, she looked at Mr. Dewels and then, in despair, looked out of the car window. She sighed and then followed up saying, "Whatever, Mr. Dewels." It was becoming more and more plausible that this seemingly "bad" situation was becoming "worse".

The drive seemed like forever, but based on the clock in the car, assuming that it was accurate, only about 2 minutes passed. The navigated streets were eerily familiar. Coming out of her despair-induced daze, Karina was now shrouded in a feeling of acquaintance, seeing buildings, houses, even trees that she had seen innumerable times before – they were pulling into the parking lot of Southview Academy. The anxiety that was relatively subsided within her had now become elevated, more than ever during this encounter. The arrogant, self-assured look on Mr. Dewels face made it obvious that evil intentions were within close reach. As he parked the car in the seemingly empty parking lot, Karina's painful recollections flooded her mind and tears slowly began to fall, just as they did during prior times she was sexually assaulted at Southview by Mr. Dewels. Mr. Dewels, now seeing his plan coming to fruition, then said, in a calm, calculating voice, "What I forgot was the good times that we had, right here, Ms. Burke. I thought since we have gotten a chance to reunite, that we could do something special before I take you home."

Filled with fear, as her monster moved closer, unbuckling his belt and leaning over to the passenger side of the car, Karina screamed while closing her tear-filled eyes, "Nooooooooo! No! Get off of me!" Opening her eyes, she saw those same evil eyes, but with darker objectives to be carried out. No more words were said, with his strength being too much for Karina to overcome and she relented, accepting that she had no way to escape this attack. As she screamed again, with a last-ditch effort of desperation with her eyes closed, she opened her eyes again and was now looking at the ceiling of her therapist's office. "Karina, Karina...it's ok. You're safe. Please calm down and breathe," said the therapist, who had abandoned typical protocols and embraced the new, troubled patient. Kerwin, was now not only awake, but crying inconsolably, seeing his mother in a way that he had never seen her before. Maternal instincts kicked in, as Karina came to herself quickly went to embrace and comfort her son. This initial visit to therapy had proven to be a drastic uncovering that Karina was not prepared for. Perhaps the pain had finally become too much and it was time for confrontation on multiple fronts.

Chapter 28

"Man, miss me with that. Are you serious? Dewels was touching on Karina? For real, man?" asked a visibly incensed Carter. "Bro, I had a hard time believing it when Gina first told me, but...I think that it really went down. The facts that she was dropping, were too on-point and had me thinking, like...like, man," responded Mel, who took another drink from his bottle with water and sliced lemons. Sitting in his car with his best friend, Mel felt that his allegiance to his friend was on full display in divulging this revelation. "All I know is that I lightweight feel like we should've seen what was going on, had a clue or something. You know?" Carter looked down slightly and nodded in agreement, simultaneously running through the stored memories of his time at Southview, trying to see what signs he could have picked up on. Conflict deepened even further on his personal admiration for Mr. Dewels. It was hard to believe that the athletic ghost that he chased through his high school years was more imposing as an alleged sexual predator.

"Yo, do you realize how crazy this is, Mel?" asked Carter. "I was at this man's neck for those records, man. I looked up to him. You looked up to him. You couldn't tell me that Dewels wasn't the man, straight up. The whole hood wanted to get like him and you're saying that he was out here doing that? Man..." Mel, reflecting in a similar fashion, replied nonverbally, nodding his head, empathizing with Carter's dilemma of seeing his childhood hero in the most negative light possible. He, too, struggled with the knowledge of this information, and knew that sharing this with Carter would not be an easy task. Despite the imploring of Regina, he was compelled to bring his friend into the fold. As difficult as this was for Mel, deep down within himself, he felt justified.

"Well...as crazy as this is, Mel...I mean, this makes this situation with Karina, this baby...it's even more of a puzzle. Like I told you before, we gotta get a test in. I'll handle my business, but if that's not me, then...I'm not trying to be caught up in this," said Carter, who raised his hands, replicating a movement of backing away. Carter understandably had increased levels of doubt upon hearing this new information. His nerves that were already sensitized had been elevated to even higher heights, hearing the traumatic detail that may have been associated with it. "And then when I think about how things went down when we did our thing, she had me thinking like I was her first. She got me good, real good. Probably set me up for all I know," said an even more skeptic Carter. "I don't want to go in on Karina, but, man, I don't know what to think, especially when I made that girl everything to me. Wish I would've never got with her, man. I wish I would've listened to you."

Carter's eyebrows lifted up in surprised reaction to Carter's last few words. "Hold on, hold on, hold on, hold on...what do you mean, C? Remember, I couldn't tell you anything. You had your mind made up. Anyway, it is what it is. That's why we're here now." "True confession, Mel – I kept trying to talk myself out of going to see that girl that day. I was like, I'll come back to practice, get the business from Coach, run a few laps, keep it moving, you know," said a contrite Carter. "I had this feeling in my gut, even worse than when we got sick from that food at that barbecue we snuck into. Yes, *that* sick." Mel, hearing those words and remembering the event that Carter just referred to, was now becoming convinced that his friend did indeed have regret. Although he knew that their friendship was a treasured one, he was never fully confident that he had a great degree of influence on Carter, as he had on him.

"Mel, it was a lot going on, man. I mean, I knew I had to do what all the young dudes were doing back then, but when I tell you that I had second, third, and a hundred thoughts. Man…" said Carter, as his words faded off with a shaking of his head. "Through all that's going on right now, though, bro, thank you for being level-headed enough to keep it real with me. Like I said, shoulda, coulda, woulda listened. How different would things be right now?" Not wanting to add to the mountain of regret that was being formed, Mel fought the urge to add an "I told you so" to the conversation, but found it hard to resist. "Well, man, put it like this, you can't say I didn't try," he said, shrugging his shoulders, with a slight chuckle. "I know you thought I was just hating on you two, but I was looking out for you at the same time. It's all good, though. We'll get through this." Carter looked up for a moment at Mel, chuckled out of a feeling of despair and disbelief, shaking his head, but then nodding, acknowledging the support that his best friend verbally recommitted to.

"There's a lot going on right now, Mel, but you gotta tell me – how did you and Gina never hook up? I mean, you two have been together like a soap opera romance all these years, and you're for real, for real when you tell me that it never went down?" asked a desperately curious Carter. Any days prior to this one, when asked that question, Mel would have shamefully found a way to change the subject or even find a creative way to insinuate that he and Regina had indeed had sex. In this circumstance, however, he knew that Carter would benefit from a reinforcement of the truth. The mark of embarrassment that Mel carried having not crossed the line of sexual intimacy with his long-time girlfriend could now potentially be a badge of honor – the sole bright spot of this dark situation. "For real, Carter," Mel said, before taking a mental audit of preparation, checking to see if he was prepared to deliver the requested truth. "Naw, man. It's been close a few times, but, nope. I can't tell you how, but we never got all the way to that point."

Intrigued, learning something from Mel that he thought he had a full grasp on, Carter wanted to know more. This was his best friend. No secrets existed – at least so he thought. Here he was in the midst of his new crisis seeking hindsight wisdom that he wish he could have exercised in years prior when it came to his relationship with Karina. "Ok, we've talked about this before, but apparently I must've let my foot off the gas on knowing the details. I thought it happened during senior year, at least. As a matter of fact, I *really* thought before summer, last year at prom ya'll...you know," he said, joining with his arms bent on either side, doing light hip-thrusts, with a sly smile. "C, I'm telling you – no. It wasn't easy and, yes, I tried. I tried, I tried, and I tried, but Gina wasn't on it, for the most part. It was funny, it was like there would be times when I was down and she wasn't and then out of nowhere she seemed like she wanted it, but something inside of me was keeping me from going there. All that to say, I don't know how, man," explained Mel. He continued, "I will say this – the even bigger miracle is the fact that all we kept hearing from our own friends, except you, was how we needed to get it over with, like it was some kind of to-do list item or something. I think, in a way, that's what kind of turned us both off from it, you know?"

Carter, in his own empathy, replied to the rhetorical question, "I get it, man, I get it. They tell you about peer pressure, but you think its just some corny afterschool special. We *lived* this. We know what it really is. I just wished I would've taken it more seriously back then." Mel, hearing his friend's confession, immediately recalled his days at the church in the classes of the "Promise to Wait" program. The program, while not the most popular outside the church walls at the time with the church youth, still held a place in his memory, slowing him from making the decision of having premarital sex. The ceremony and curriculum that he was forced by his mother to participate in was far from the most exciting. A combination of bible verses, weekly homework assignments, and a variety of guest speakers were spread over the multiple-month program. One speaker, however, stood out from the rest. Their words echoed in his memories.

"I didn't know what I was doing. I was excited, I was nervous, I was...I didn't know what I was, to be honest. All I knew was that I was about to get some, as they said," said the speaker. "There wasn't a bible verse that could've stopped me from getting with that girl, and I knew them all. I practically memorized 1 Corinthians 6 and 7, tattooed on my brain. I had the holiest of training from my church and heard it all, how bad it was and how I should wait. My body, though, as a young teenager, knew what it wanted." His words were sincere and were intended to create a bond with the youth group. This particular session was set only with the high schoolers, with the content expected to be a bit more explicit than normal. It was a tactic that Mel's mother caught fire from some of the church members for, but nonetheless still received the final push of support from their pastor. This particular session already was coming off as the most engaging, as it was being led by a man who was well known in the area. While there was a visible gap in their ages, the words came from a sincere place.

The speaker continued, "Her name was...well, her name don't matter. All that matters was she was fine! I met her at a school dance from my rival school and she was all that! One thing after another and we knew we wanted each other. Back in my day, we had a spot that people would go up to and, uh…after that prom…well, just know we didn't have 'after-prom' like y'all do now. We had to make some'm up. At that age, I knew what I wanted, you know?" The young men in the room nodded, with some looking at the young ladies in the room, who gave looks of rolled eyes in response, appearing justified in their own assumptions. The speaker, seeing that he had the audience captive, looked at one of the young teenage boys an asked, "Say, man, tell me this? Have you been tempted to…you know?" He gave a look that was indicative of the absent words. The response to the question was slow, but deliberate. Aware of his environment, he answered, cautiously, "Well, I could've but, I fell back. Wasn't trying to get into all of that."

The speaker, knowing that he was being given a response out of caution, gave back an incredulous look, but immediately gave an understanding nod. "I feel you, little bro. Just know this – if…no, *when* you get the urge, that feeling…its normal. As normal as…as normal as y'all wanting candy from the corner store. As normal as breathing. As normal as...as normal as wanting to want that last piece of Sweet Potato Pie at Thanksgiving." "What about Pumpkin Pie? We eat Pumpkin Pie at Thanksgiving. Its pretty much the same right?" interjected a teenager in the group. With a confused look, he responded, "It ain't the same, but if that's what floats your boat, then you get what I'm saying, man." The confused look was mirrored by a majority of the attendees of the room, including the group leader, and even Mel's mother who stood in the back, astounded that the simple example would extract such an unpopular question for clarity.

The speaker, in attempt to not lose the audience any further, knew he had to get the subject matter back on track. "Ok, y'all, ease up on the young fella. But, yeah, my point is that it's natural to have the itch to want to have, you know..." Mel's mother interjected, to fill the empty air that concluded the trailed off words, "Sex. It's natural to have that urge, even though you all are not ready for it, to wonder about sex. And that is why we're having this talk tonight." She extended her right hand to the speaker, seemingly returning the invisible microphone and resetting the attention. He took the cue and continued on his trajectory, after a slight clearing of his throat. "So look, y'all, let me get down to it, because my time's almost up. One of the biggest mistakes they made when I was your age, was making us think that we were tripping for thinking about sex. They never explained anything. All they did was just drop the condemnation of God on us for having these moments, especially since we weren't married. But who's getting married at 17, 18 years old? We're in the hood, not some place where kids are getting married off as soon as you finish learning your timetables." He laughed and was soon joined by the audience. His charisma and ability to relate had recaptured the audience and even brought a chuckle to the oft-serious group leader and even Mrs. Gaines.

"But real talk, like I said, you can know all of the scriptures there are to know. Become a pope, minister, deacon, Pharisee, Sadducee – you can be one of the twelve disciples for all I care. You need to know the natural truth! I didn't know what that was until...well, until the young lady I got with...she and I had a kid," explained the speaker, now seemingly emotionally-drained. "We are almost fresh out of school. I was an athlete – a jump-out-of-gym athlete. I was supposed to go to college, hoop, and live that life. You couldn't tell me nothing! Instead, I made a decision that would change my life, her life, and the life of someone who had absolutely nothing to do with it. Just that quick." He concluded almost simultaneously snapping his fingers. There was a captivated silence in the room, which minimized almost completely the usual chit chatter that could be heard when almost any other speaker was in the room.

The moment was shifted, when a young man's hand was raised with a question, "So what happened next? Did you take care of the baby or...did you "take care" of the baby?" Several of the young girls in the room, including Mrs. Gaines, shot visual daggers in the asker of the question's direction. The young men, not seeking to even be suspected of having a similar platter of options, averted their gaze, in hopes that the moment would pass quickly. Seeing the immediate reaction across the room, the speaker felt sympathy for the young man, and responded quickly, "Even at my most naïve, man, that was *not* an option. Yeah, things were changing – like "change" change, but that was not something I was even thinking about. That life...my unborn son at the time...he had absolutely nothing to do with what got him here. Absolutely not."

"So, to get to the point, my girl ended up having my son. While I'm proud to say that I saw everything through, for reasons that she and I agreed to, I have never met him. I know that I'm not perfect, but the topic isn't fatherhood, it's about the decision to have sex. If I could do it all over again, I definitely would've fallen back," confessed the speaker. "If y'all only understood how much more life you have in front of you...sex is just a distraction. The pressure that is around you all the time, I can only imagine how bad it is now. Back in my days, that's all the fellas talked about. If I could say one thing, and I know you've heard it before – just wait." In an effort to reemphasize his point, he chose silence to set in, allowing his message to permeate the young vessels who sat before him.

"Just wait – whatever it is that God has for you is so much greater than what you call yourself trying to get into. The scriptures that Mrs. Gaines and all of the people in your church try to school you on – listen to them," he quickly advised. One of the young ladies in the room interjected, "I wish you would tell these boys. I mean, scriptures is cool, but I just don't feel the need to become someone's baby mama, especially when all it does is make you have to be stay in this hood and your life is on stuck." Other girls within the room agreed and murmured their empathy, reflecting similar sentiments throughout the room. Acknowledging the request, he replied, reiterating his message towards the boys in the room, "Fellas *and* young ladies, when I tell you that we are more than a generation of baby daddies and baby mommas…it all starts with the decision to hold off on sex and, instead, focus on doing things the right way. And, yes, that starts with marriage. If you can't marry her, then sex…" He motioned his thumb across his neck, signaling how bad the decision would be. Averted gazes cascaded throughout the room from several of the boys in the room.

Feeling a divine obligation and knowing that this was potentially his last plea he could give to his young, impressionable audience, the speaker added, "And one last thing, everybody. I…I know this may…sound corny, even weak, but check this out – sometimes, all you will have *is* prayer. I promise you, you'll find yourself in some crazy situations and...I know I was talking about scriptures and all of that, but if you take anything from what I'm giving you today – don't be afraid to call on the name of Jesus! Probably the last thing you think you'll want to do when you're all worked up or feeling like gettin' into something that you shouldn't but..." He hesitated. Looking at the eyes of the young audience that he held captive up that point, he could see that a line was being drawn in the sand, with some having taken back their investment of interest, while others chose to remain ready to receive the final delivery of wisdom. Knowing that his rate of success had seemingly been reduced, he looked to the inquisitive eyes of those who he could discern chosen to remain aligned with his well-intended message. Inside he prayed that he did the right thing by adding those last few words, instead of opting to end his speaking engagement.

"Anyway, my time is up," the speaker said with a sigh of hope. "Mrs. Gaines, thank you again for having me. You have some real cool kids here. Really appreciate you allowing me to share my story." One of the teenage boys enthusiastically asked, "Mrs. Gaines, can he come back? I wanna know more." Mrs. Gaines, responded, "Ok, Carter. We'll see if it can happen. People have schedules, so we'll see." The speaker seemed anxious to accommodate the request, although he knew the decision would be left to the program administrator. His message resonated with quite a few in the group and it showed in the reactions given.

"Alright, well...now we got all of that out, what's the move?" asked a resolved Mel, in an effort to move the conversation forward, having returned to his present situation. "The move? Man, I don't know. I got a possible baby, baby mama, and you just dropped the bomb on me that my childhood sports hero might have been touching on kids, including her? Your guess is as good as mine right now," replied Carter, who was understandably without a plan in mind at the moment. He leaned back in the seat, with both of his palms on his face, wishing that the answers would magically come to him. "Mel, I really just...don't...know. You always got something for me. What should I do, bro?" Carter said through his palms, still on his face. Mel responded with instinct, but unknowingly said to his friend, "Carter...bro, we gotta pray. I'm saying, if there was ever a time you needed to call on the name of Jesus, it's now man." "Mel, you sound like we're about to open up the sanctuary, have Pastor hollering, the choir coming down the center aisle, with those gold collection plates in hand. Come on, man," responded a sarcastic Carter.

But before he could further respond to Mel, he quickly cycled through what alternatives he had to fall on in this moment. This situation went above beyond anything that he ever imagined he would have to go through in his young life. His hoop dreams were quickly becoming vaporized as the possibility of being a young father was becoming more and more of a possibility. Maybe prayer was the only thing left to do. He always had been told of the power of prayer, but never really thought that he would have to lean on it as his last resort. With all of those thoughts, he relented to Mel. After what sounded to be a defeated sigh, he said, "Look, I'm not even going to front. I don't know what to say, I have no clue where to start. I'll pray, man, but you're gonna have to lead the way. Not like I have any other options on the table, right? Just don't have me looking all awkward like you did your little man last night at the church.: He offered a chuckle to provide a brief moment of brevity between them both. Mel laughed to hopefully aid in easing tensions.

"See, that's what I'm saying. This certainly isn't the time to get into it all like that, but take it from me – you've gotta stop acting like prayer is the last resort or last line of defense and go ahead and make it your first line of offense. I'm believing right along with you, bro. You down?" asked Mel, hoping that his offer would not be rescinded. Carter looked at his friend, gave a slight, somewhat relenting nod, then closed his eyes while clasping his hands in front of his forehead, allowing it to lean on the steering wheel of the car. Mel, took his cue, closed his own eyes, clasped his hands in his lap, and began his prayer.

"Lord…I know that you hear us, me and Carter. My friend has a situation that I know You know about. You also know that he does not know what to do. All we know is that you are in control and he…I mean, we need You. He's pouring himself out, doing the right thing, so we pray Your will..." Carter, hearing the sincere intercession that his friend was providing was filled with a combination of faith and hope that was quickly being counteracted by fear. The words "Your will" shook him, as he knew from his teachings at church that "His will" did not always match his own will. What if the "will" that they were praying for ended up with him being the father to Karina's child? He knew the possibility was there, but knew his alternatives had been taken to zero. And so, he returned himself to the prayer for which was being spoken on his behalf to God. "...and we know that through it all, faith without works is dead, so please work it out, Lord. Thank you for hearing our prayer and we're believing it to work out best, in the name of Jesus. Amen." Mel concluded the prayer but stayed in his prayerful position, as Carter did the same. The car had become quiet, as the words given had reached their limit and a solitary tear began to roll down Carter's face. He knew that it sounded good to say he had faith, but he could not escape the fear of this paternal unknown. If this "faith" did not work, he wondered if he might see his dreams end up being dead.

Chapter 29

"And I want to thank you again for stopping by Detective Price," said Pastor Kingsley. "We prayerfully hope that we all can get to the bottom of all of this and that healing can finally begin. If we get any new information, I'll call you back at the number on your business card." "Please do," responded Detective Price, feeling convinced that she was drawing closer to resolution and that Pastor Kingsley may likely be the helping hand she would need. Knowing his connection with the community, she thought it best to take what some of her peers may have considered an unconventional route and create an unofficial alliance. Having completed her meeting with Regina earlier in the day, each step that she took was intentional and appeared to expedite closure of the matter. "Have a blessed day, Pastor, and thank you again for your time," concluded Detective Price, as she exited the room, as Pastor Kingsley held open the door for her departure.

As Pastor Kinglsey walked back to his desk, preparing to resume his message for tomorrow's service, a continuation of a series that he had begun, he heard a knock on his door. Letting out an inaudible sigh of frustration, he took off his glasses, placed them on his desk and responded, "Yes, please come on in." As the door slowly opened up, Pastor Kinglsey did what he could to improve his disposition, as it was one of the elders of the church paying him a visit. "Pastor, I'm sorry to disturb you. I know that you are continuing your 'Keep on A.S.K.ing' series, but I was hoping that you had a minute. I had another one of those dreams and I thought it best to let you know about it," the elder humbly said, standing a few feet away from the pastor's desk. "Sure, Elder. Have a seat. It's no trouble at all. When it comes to your prophetic visions, I can't ignore the divine revelation that usually comes with it. What's going on?" asked Pastor Kingsley.

The interest that he had to hear the elder's words was sincere. Having ordained his team of elders and ministers, he served as best as he could as a confirmer of their divine gifts. Recognizing the divine gifts of those who he ordained, Pastor Kingsley still thought it best to encourage them to consecrate and pray, allowing them to develop their own understanding of the gifts that he already saw were in their possession. In the classes that he held prior to the ordination, he concluded each session with a prayer and the same message, rarely deviating in the words used: “It’s one thing to answer the call, but totally another to actually live out the call. We’ve got work to do!” He knew that he had to reiterate that the active roles in the church were not to serve only as the carrying of a title, but the carrying out of works within the church. Being careful in his assigning of leadership within his church, he took no chances in his constructing leadership team, striving to create a group who took the call to spiritual action as serious as he did.

While there were some who thought that his designation of said gifts were exaggerated and not as divinely infused as he proclaimed, he kept record of certain manifestations that proved his discernment to be accurate. Blessed Hope Missionary Church services had a number of given prophecies and healings, many of which resulted in instances of testimony where the church bore witness to “the Holy Ghost putting in work through His lil’ ol’ vessels”, as put by Pastor Kingsley. With a customary shout and an inspired sound backing from the church band, these instances had become welcomed moments, creating anticipation for the church body and even drawing interest from onlookers near and far, who would critique the wonders, but find themselves drawn in even closer. Pastor Kingsley was steadfast in his course of action, heeding to the thought that the attention would draw in even more souls, more people to help in the mission.

Confident of this elder's ability to have and interpret visions, he was anxious to hear what was to be shared. "Pastor, this dream was…it was something else, I tell you," the elder stated, starting their narrative. "I found myself in a school. It was a school that looked real similar to the one I used to teach at. It was familiar, almost as if I had never left. My babies were gone for the day and I was gathering my things to get ready to go home." There was a pause. The silence was to take a break from the heaviness that was to follow. As the room sat in quiet, Pastor Kingsley sat with lightly clasped hands on his desk, exercising patience and wisdom, allowing the dream recollection to continue. While the interruption in his day appeared at first to be a setback, he began to feel as if this was yet another one of those divine moments he bragged in gratitude about to anyone whom he spoke with.

As seconds passed, the story continued. “I’m almost all packed and then I...I heard screams. Loud screams. So, I dropped everything and ran out to the hallway. The hallways were dark, pitch-black. The only lights that were on were the emergency flood lights for some reason. The screams continued and were piercing my very soul, Pastor. They sounded like different girls, quite a few of them. I tried to narrow them down to how many there were and from which rooms they were coming from, but it became too difficult. And then...” Another pause ensued. Again, Pastor Kingsley sat patient, knowing that the reward for his willingness to wait for the unfolding of this revelation would be more than worth it. In a mere few seconds, his patience was rewarded as the elder’s recollection of the dream continued. “As I walked down the hallway, barely guided by the flood lights, I started to narrow the screams to one classroom at the end. The closer I approached the classroom, it was familiar to me for some reason or another. The room had a red tinge coming from it, and got even brighter as I got closer. So I looked in to see what was going on. What I saw, or should I say, *who* I saw caught me off guard, even though I probably shouldn't have been too surprised."

The intrigue incited an immediate question from Pastor Kingsley, who was unable to hold his peace with the elevated suspense given from the place in the narrative. His eyes slightly widened, inviting for a continuation of the elder's description of what was growing to be a potentially revelatory vision, as he predicted. "What did you see? I mean, was it someone you knew or something...something...something that makes it hard to give utterance," asked Pastor Kingsley, slyly referring to the revered testimony he often referred to in his leadership classes. "Oh, I am going to do more than utter, sir. I saw the girls who were screaming. They were all bound in their desks, in a classroom that seemingly had no back wall. I tried to count how many little girls in there and what age they were. I'd say there was about 40, if I had to guess, but it was hard to tell." Pastor Kingsley, immediately implementing his wisdom of numerology interrupted, "Sounds like you're speaking on trials, if 40 was the true number you saw. Keep going, elder."

The elder colluded with Pastor Kingsley's astute interruption with a quick nod and then continued in the detailing of the dream. "I tried to get into the room, but the door was locked and there was heat coming through the doorknob. My hand was burned trying to open it. I looked in the room and saw this demonic-looking figure at the front of the classroom. He looked insatiable, almost as if his hunger, lusts...whatever it was that drove him, wasn't being met and he paced and paced the front of the room, salivating, like an animal," described the elder. "Most disturbing part, aside from hearing the screams and seeing this disgusting, crazy-looking thing walking around was when it, he, or whatever saw me, they quickly went over to a coat hanger at the far side of the classroom, picked up and put on a bodysuit that resembled what would look like a shed skin. It was a whole outfit, Pastor. I mean, like a whole outfit that made him look like a human. A teacher, in fact. As soon as he put the skin on, I immediately recognized this...this...this creature," as the words of this excerpt slowed, a deep breath was taken, in hopes of energizing the next leg of this disturbing vision. “Pastor...I saw Atman. Once he had his skin on, it was Atman.” Pastor Kingsley sat confused, with a look intertwined with disappointment for what immediately came across as an anticlimactic moment. “Wh...who is that? Atman,” he asked in audible confusion.

“Pastor...Atman Dewels. The teacher that everybody in the community loves. Every woman out here getting loose and throwing themselves at him and all these kids looked up to him because he knows how to dribble a ball real good. You know who Atman is, sir,” explained the elder, whose confusion began to evolve into unbelief. His unbelief was rivaling the confidence that he had at the beginning of this eerie dream being shared that revelation was on the brink. Still, he compelled himself to listen more, being open to see what more there was to uncover in the dream that his prophetic elder was confiding in him. “So, Pastor, as I was looking at the creature-turned-Atman, he looked back at me, pointed at the girls in the room, which, when I looked in the direction that he was pointing, turned from the forty into just one. The young girl – I looked at her, trying to recognize her. Her face changed a few times. All of the faces looked so familiar, even with the screams that were coming out. It bothered me, because I couldn't get in and the fact that all of the faces were so familiar. And you know that I don't forget faces, as long as I was teaching," continued the elder, with Pastor Kingsley nodding in agreement.

"And so in all of this going on, I prayed for strength, called on the name of Jesus to be able to open the door and rescue that poor girl or those girls, whatever she was. Atman looked concerned, almost as if he knew that his time was up and this madness was about to end. Eyes got wide, looking frantic and carrying on. It was then that I managed to open the door. When the door swung open, Atman shrieked and ran like he stole something, towards the infinite darkness in the back of the classroom. The girl that I saw, she faded away, but the screaming ceased. I heard her speak and the words I heard were 'it's not just me'. I still hear it as clear as day, Pastor. Haunting me as I tell you this. And then...then I woke up," concluded the elder, exhibiting relief in sharing the dream.

Pastor Kingsley, still processing the incredible dream shared by one of his trusted elders, then took time to formulate questions to ask for clarity, trying hard not to jump to conclusions or appear to be doubtful of the account's validity. Placing his hands in fists, propping up his head, he breathed intentionally, exuding calm as best as he could. "Elder, let me ask you this – with all of that you said, what familiarity do you have with Mr. Dewels?" "You mean, Atman?" asked the elder. "Yes, Atman. As a matter of fact, I thought that his name was David. Where's this Atman come from? Sounds like you got some history on this man that you haven't explained yet. Let me know something." The invite was immediately, readily accepted by the elder. As unexpected as it may have initially seemed, there was a preparedness that would now surface in this conversation.

"So, Pastor, remember when you started your series on names and their meanings? You broke down, from top to bottom how names in the bible mean something. Well, I was intrigued. I was so intrigued that I looked up some names. I looked up family members, friends, and then I thought to look up people that, Lord, forgive me,

I felt some kind of way about. I looked up Atman and you know what I found? His name wasn't in the bible, but I kept digging and found that it came from Hindu culture and his name meant, get this – soul!" Pastor Kingsley wanted to respond to the elder's declarative words with wonder, amazement, or even fundamental understanding, but found himself still as perplexed as he was initially. He responded, finally providing response after seconds passed, seemingly imitating what felt like minutes, "I'm not going to act as if I really know what all of this means, Elder. Feel free to break it down for me. Treat me like I'm one of your students, if you have to." He leaned back in his chair, with hands open and extended, preparing for the invited lesson.

"Pastor, take his name, his first and last, and it literally means, or at least sounds like, 'soul duels'. That man has a battle going on, a conflict within himself. Everybody sees this great, handsome man who can do no wrong, but inside is contained an evil being that is the direct opposite. This is right in line with the seventh chapter in Romans when Paul is taking about his inner conflict. Now Atman is no Paul, and, in my book, might be worse even than Saul, but his name, Pastor, tells me that he has some serious issues. With this dream that I had, I just know that his time is coming to be exposed. I never crusaded to be the one to do the exposing, but I always knew that his day would come. I always knew." After explaining as best as possible, Pastor Kingsley appeared to be caught up to speed on what he needed to know from the information that was shared. He used strong discretion before formulating a response, discerning on how much he should share about related information that he had just received before the impromptu meeting.

"Elder, I'm going to share some very, very sensitive information with you. Based on your timing – your divine timing – I'm sure that not much will surprise you with what you are about to hear," started Pastor Kingsley. He thought, due to the timing of the last and current visitors that it was more than likely that the revelation in his next few sentences would not be too extraordinary. "Right before you came on in here, a detective was here. She was here about a young lady who grew up in our community who appears to have been messed with and had a child behind it. When I tell you..." The elder interrupted, "Pastor, you're talking about Karina...I can't think of her last name to save my life, but you're talking about Karina, aren't you?" Pastor Kingsley sat back, with widened eyes, in astonishment. To his knowledge, the information of this situation had been close to the vest since its introduction from the day prior. Could it have been neighborhood blotter information already, becoming the hot topic of all of the current conversation tracks, even taking residence in his own church? He knew immediately he had to get to the bottom of knowing how the identity of the alleged victim involved was already known.

"Ok, Elder, you know you have to let me know how in the *world* do you know *anything* about Karina. Are people already bumping their gums about this young lady? We've got to shut this down, especially if its here at Blessed Hope," said Pastor Kingsley, with evident concern in his voice. "Word of knowledge, Pastor, word of knowledge. In my vision, of the faces that kept changing on the girl's face in that classroom, it was her face that I saw the most of. It was almost as if, now that you mention it, I was supposed to know that she probably got the worst of whatever Atman was doing. And now that I think more about it, I remember her *very* well. After I retired, she was a classmate of my grandson, DJ. And as I remember her – Lord have mercy," exclaimed the elder, seemingly having yet another revelation while speaking.

"Pastor, I know that what we believe, what we know in the Spirit won't be something that they'll let us use in court, but I'm telling you, I know what that man did to that little girl and *when* it happened. You know DJ didn't get in too much trouble to the point where he had to go to detention often, but I remember seeing that girl in detention when I had to pick him up one day. Make matters even worse, when I saw her and DJ and I were leaving that room – Lord knows I wish that I didn't leave that girl in that room by herself with him. I knew better. I knew better! I...I...oh that poor baby! I know that man did something to her," said a now-repentant elder. The realization was deepening and was ballooning a remorse for an event that was resurfacing in recollection. Pastor Kingsley, now being compelled to take up his office as counselor, saw the face of his prophetic elder and spoke up to provide encouragement. Knowing that there was little to know way of being able to be sure that such an atrocious crime would take place, he wanted to alleviate the guilt that seemed to be building up on their conscience.

"Look, Elder, I don't want or need for you to give yourself a first-class seat on the guilt express. I know that I affirmed your ability to see things, but remember, we know in part. You *cannot*, and *will* not, beat yourself up for something that you had no idea was going to happen. Now what we're going to do is get things going in the here and now. I don't know what it'll mean, if anything, to the detective, but we might need to get you hooked up with her so you can share something. You know what, as a matter of fact..." Pastor Kingsley interrupted himself, picking up the business card just left behind by Detective Price. He then picked up his phone and dialed the number listed on the bottom right-hand corner.

While doing this, enacting ringing in his ear, the elder immediately mentioned, "The poor girl left the area and now it all makes sense. We have got to do something. For that man to do that to that little girl...and to have a kid behind it, too?" As the rhetorical question was asked, the phone was answered by Detective Price, responding with "hello" in Pastor Kingsley's ear. He quickly responded, "Detective Price, I'm so sorry to bother you, but I do have, what I think, could be some valuable information, perhaps just to Mr. Dewels' character. If you can, please come back to the church. I have an elder here who I think you will want to hear from. Her name is Elder Janice Murdock."

Chapter 30

"I still don't think that this was a good idea, Mel," said a still-skeptical Regina, with crossed arms and a tense tone to her usually optimistic voice. They were at the same diner they used to frequent as high school students, under less than enjoyable circumstances. Mel sat across from her in the familiar booth just as uneasy, even questioning himself if this indeed was the right thing to do in pushing for this meeting between his best friend and one-time adversary. A few booths over from them sat Carter and Karina. Finally, Karina was able to get an in-person meeting with Carter and her former classmates. This was far from the reunion anybody would have wanted, or much less expected, having dredged up history, bringing back dark revelations that were likely to change the trajectories of many.

"What do you think that they're talking about?" asked Regina, breaking the silence that followed her previous statement. Willing to now respond, seeing a slight relent in his booth-mate, Mel responded, "Who knows? I just hope they can figure this out.

Shouldn't be too crazy, though. Not like we're in court preceding for child support or something." Regina agreed, responding, "That's true. Fact is, we still don't know if he's even the father. I'd be lying if I didn't say that I still can't believe this is happening." Her shock never waned from the onset of this recent chain of events. Feeling torn as a result of a situation between two of her friends, with the ambiguity of not knowing the absolute facts. She felt an obligation to the matter, but was unsure on where she would be of any good to anyone involved. At the very least, she felt she should be here for the long-awaited meet-up. While looking at the all-too familiar dinner menu, Regina followed up by saying, "I'm sure we'll know what's up soon enough. Just can't wait for this all to get figured out. I miss us just being cool, being young, enjoying life."

Mel empathized with Regina. As often as he and Karina were in opposition, he longed for the days from only a few years ago where they priorities went no further than the next school dance, an upcoming test, or whatever chores they were tasked with by their parents at home. Unbeknownst to them was the internal struggle that Karina struggled with for some of the time they knew each other. He was amazed at the inordinate amount of sympathy that had amassed in the last 24 hours since this situation had made itself known. “Real talk, Gina, I hope the best for everybody, even your girl. Not to mention her son. He doesn't have anything to do with it and deserves a father, you know?” Regina nodded in solemn agreement, while both went over the menu, for what seemed to be the hundredth time while taking infrequent sips of the water provided upon their arrival.

Meanwhile, the conversation between Carter and Karina was not any lighter. “So…” began a hesitant Carter. “So…how have you been, Karina. Long time, huh?” Karina, feeling equally awkward, did her best to respond in a way that did not further exacerbate the uneasiness. “Well, you know…just been living, taking care of my son. Been trying to get myself together. Mom's tripping like all the time. Looking at going back to school, hopefully, but…well, I got a lot going on. Typical almost-20-year-old stuff, right?” she asked rhetorically, offering her brand of dry humor. Carter, interpreting his former flame’s attempt to incite humor as her tried and true coping mechanism, thought quickly to add to her words to try to ease the tension of the moment. "Yup, real typical. Like anything is typical nowadays," he said, combined with a slight chuckle. "But anyway, about that taking care of your son part – I wanna know more about little man. I'm still taking it all in that you're a mom and..." Karina leaned in with feigned interest, "And what? You're the daddy? Yeah, it's possible, C."

Carter contended defensively, still making sure that his guard wasn't visibly let down for Karina to see. He was worried that his empathy or willingness to connect in this thrown-together late-afternoon meeting might be seen as an acceptance of the unconfirmed paternal role. The questions still swirled in his head on what the true answer was. The conversation that he had with Mel was still fresh in his mind, as well as the words of the prayer that it was capped off with. "Is this God's will?" The question still took up residence in his mind and only repeated more while sitting in the diner booth. As great as prayer sounded and was supposed to be, his response was definitely going to be one where his emotions were going to be known, without filter. "It's possible? Karina, for real, if it *is* possible, why am I just now sitting here at the diner, kid's like 3 years old, being told about it now? You can't be serious. I mean, it wasn't like I had even a clue. You come through, blowing up people's phones, trying to find me…"

Karina interrupted, seemingly not unprepared for the words received from Carter, "And that's why I came back, finally. You think I asked to be moved up out of the city, away from everybody, away from you? My mom is the main reason for all of this. I wanted to talk to you and let you know what was going on, what happened. Before I could say anything…" Carter matched the interruption with one of his own, somehow managing to keep his voice from elevating. He knew that with the size and acoustics of the diner that their words could easily be heard. "You hit me with that sad, confusing, random phone call and left me hanging. I get it, Karina. Look, I was hurt, but I moved on. I hooped harder, got my mind as right as I could and kept it pushing. I did all of this, clueless about this. *All* of this."

Karina slowed in her response. She considered if she were to reveal what she knew to be the reason why all of these revelations had suddenly surfaced, as Carter just referenced. Looking in relatively close distance, she saw Regina and Mel placing their orders, with a server who was distinctly familiar. The unfamiliarity subsided as the order was being written down and they walked away. In her own mind, Karina reedited her words to Carter, having been taken back to a memory that she now felt was long-overdue in sharing. “OK, Carter, look...I hear all of that, and please know, I'm sorry. I'm sorry for how everything happened. I'm sorry for how quick everything was. I'm sorry that it all came to...came to this. But I have something else to tell you about.” The same server who just seconds before was taking Mel and Regina's order came to their table. “Hey, Carter,” she said with a smile, then turning her attention to both, while maintaining her pleasant disposition. “What can I get you two to eat?”

Karina and the server looked at each other, with the brief silence interrupted by a question. “I'm sure I know you. You have a familiar face and I'm usually good with faces. Do I know you?” asked the server. "Probably not. I guess I just have that kind of face," responded Karina. "I'm good for now, though. I'm really not hungry. Water's good for now." "Same here, I'm good, too," added Carter. The server, feeling that this was a serious moment, put away her notepad and said, "Well, ok. Look, I'll bring you a couple of U.C. Milkshake specials on the house. Can't have this community's next big thing sitting here sipping on water." Before either could turn down the complimentary service, the server went on her way to input the round of orders she just corralled from the tables.

"Man, they stay filling me up on milkshakes here. Good thing I'm not lactose-intolerant," said Carter while shaking his head, still humbled that his athletic star was still visibly on the rise. Seeing this, Karina felt even more pushed to share a buried moment that happened just years prior. "I wasn't even planning on talking about this, but, look, Carter...remember that night I was supposed to meet you after that Classic tournament game, here at the diner?" asked Karina. "Yeah...what about it," responded a . confused Carter. "That server. That same one that just took our order...she was here that night, and um...." Karina paused, feeling slight mental trauma in her recollection, but pushed to resume. "I did come to the diner and I was just about to walk in, but I saw..." Before she could complete her sentence, Carter quickly made sense of the moment. He jumped in and they both said, almost simultaneously, "Mr. Dewels." Carter nodded in understanding, while Karina was both confused and appreciative for what appeared to be a lifting of yet another heavy burden from her emotional vault. "Yeah...I saw him and then..." Carter again jumped in, hoping to spare Karina the energy and hurt, pushing back his justified frustrations, instead opting to exercise momentary compassion. "Karina, I know. I'm hip to what happened with Dewels. Dude's a monster and I don't mean on the court. You don't have to explain."

What seemed like a serendipitous moment, Karina happened to look over at her old best friend and one-time adversary, Regina and Mel, who shared a brief look The look was one of like compassion, knowing that the recent revelations were borne of pain. Pain that was not asked for, nor in any way deserved. With all of these years having passed, in this moment, Karina was strongly reminded of the unique bond she had with these three. The good times shared from their times at Southview up until their unforeseen separation flooded her mind, forcing tears to make their way out almost immediately, as she looked down at the table. The shedding of tears was a culmination of what she felt to be a failed holding in of years of pain. Never did Karina believe that she had anyone in her corner, anyone who would support, much less believe her. She felt both upset for not allowing her friends to show her their support and also for another reason she felt even more obligated to share with Carter.

Fighting through the busted reservoir of tears, Karina looked up at Carter, and said, with genuine resolve, “Carter, my mom is behind all of this. I don't know if you’re my son’s father, but...my mom is plotting. I’ve gotta tell you everything.” Carter sat shocked, doing all he could to brave himself for the confession to follow. He did not think this situation could get any stranger or worse.

Chapter 31

"Something's gotta shake, Karina. These bills are not gonna pay themselves. And if you do not get that boy calmed down. He's going to make sure this headache won't go away," said a frustrated Ms. Burke. "Kerwin will be fine, Mom. His ears are still coming off of the ear infection. I just gave him his medicine. He'll be fine," assured a tired Karina. It was a long day for both Karina and her mom, the elder having just come in from a double-shift at work and trying to wind down her work week. Coming into the house, reviewing new bills, some compounded with final notices, Ms. Burke' frustrations were kindled. The weekends were often not the celebrated space of time for this household, as the finances never seemed to overtake, much less survive, the mounting debt that accumulated week after week.

"Look at this – light bill, gas bill, water bill with a shut-off notice. Cable bill just increased for no reason. I'm not even here half the time to watch anything, but I'm sure you're caught up on your shows. DVRs full on your little shows, alone," complained Ms.

Burke. "Gotta pay them with the internet attached to it. Car note that I didn't want is falling behind, already." Having heard this detailed roll-out of household finances before, Karina did her best to not immediately respond. The weekly repetition of the struggle to pay the incoming bills was a lot to bear, not only for her mom, but for her, too, as she stayed at home to watch Kerwin, making her unable to work. To avoid the high costs of childcare, after earning her GED, both Karina and her mom agreed that until he got to school-age, this would be their plan. Financially, however, this plan was not paying off as well as they imagined. Karina, sitting on the couch in their living room, sat listening to her mom upon her return from work, but knew that eventually the focus would be recast on her for lack of financial contribution.

"And the hospital is up on my behind again for Kerwin's bills. That little boy is the most expensive thing we have here," said Ms. Burke, while gesturing her hand towards his room. Karina, now pushed by offense, looked up and responded with an incredulous look, "That 'thing' is my son, Mom. And I'm sorry that these bills are so high, but..." Ms. Burke interrupted, reloading her ammunition for verbal onslaught, “Sorry for what? That you couldn’t keep your legs closed? It’s that very reason why we're in the mess we’re in now. Don’t get me wrong, Karina, I love that little boy, but he didn’t ask to be here, and…and neither did I.” The tension of the moment incited a heavy-weighing silence in the room following those words. Karina saw her mom as a serviceable grandmother to her son, but could sometimes feel the subtle resentment that just came out in her words in this moment. It was a resentment that hung over her, seemingly from the day that they were turned around from her trip to potentially terminate her pregnancy. While Karina resolved in her heart that the twist of fate experienced that day led to the right thing happening, she could not precisely conclude that her mother felt the same way.

Karina's hurt bubbled up a reminder she felt compelled to respond with, somehow remembering to keep her volume low for Kerwin to have a chance to finally fall asleep. She stood up and said, “Couldn’t keep my legs closed? Yeah, mom, that’s it. I couldn’t keep them closed because in one instance they were forced open. Remember that?” Ms. Burke stood undaunted and responded, stepping closer towards Karina, "You can keep this guessing game of 'who's the daddy' going on all that you like, but there's no telling what you did to make that man want you like that. And that's even if you were telling the truth about that, with your fast self. You...you...girl you just don't know!" "Know what, Mom? That Kerwin's father might not be Carter that it might be from my rapist teacher? That my beautiful little boy wasn't the result of teenage love but from my seventh-grade teacher having his way with me? Yeah, Mom...I guess that I don't know," responded an emboldened Karina, as she sat back down, nor knowing what else could be said. Her frustration went beyond that of undetermined paternity for her son. Her mother not acknowledging the sexual assault that potentially brought Kerwin to life caused a deep-seated pain. The pain was the fact that while her mother believed her enough to remove her from the school where her attacker was under the pretense of bullying, she never pressed charges or considered all that possibly resulted from the attacks after the fact.

"Girl, if you don't stop with all of that 'woe is me' mess. All I'm saying is that you need to step it up. Contribute. You have money sitting right up under you and you don't even know it. *That's* what you don't know, with your naïve self," responded Ms. Burke. "Mom, I've tried. You know I've tried. I filled out the forms. The case worker keeps putting me off. Even they said they don't know if I'll get approved. There's no job that I can get that won't block me from any assistance or stamps that they'll give," said Karina, clearly increasing in frustration, still trying to keep her voice from being heard in the other room by Kerwin. "You think I'm happy the way things are. If it were up to me, I'd take Kerwin and leave right now..." "Karina, shup up and listen, for once in your life," said Ms. Burke, as she grabbed her daughter's shoulders, almost seemingly preparing to shake her. "I *said* that you have money sitting right up under you, girl, and you need to work on getting at it." Confused, Karina looked in her mother's eyes, not phased by her shoulder's being gripped, but more confused by the cryptic message being spoken.

Karina's eyes non-verbally served as an invitation for her mother to continue in her explanation of her mysterious message. "Karina, you had a baby. The baby has a father. The father, from what *you* first told me is that boy you went to school with," started Ms. Burke. Karina, still trying to follow along with her mother's ambiguous reasoning, nodded and said, "If you're talking about Carter, yes, Mom, he *might* be Kerwin's fa…" Ms. Burke interrupted immediately and resumed her explanation, "Like I said, you said he was the father and from what I've been seeing in the news, he is about to go to play basketball professionally. Girl, something good might come out of this after all, if you play your cards right. All these bills, us barely making ends meet…" Karina stood back astonished, stepping back from her mother after hearing what she had to say. "So let me get this straight. The same guy you kept me from telling that he had a child, that you dogged me out for opening up my legs to – you want me to get up in his face and tell him 'Hey you're a daddy now. Here's your son. Now where them dollars at?' That's what you want me to do, Mom?" asked an increasingly incensed Karina. "So now I have a lottery ticket to become a basketball wife and everything's all good, huh?" Ms. Burke shook her head and sighed, "What part of marrying did you hear in anyth…" Karina left no room for her mother to speak, following up, "And on top of all that, Mom, you still refuse to accept that Mr. Dewels might be…"

Before the next words could exit her mouth, Ms. Burke stepped forward towards her daughter, in an effort to disallow the continuance of the words to follow, preparing her right hand to begin a backhand motion. "Girl, bring that man's name up one more time," threatening to strike Karina in the escalating moment. This continued to be a staying point in the uncomfortable relationship between the two of them. Karina continued to be haunted, not only by the assault, but even more that her mother simply moved them away and refused to further address the matter. Karina never felt supported and found herself being suspicious of her mother's intentions. While she was grateful that her mother was quick to remove her from Southview in response to her allegation of being bullied, she found it odd that she did not take as swift an action when it came to her finally admitting that she had been assaulted by her former teacher in multiple instances. Karina also could not understand how her mother expressed more reaction when it came to having sex with Carter, placing more responsibility on her in both instances. As a result, Karina always felt that her mother found more cause to blame her, rather than advocating for her as she hoped she would. The push to now "cash-in" on her former boyfriend's rising athletic fame repulsed her and appeared to be the last straw for Karina.

"Karina, look – the bottom line is we have bills. I mean *bills* bills. At this rate, I don't know how much longer we have until these places stop giving us extensions and start pulling up to cut off stuff. What you gon' do?" asked Ms. Burke, concluding with her ultimatum to Karina. As if the dam holding the sounds of their argument had finally broken, the cries of Kerwin came from the other room, still feeling slight effects from the ear infection that had not completely left. This was one of the rare times where, for Karina, the cries of her ailing son was a welcome exit from the draining back-and-forth she was engaged in with her mother. "Mom…I gotta go get Kerwin, before he's up all night. Can we talk about this later?" asked Karina, trying to disguise her relief for this great escape. Ms. Burke cut her eye, turning her head, while shaking in a feeling of extended frustration. As Karina left to console her son, the sleep that Ms. Burke was anxious for before the exchange with her daughter felt a far ways off. Now consumed with thoughts of how to persuade

Karina to push the issue of paternity towards her daughter's boyfriend from prior years. These suggestions ran through her mind, all while taking herself to sit in the small kitchen at the table, covered with small stacks of the bills she brought up in the debate with Karina.

The aggressive, unrelenting demeanor for Ms. Burke stood guard for feelings that she dared not to share with Karina, or anyone else for that matter. Her lack of acknowledgement of the sexual assault Karina suffered was not a difficult talking point so much because of the pain and potential pregnancy that ensued. Beneath the surface was a deeper resentment, one that seemed to still fester, even after the passing of years. For several years, she parented Karina, working as hard as she could to provide and have her daughter in need of nothing. Through the years, however, she felt the sting of loneliness, wanting to one day be with a man who could be her perfect match, perhaps marrying her and being a father-figure to Karina. With little to no time to date during most of Karina's childhood, due to her busy work schedule, her scope for prospective men was small. Typically, the only men she would see would be unattractive to her in one way or another.

However, there was one. One who caught her eye and her heart – or so she thought. Just the mere memory of this man drew up fantasies of what could have been, or in Ms. Burke mind, should have been. They were close in age, having familiarity from their younger years in the city, going to different schools, but not being closely connected. She stood afar, too shy to approach, and yet she felt not compelling enough in beauty to elicit the attention of her rare crush, especially as he had the eye of almost every woman of varying ages keeping close tabs on him. It would not be until a chance encounter, as Karina was entering her eighth grade year that Ms. Burke was finally able to have a date with this man she had long-admired. While she felt accomplished, finally having the sole attention of a man, specifically a man whom she longed for and seemingly had mutual interest in her, it was her woman's intuition that triggered while she sat at the restaurant that troubled her. Something inside of her, as she sipped on her Shirley Temple, caused her to know that this feeling of potential bliss was not meant to last. Looking into His eyes as he trapped the feeling would not shake loose, as hard as she tried.

It was no less than a week later that Karina came home in a frenzy, crying that she had been bullied and did not want to go to Southview any more. As odd and out of place as it was for her daughter to make such a bold declaration, Ms. Burke began to feel that perhaps this was what would disrupt her pursuit of relational bliss. The only thing in her life that she prioritized more than anything else was the well-being of Karina. Without any further questioning, feeling the need to take immediate action and confident that her daughter would not say anything even remotely dishonest, especially to this magnitude, Ms. Burke turned her focus away from her dating interests and solely on Karina. Withdrawing her from the school, she simultaneously felt convicted that she had taken her attention on being the parent that Karina needed, feeling guilty for her daughter suffering such pain and not being aware of it. Additionally, she called the man days later, breaking off the early-sprouting relationship. Disappointed, she knew in her heart that she was doing the right thing.

Still, to this moment, Ms. Burke wondered what could have been. If she had proceeded and not deprioritized herself in that one instance and pursued what she felt to be love that stood in front of her. This evening, coming home from work, faced with several bills with no clear path to payment, she found herself dueling in her own mind, considering potential what-ifs. Ms. Burke did not mind being a strong woman, but could not help but question if she could be that same woman, perhaps standing at the side of the last man she thought would be the one.

Pulling out her phone, she looked at a website featuring athletes from her hometown. The website had been bookmarked for some time with her attention drawn as recently as a few days ago because of the image seen upon opening the page. The homepage featured Carter, showing him dunking with the title "U.C. The Next Big Thing" emblazoned across. Another window she had opened from the site however, is where she now turned her focus, featuring archived athletes. The headline said 'Where Are They Now?"

Looking at this page, she let out a sigh, while shaking her head. “David…why? You had a whole woman in front of you, a good woman, and you chose my little girl?” in almost immediate succession, tears fell from her face, with any sounds she was making in sorrow being drowned by a still-inconsolable Kerwin, being comforted by Karina.

Chapter 32

"So you're going to not believe me over...over some journal, Angela? You can't be serious," said David, with an incredulous tone. "You can't give me one shred of proof that would even put me in proximity of doing anything to that girl or anybody. Stop this nonsense!" Angela sat at her desk in her home office, flustered. Detective Price having left just moments before set a raging fire between the married couple. The revelation of the evidence given by the journal found at the school was just shared by Angela, as David was confounded as to where the push came for him to be questioned about Karina and alleged sexual assaults. "You call it nonsense, but it was enough for police to come to our home and ask question after question, figuring out what's really going on, David. As smart as you are, don't you see this is bigger than some misunderstanding?" asked Angela, still sitting with her hands at both sides of her face, doing intentional breathing to attempt to keep herself calm.

“Bigger, yes. Another allegation, another attempt at slander…” started David. Angela abruptly interrupted, however, “That's the point – ‘another'. David, how many times do we need to go through this. Your career, my career has been at risk because of these allegations. I'm starting to think…” “Starting to think what, Angela? I've told you – I didn't do it. Not then, nor with her, nor with anybody! What more do I, *your* husband, have to say for you to believe me?” He said these words, deescalating his tone and setting himself on one knee, in front of Angela. He was confident that his charm would bring needed peace to the chaos that was elevating between them. In his time of marriage, David was able to assert himself to Angela in a way that would ultimately reset her, taking her to the early days of their courtship. It was a ploy that Angela was all-too familiar with, but found herself always struggling to counteract, even in her best efforts. It was David’s charm and charisma that held staying power with her. Unfortunately, she knew that to be the same for all of the women who unapologetically sought her husband – before and after their nuptials.

"David...get up. Get up and stop...stop trying to finesse yourself out of this," said a resolved Angela. "This one is different. There's possibly a child involved. A whole child! A child that doesn't know his father and is just...just out here, not knowing what's going on."

"What does a child have to do with me when I didn't touch anyone, Angela? Again, why don't you believe me," asked a seemingly desperate David. He was coming to realize that his go-to moves were being deflected by a now-impervious version of his wife. Silence cascaded throughout the room, eerily assimilating with the tension that had built and only escalated with the post-interview conversation that ensued. The married couple had reached a stalemate in their debate, neither seeking to lose ground in their position. Regaining his original stance, slowly and in shock, David stood silent, surprised that the grace he usually garnered in these situations was not being offered from his wife. He had come to realize that this particular instance was indeed different.

He went to his own desk, pulling out the bottom drawer a bottle of cognac that he frequently indulged in during times of stress or unwanted pressure. The cool, calm, resourceful Mr. Dewels of past years had slowly transitioned into an opposite figure. Years of frustration from fighting the allegations of sexual improprieties in recent years, dealing with ailments from injuries suffered during his athletic career, and seeing his marriage struggling all provided compelling reasoning to turn to the dark alcoholic anesthetic. David was never one to drink more than what was expected in social settings, feeling unbothered and in control of even the most challenging of scenarios. However, the pressure to hit the game-winning shot or to ensure his class' test scores were optimal stood miniscule to the obvious challenge of reality that he was being confronted with today. David looked at the small glass that sat on his desk. He usually used it for water to take with his pain prescriptions when in view of his wife. In other times of Angela's absence, it served as his partner-in-crime to partake in the secluded bottle of cognac in which a dependence developed. This time, however, he looked away from the glass and saw this as a justified occasion to consume directly from the bottle.

Having followed him to his desk moments later and seeing her husband with the bottle in hand, Angela immediately commented.

"David, this is the last thing you need right now. Our counselor, your sponsor...everybody is making it clear that you need help. *We* need help! Come on, now," chided Angela. Having placed the bottle back down on the desk with enough force to where small drops flew out of the bottle opening, David felt a small surge of relief from the alcoholic elixir, but saw his wife standing before him, anchoring him in the reality from which he was trying to escape. He responded, fiercely, "The last thing that I need is my own wife not believing me, taking the word of people who have some hidden agenda against me, and..." "And? And what else, David? Do we need to rehash the times I caught you, yes, caught you going out on me with other women?" interrupted Angela. "You validate everything that you do in one way or another. You can never be wrong. There is always a reason, always a justification. Everyone is out to get David, right?"

David readily responded, "Again, you rehash my past mistakes. Mistakes, Angela! For someone who carries themselves so graceful, you surely lack that when it comes to me. I have apologized and begged and groveled and been relentless in telling you that I messed up. When does it end?" Angela, feeling at a loss on how to respond, stood speechless, disrupting the rhythm of the verbal tennis match, and exited, bee-lining towards the living room. Having his motor skills slightly slowed by his oft-injured knee and the drink that he indulged in moment before, David was slow in his reaction to attempt to follow Angela. A combination of her determined walk and desire to respond, Angela returned to David's office, which halted him from moving any further. In her hand was a manila folder, which had written on the front of it in capital letters, "D.J.". Frustrated by the sight of the folder, David let out an exasperated sigh and prepared to remark on the all-too familiar folder, but Angela immediately spoke. "This, David. This is the only excuse that I see that lies underneath so much of what we are going through now. Then again, I don't know if me having our son or any child for that matter would change the ugly, sickened man that you are in any way. You...you need help!" said Angela, as she pressed the folder into her husband's chest and proceeded to walk out of the room.

The room had become a miniature arena of verbal rage, with the exchanges escalating with each shot taken by one at the other. The pressure had built up and still lingered, even with the exit of one of the combatants. David held the folder that had been forcefully delivered and looked at the scripted name of the child that he had aspired to have with Angela. It was true that the inability to have a child had bore a heavy toll on their relationship. It was a dream that they shared even prior to their marriage, as they both prioritized having a family. The folder usually was nestled behind the framed photographs that sat on the top bookshelf in the living room, secured as a filing of regret and disappointment that the couple shared and often lamented over. The paper-clipped ultrasound had begun to fray on the edges, but the day that they were given it was still fresh in David's mind.

David had now become entrenched in a solemn mood, reflective of not only the unexpected loss of their son, but of the allegations of which he was now up against. The times of infidelity that Angela brought up, were not only due to the loss of D.J., but also was a continued struggle within himself to remain committed to his relationship. While he seemingly was able to keep things together with ease, David often found himself caught in internal conflict, enamored with the frequent overtures from women, dating back to his years as a high school star athlete. While he had made a public declaration of matrimony with Angela, his commitment to remain faithful was always loosely kept intact at best. The smooth vernacular and calming disposition always kept Angela at bay, even causing her to not question her husband's suspicious behavior. She, as many other women in David's past and present path, had fallen victim to his persuasive tact, calmed into an almost hypnotic state that had become terribly challenging to overcome.

While David was confident in his influence and ability to navigate the psyche of the women whom he interacted with, his nerves in this moment compelled him to reach for his bottle of cognac for another comforting round of consumption, while also picking up a portrait paperweight of he and Angela from their engagement years ago. It was a brass heart, that was a customized engagement gift presented originally in a set of two, with each partner keeping one at their respective desks. He glanced fondly at the keepsake, while putting the bottle back down on his desk, with the realization beginning to sink in even further that the security blanket which he was covered by comfortably for the majority of his life was beginning to be forcibly pulled away from him. While Angela was aware and forgiving of his cheating ways throughout their marriage, could the revelation of his sexual assaults of his former student be the last straw? He pondered if the evidence and items mentioned in the meeting with Detective Price could actually be the final remnant of grace that he could hang on to. Never before had his darkest secret, held in co-ownership with his victim and the school where he formerly taught, was so close to taking his life to disastrous levels he never imagined it would.

"Angela...listen," said David, finally uttering words to his wife, who had since gone to their bedroom. He was able to determine her location, following the cries and sniffles that could be heard down the staircase. Following the sound, he struggled up the stairs with trepidation, nervous that this attempt to calm Angela would be thwarted as it was moments ago. Walking into the bedroom, he continued, "I know that things may look a way. I think it only fair to share with you why I left Southview when I did. If you would allow me, you deserve to know the truth. The real truth." He sat on the bed and nestled her hands between his, attempting to create a safe space to deliver his perspective and further defend his stance. Angela still did not look up at her husband, slowing down in her tears, but still embattled on whether or not to allow subsequent words to follow. Many times before she found herself in this same position and David carried an undefeated record, managing to win her forgiveness and earn a clean slate, time after time. She pondered if this would be another surefire loss and blow to her damaged self-worth.

“David,” Angela replied softly, temporarily absent of tears. “You're already drunk or delusional or both, for all I know. I know why you left Southview. That ‘secret’ board meeting exploded and ran through the entire community. Even your smoothness can't outdo when people start talking.” Angela’s words pierced the usually impenetrable armor that was usually a mainstay for her husband. The emotion behind her words carried a different weight and impact. The plan to reiterate his denial was seemingly faltering. He stood speechless as her verbal preemptive strike continued. “David, honestly, I've chosen for a long time to overlook the narcissist that somehow I've come to love. I even tried to believe the lies that you clung to and adopt it as my truth, too," she said, almost choking on her words while her tears remained barely walled behind her squinted eyelids. "You need help, David! Somehow in all of this, I committed myself to be your hero, but I can only do so much. I'm done, David. I'm done!"

The room had gone quiet almost immediately. The silence had taken hold between Angela and David in way like no other time before. While David acknowledged Angela as a woman who could hold her own, independent in her thinking and unafraid to speak her mind when she felt necessary, this was a side that was unfamiliar to him. The smooth resolve he would often employ was reduced to a solemn and shocked state. In his own mind, David never before felt so devoid of control. Always a confident controller of the narrative, he had come to realize that this scenario was unlike any he had yet experienced before. At his core, he felt as if he had let down his sole supporter. Even in a shaken, unfamiliar plot in their timeline, he boldly extended his right hand to Angela.

“If the next words out of your mouth are simply how you didn't do this or didn't do that or how this is all just a set up,” started a wary Angela. “Then keep your hands away from me.” “What if I were to tell you that...that I want to make things right. Right for you, right for me...right for even this gir-.“ He quickly corrected himself, resuming his contrite tone. “For the young lady making these allegations.” Angela added her own correction, retorting, “Her name is Karina. Her name is Karina! Can you please, for once in your life, acknowledge beyond your narcissism that her name is Karina?” “Karina, yes. Karina Burke,” conceded David. He walked away, turning to a dimply lit corner of the room, shrouded in what seemed to be shame, preceding confession. “Angela...it’s time. It’s time that I just bare my soul to you. Full transparency. You deserve that. You deserve that much.”

Angela, realized that there was a contrite sound to her husband. Her naiveté had subsided long ago and she awaited the day when his suave persona would be yielded, giving her full visibility of who he was and the potentially dark secrets he held within. She awaited his following words, hoping that this moment was as true as perceived, and not a clever guise that he had been known to resort to, yet again evading the revelation of the unknown. "I love you, Angela. I hope you know that. With that love comes the need for you to know that...that there's a battle raging within me. It's a back and forth that I cannot explain, that I have dealt with since...since I was a kid. I won't be foolish to try to explain away everything to whatever turning point in my life that may have caused this. What I will say is this – did I do some things that weren't right? Perhaps. Could it have involved Karina?" Angela awaited the inevitable confession. While she knew in her heart that the allegations were more to her as confirmations, she needed to hear it from her husband. Angela found herself in the court-like precedent of being innocent until proven guilty. She did not want to believe that David could have done such a thing, but the reality proved to be to looming to deny.

As Angela waited, the question just asked by David, supposedly spoken to create an extended path to his admittance of the allegations remained in place, followed by silence. David instead took a deep breath and exhaled, as if preparing to speak something that he knew would change everything in his life, leading him to place he avoided for so long, both physically and emotionally. As put-together as he was perceived by all who observed him, David fought several internal conflicts, many of which he self-diagnosed to be the root of his struggles. The issues that he sourced as the foundation of the man he had become overwhelmed him and he only came to such a realization preceding his actions the he knew to be morally corrupt, but satisfying to a dark side that had developed, much of which in secret. This moment was proving to potentially be a watershed moment, or at least one where he could come one step closer to repentance, witnessed by his wife, no less.

Angela, discerning that the pregnant pause was a gateway to her husband preparing to unload a burden that he carried and desired so much to be loosed of, let go of the ire that she had built up within her as this chain of events unfolded in their home. She stood up, now overwhelmed with compassion, and slowly approached her husband, who stood in the corner, still draped in mysterious solitude. This was a moment she had prayed for. As she was raised in the church and drawn away since their relationship blossomed, she felt a darkness that bound her and was inexplicable. In recent years she would make time when alone in the house to pray. Her prayers were at first repetitions of her desire to be a mother. With each prayer, she felt further and further away from what she and David desired. Yet, in recent months, she found herself in a place of acceptance that, for reasons beyond what she knew or chose to accept, the destiny of having a child was not to be.

Angela's countenance had suffered with this internal revelation. While she carried herself proudly, having success in her own right and having a resume of noted professional exploits that made her, too, the envy of many in the community, even before her marriage. Still, having the title of "mother" continue to elude to her was a dark cloud that refused to depart. The disappointment was broadened by a husband who she suspected waned in his faithfulness, but now the divine hint that having a family with David was not to be. In this tumultuous moment, Angela held a thin-veiled sliver of hope that this may be the bridge that they could cross together and reroute themselves in a way that even she herself could not imagine. All she knew was that change had to come and this moment, as eerie and life-changing as it was building up by the seconds to be, was likely it.

"David, I want you to know," started Angela, as she placed her left hand on his right shoulder. "That you have my absolute sup..." Angela was interrupted by a sudden movement by David. He turned quickly, using his left hand to strike his unassuming wife in her head, instantly causing her to lose consciousness. David, himself, stood in shock, looking at his wife, then looking at his left hand that held the brass heart paperweight even he himself did not realize he still was carrying from his desk. He dropped the object, wondering what he had done and how he could explain this to anyone who would ask. His resolve had completely unfolded, having completely sobered up and now forced to figure out what to do next. "Angela...Angela...I'm sorry. I'm sorry!" After his confession to his unconscious wife, he cried inconsolably, falling to the floor next to her.

Chapter 33

"On everything, Mel, I think I'm going to have to see Dewels, bro," exclaimed Carter. "Dude went from hero to zero in record time. Got a whole son out here and the way it all came about...scandalous, man." "*Might* have a son. That's why we're here right now, C," Mel said, correcting his best friend. The two sat in the office of Pastor Kingsley, the agreed upon neutral ground for an arranged paternity test. In a swift sequence of events, and somewhat informal manner, the involved parties all agreed to prioritize determining if Carter was truly Kerwin's father. While it was an agreed upon initiative between Karina and Carter, there still remained the question around the possibility of the paternity of Mr. Dewels. Detective Price, privy to this meeting and its purpose, pledged to the involved teenagers and Pastor Kingsley that she would do all she could to get Mr. Dewels to the meeting. She insinuated that as a trusted community leader, meeting with Pastor Kingsley could be a bridge to a solution for the troubled matter. At least that is what she explained when she visited the Dewels' home the day before. The tenured detective knew that it was a longshot, but thought to speak to the better nature of the accused Mr. Dewels, leaving a proposed

DNA test out of the spoken proposal, as to not push him out of the meeting before he would even agree to arrive.

Meanwhile, Karina sat in the parking lot with Pastor Chris who was stationed, per Pastor Kingsley's request. There was an uneasy silence this Sunday afternoon, intermittently interrupted by Karina's vibrating cell phone. Chris could not see the caller ID because of the privacy screen, but he could tell that the caller was having an effect on Karina. "Calling again, huh? Your phone is the hotline, apparently," he said with a forced chuckle. "It's just a wrong number. They'll stop calling. I hope so, anyway. This is getting annoying," replied Karina, uneasily. While the visibility of her phone screen was limited, Chris knew that the caller was more than likely not a wrong number, but someone who she was doing all she could avoid. It did not take his gift of discernment to conclude that whoever was calling was someone Karina had no intention of talking with in this moment.

Karina's discomfort in the moment only increased with each call that came through. Feeling the pressure of finally seeing the moment of revelation of Carter's possible paternity, she knew that there was no turning back. When the idea was suggested to her to have this meeting, she was mixed simultaneously with both excitement and fear of the discovery of truth. Karina could not help but weigh the possibilities and the future that would lie ahead with each. Assured that Kerwin's father was either Carter or Mr. Dewels, having only Carter take the test would be enough for her to know the answer she had sought for so long. The likelihood that the other possible father being actually willing to cooperate and take the test seemed low and her now apparent PTSD from his abuse still kept her from wanting to confront her abuser, even years later.

"So," Chris started awkwardly. "What did you think of the message today at church?" "Well...to be honest, I really wasn't paying a lot of attention," responded a timid Karina. "It's been a while since I've been at the church. Actually, it's been a while since I've been at *any* church." Chris responded, first with a short laugh, unsure of where to go next with the conversation, "Yeah, yeah...of course. Most people are kind of at a loss when it's someone other than Pastor Kingsley preaching. I guess we all can get like that sometimes. And with all of this going on...I can't even imagine." Karina appreciated Pastor Chris' attempt to ease the tension that had become the standard for the day. She woke up knowing that it would be a challenging day, but the support that she received from Pastor Kingsley and the church staff was the most feeling of support that she had felt in a long time. This was especially meaningful to her as she yearned to have even a semblance of this support from her mother.

"I will say this, though," said Karina to Chris, who was grateful that she had picked up the reigns of the broken conversation. "I can't say enough how much I appreciate you all for doing this. I mean, you all didn't have to do any of this and..." She stopped mid-sentence, holding back tears, but managing to muster up a smile, emitting her gratitude. Chris nodded in understanding and offered a slight smile in return. As complicated as this matter had become, he understood how vital it was to be there in any way that he could for Karina and Carter. While many saw this as yet another potential case of teen pregnancy with hoop dream implications on the line, Chris realized from his own experience how life-changing this could be. His heart was also sympathetic to the sexual assault that he was explained that Karina suffered, having heard several similar instances in his upbringing, in his own family to both men and women. He carried the sentiment that if he could help her in any way, it could be a way to pay tribute to those whom he could not help directly.

At that moment, a text message came through on Karina's phone. It was Carter.

"You good?"

Nonverbally excusing herself from the conversation with Pastor Chris, she responded, trying to provide short correspondence.

"Yeah. Just waiting to get this done. How are you?"

"NGL – haven't felt BGs like this in a while. Probably our first date."

Karina smiled and replied with a smiley face emoji before typing more of a response. She did not return to reignite her old relationship with Carter. It even surprised her that he would make such a comment. Still, Karina remembering how much Carter cared for her quickly understood that it was very possible that the feelings he had for her quite possibly never went away.

"LOL. Just pretend it's the city championship and you have to go out and hoop like your life depends on it."

She knew that if she could relax him with a basketball scenario, then the chances were likely that he would find calm and be eased as the all waited for the mystery to end. The response that she received from Carter did catch her off guard a bit.

"Well my life does depend on it fr fr. And so does yours. We'll see what happens."

Carter turned to Mel after sending the text and let out a sigh. "I already know what that sigh means, or at least I think I do. What's up?" asked Mel. "Bro, I know it sounds crazy, but...but I think I'm falling for this girl again," responded a confused-sounding Carter. His friend responded in an unbothered manner, "And? C, she was kinda your high school sweetheart. I know there was a time when I was one-hundred percent against y'all, but you loved that girl, and I gave up trying to talk you out of it. As a matter of fact, it's not like you would listen to me anyway." Mel concluded with a laugh that would be shared lightly by Carter. Carter added further explanation to his commentary, "No, for real, Mel. I'm saying, what I'm supposed to think? Karina bounced on me and I went right on my hoop grind back, going hard. She comes back and I'm supposed to just drop everything for her..." "No, but if this little boy is yours, *something's* gotta shake though, right?" interrupted Mel. "We talked about this. We *prayed* about this! It may not be a 'happily ever after' with Karina, but, like we said, we gotta handle business if he's yours, right?"

Carter nodded solemnly in immediate response to Mel. Looking across the office at the door, he anxiously awaited the arrival of Pastor Kingsley. The sooner he would arrive, the sooner, Carter felt, they would get closer to settling the built-up anxieties that continued to elevate as each second ticked away. He knew that, although it came across selfish, his own future was potentially set to be altered, maybe even away from his predestined hoop dreams.

While staying the course in school would not be instantly impossible, Carter knew that fatherhood would have to become the top priority. He had not yet resolved himself to telling his mother, who usually was the first outside of Mel to know any happenings in his life. Carter wanted to be absolutely sure of where he fit in this complicated equation before he would deliver news of this magnitude. Dropping his eyes down he saw another text message coming through, but before he could read it, the office door began to open.

As both Mel and Carter's attention turned to the entryway, they anticipated Pastor Kingsley finally making his way to the culminating gathering. To both of their surprise, the figure that walked in was Detective Price. She moved past a customary greeting and led with a question, with urgency, "Where is Pastor Kingsley? We have a bit of an emergency." Both young men shrugged their shoulders, expressing both a lack of information and a curiosity as to what was behind the question. While Carter went to see what the text message that he just received said, Mel took lead in verbally responding, "We've been waiting here for him like they told us to. I guess he'll be here any minute. You know how hard it is for him to escape all the people that run up on him after church. Is something wrong?" Detective Price looked troubled, but was slow to respond. Mel could tell that whatever it was, there was something bad behind it.

Reading the received text message, expecting further communication from Karina, Carter read and saw that the sender was someone else. He noticed that it was a group message, including Carter and Karina, coming from Regina.

"Hey, Dewels is on the run. Word is he left town and is trying to get away."

Looking at his own phone, Mel saw the same message. "Wow," he exclaimed. This was seemingly confirmation to Detective Price that whatever news she harbored had beaten her to the destination. Looking at the faces of Mel and Carter, she was tempted to divulge details, but held the news within. Doing her best to hold her resolve, she said, "OK, um…I'm going to go and try to get Pastor here, so we can get..." "Get going on a plan to figure out how to keep this man from killing himself at Southview? Am I right?" asked a pensive-sounding Pastor Kingsley as he walked into the office, visibly as troubled as Detective Price. "How did you..." began Detective Price, who verbalized the same curiosity of Mel and Carter. Pastor Kinglsey, interrupted calmly, "Just because I'm not *in* the streets, doesn't meant that my ears are deaf to when they're talking."

As usual, Pastor Kingsley had insight into a neighborhood matter that was barely fresh off of the police scanner. "And since this young man is caught up in this situation, I don't think it makes any sense not to let him in on what's going on," said Pastor Kingsley, allowing his eyes to indicate he was referring to Carter. "From what I was told, the man was sitting in his car, drunk out of his mind with a gun in the parking lot, and then..." "Pastor, this is a fluid situation, that we cannot..." interrupted Detective Price, who would in turn be stopped again by Pastor Kingsley. "Young lady, I respect your role and thank you and the department for what you all do, but, as the young folks say, sometimes we have to just keep it real. This isn't going over the pulpit and the news is already on its way to the streets. I think it best just to talk and get it out now," he said as he made his way to his leather desk chair behind his desk.

Detective Price put up her hands in feigned surrender and took a half step back, relenting to the Pastor's words. Both Mel and Carter sat as observers, mimicking spectators at a tennis match, watching the discussion volleying between the two communicators. Finally landing eyes on Pastor Kingsley, and seeing that he had they and Detective Price's full attention, he continued his narrative of what he was informed about Mr. Dewels. "They think that he sat in the parking lot overnight in his car. When they approached the car, he stepped out holding a gun to his head. Apparently, he had quite of bit in him and somehow the officers got to him. There was a little struggle, so the gun went off and, uh...let's just say that the bullet was flirting real close to his manhood. Got pretty messy from what they said. Almost became a eunuch on the spot. They had to get him to the hospital, trying to keep him from bleeding out."

The reactions in the room were immediate and varied between each person. Mel sat in shock, with his mouth slightly open, and grabbing his own self, as if he himself had been the one shot in the given story. Detective Price slowly shook her head and let out an uncomfortable sigh, looking down at the office floor, still in unbelief of the raw and uncut account just given by Pastor Kinglsey. Carter, on the other hand, had a slight smirk and immediate words in response to the graphic tale he was just told. "Man, ain't God good? Got a rapist and pedo the justice he deserved. Took a little time, but He showed up and shot him up. Now *that's* what's up!" "Boy, God ain't in none of this mess! Stop with all of that nonsense," Pastor Kingsley said, chastising Carter. "I know this whole situation is a lot for you and Karina, but last thing we're gonna do is wish ill on another man, regardless of what allegations are still to be settled. Today is about peace and resolution."

"Peace? Pastor, for real?" asked an incredulous Carter. "No disrespect, but what peace is there to get from a rapist teacher that, for all we know, got one of his victims pregnant. And who's to say who else he did this to? He was probably touching on all kind of girls…maybe even little boys, too. Karma was going to hit him one way or another. Right?" He asked the question looking for support from anyone in the room, coming into agreement with his thought that justice had been indiscriminately served. "Son," started Pastor Kingsley, who felt the need to lessen his now-stern tone, to one of a father figure determined to get through to the impassioned Carter. "Two things wrong with what you just said. One we don't do karma or the law of attraction or any of that stuff. We believe on the Word of God and "karma" is nowhere to be found in any of the 66 books, you believe me when I tell you that. And the other point, son, is that, as hard as it may seem to do now, forgiveness has to be in the mix of all of this. This meeting that we're having today, other than reading off a DNA test result, is about clearing the air and getting everybody right."

Carter listened intently, with the smirk he briefly had permanently disappeared from his face. Though he knew what Pastor Kingsley had shared was right, he did not want to hear it. The man who he once looked up to and served as the measuring stick for the star basketball player that he strived to be had betrayed him and the whole community. Forgiveness was not a word that he was willing to put into action, much less listen to, even from the highly-respected Pastor Kingsley. Still, he muted his speech, choosing to not engage any further in debate with the man who was kind enough to corral as many as he could to attain resolution. Mel, sensing the heaviness in the room only increasing in weight, spoke up in his overt awkwardness, offering up words to help progress the moment, "So, with all that happened, are we still good to meet with those who could make it? I mean, finding out where Karina and Carter stand is still important to find out, right?"

Detective Price, in alignment with Mel, chimed in, "I think that we could still get that part addressed. Mr. Dewels' presence here was more in a kind of counseling capacity, so, with Pastor Kingsley's blessing, I think we could press on. Did the results arrive yet, Pastor?" "Let me call and check with my assistant to see if the package arrived. As much money as we paid for this, it better be here with a copy of Noah's blueprints to the ark," responded Pastor Kingsley, with a humorous attempt to break the solemn tone of the room. The joke fell flat, as Carter still sat stewing in his chastisement and both Mel and Detective Price shared an awkward, mutual look at each other. The test result was expected to be delivered in time for the meeting, but the company they contracted said that they could not guarantee an expected time of delivery. Still, everyone held out hope that the answer would arrive this day.

As everyone in the room awaited the status update of the DNA test results , the office door swung open and in came Karina, with shock in her face. She immediately approached Carter saying, repeatedly, "I'm sorry. I am so sorry, Carter, I promise, I did not mean for this to happen." With all confused in the office, Carter, with a puzzled look on his face, immediately responded, "Look, Karina, I already told you, if I'm the father…" "No, C. Listen," interrupted Karina. "Outside in the parking lot is a bunch of news reporters and they're here….they're here looking for…you." Mel, intrigued himself, wanting to understand, asked, "How do you know they're looking for Carter?" Pastor Chris followed in, shortly behind, slightly out of breath, and replied, "Because all of the questions they asked Karina was about if 'the next big thing' was the father to her baby. Pastor, security is at the doors, keeping them out as best as they can. They are relentless!"

"Hold up, so I am the father? How you know already?" asked a shocked, but slightly composed Carter. How did you get the results, but Pastor didn't?" Karina, already feeling guilty for everything culminating to this long-awaited moment, looked away, not wanting to shed light on the truth she knew it to be. "Karina, for real. You know dealing with reporters is nothing to me, but I'm saying, how do they know that I'm Kerwin's father already? Did you tell them?" asked Carter. Before he could get his response, Pastor Kingsley ended his call, overhearing the commotion and thought to double-down on the given question. "Young lady, I just got off of the phone and was informed that we won't get the results to the test for at least two more days. Please tell me why I have news reporters ready to bust down my doors for a reason other than pointing fingers at me and my church as they have for long enough."

"Carter, it's my Mom, I know it!" replied Karina, in a semi-outburst. "She had it in her mind to tell the world that Kerwin was yours because...because you're on your way to the league. I promise, this was not at all my idea. I wouldn't do you like this." "What? What you mean you wouldn't do me like that?" asked a visibly incensed Carter. "You left me in the dark all of this time, and now I'm some kind of lottery ticket? Well, you can run your game on someone else, because I'm tired of being played like th..." "Whoa, whoa, whoa, Carter. Hold up," said Pastor Chris, trying to calm Carter down. "I know that 'crazy' just went 'crazier', but I think she's telling the truth. I was just in the car with her that whole time waiting and there's no time that she could've reach out to these news outlets. As a matter of fact, she was receiving calls and not answering them...come to think of it, that still sounds a little suspect, I have to admit."

"Let's nip this in the bud, everybody. I find it hard to belie- no, I *know* that no one in this room is why those reporters are here. Young lady, I believe you, but Carter isn't going to the league – yet, anyway. Are you sure your mother would plot something like this?"

asked Pastor Kinglsey. "I'm almost 100% sure, Pastor. You all don't know my mom like I do," replied Karina, with a frustrated look on her face. Detective Price's phone began to ring. She took the call and immediately went to a far corner of the office to hear better in the midst of the discussion in the room. Knowing that he had to do what he could to take command of the escalating situation, Pastor Kingsley stood up in the room, at his desk. "Ok, everybody, let's handle what we can here. For one, we don't have the results yet, so we have to reschedule this meeting. In the meantime, we have to figure out how to get these reporters from 'round here. We still have people trying to get out of the church. Chris, if you can get security to go out to those reporters and get them to back off, I think that will take care of that." Pastor Chris immediately left the room to honor his spiritual father's instruction.

Pastor Kingsley continued, "Now, as far as Dewels, I know he was supposed to be here, but..." "He is about to die. That was one of the officers from the hospital and they told me that the amount of blood that he is losing...it's not looking too good for him." The room went eerily silent. The five who remained in Pastor Kinglsey's office stood unsure of how to really feel about the dire and potentially deadly news about the man who had been the catalyst of the day's gathering. Even Pastor Kingsley, usually the source of wisdom in virtually all situations, sat confused as to how to proceed. Arguably, the most torn in the room was Karina, who at one point stood resolute that the most important matter to her was determining the paternity of Kerwin. Now she begun to have feelings of anger, seeing that her assailant had seemingly found a way to escape his day of atonement. While she knew the likelihood of him showing up to the meeting was low, she held out hope that she could confront him, with the help of the exclusive group in attendance. Now she stood bewildered, not knowing what to do.

After the cascaded silence, Detective Price continued and said, "And I don't know how to say this, but..." She paused, being careful, as she was unsure how to deliver the following words and what the reaction within the room would be. Taking a deep breath and clutching her cross pendant, she continued, "He wants to see you, Karina. He asked if you would come to the hospital to see him. He says he has something to tell you." Silence resumed amongst the group. All eyes in the room slowly began to fall on Karina, as they wondered what she would do, what she would say. This day of hoped for closure and revelation had quickly turned into one of increased questions and confusion.

Lightning Source UK Ltd.
Milton Keynes UK
UKHW010806051222
413416UK00018B/1009